TERRIBILITA

BEN WYCKOFF SHORE

Cinder Block Publishing

Cinder Block Publishing

FIRST EDITION

ISBN: 978-0-578-63203-2

For Marian

1

Genoa, Italy — 1881. The boy pulled the blind old man through the garden and up the hill to their favorite talking spot. He guided the old man's steps with matter-of-fact directions. He took his charge very seriously as it was his responsibility to get his grandfather to the talking spot on top of the hill.

The talking spot atop the hill had two perpendicular slabs of rock for sitting that opened generously to a view of the Port of Genoa, just a league south of their modest family farm. The old man could no longer see the coast, but he could feel the sun and taste the salt.

They had been coming to this talking spot for as long as the boy could remember. He loved listening to his grandfather's stories of revolution and adventure and gazing out over the bustling port. The boy had noticed more and more steamers coming in and out of the port over the years. There was something dreary and monotonous about them, and he preferred the old, proud clipper ships that gracefully heeled against the southerly winds as they beat into the Mediterranean. He liked to draw the clipper ships, and this perch furnished the flint to spark his sketches.

When they reached the talking spot, the boy saw six clippers in the port on this day and many cutters, schooners, barques, brigs, and steamers. Good. This is good for his father's business, the boy thought.

"Lucca, I want to tell you an important story today," the old man started and then paused.

"Can you tell the one about the riots in Nice again, Grandpa?" Lucca loved this story because it also featured his father, Enzo, who was sixteen at the time, only four years older than himself.

"No," the old man said brusquely. Lucca blushed and averted his gaze in embarrassment. "This is not a story you've heard before, Lucca, but it needs telling. It is not a happy story, but it is an important story for our family. I sense there will not be many more opportunities for me to tell you this story, so you need to listen with care, Lucca. This is the story of the Battle of Solferino."

The boy was rapt in attention.

2

I t was evening. Enzo Ferrando entered his modest family home, traversed the foyer in two bounds, and went to work in the kitchen with the washbasin, scrubbing his hands free of the day's toils. He looked up out the back window and into the garden and saw his blind old father and young son coming back to the house after one of their rituals.

He noticed how hesitant his father's steps had become, and for an instant he could barely recognize the old war hero whom all of Italy once called "The Bull." Antoni "il Toro" Ferrando, who had served so faithfully under Garibaldi fighting for Italian unification. The Bull, the giant whose unyielding will had helped inspire victories for the Italian revolutionaries at Vese and Como and the hill of Calatifimi. Now he was the Old Bull. What has age done to you, old man?

Enzo himself had grown up on the Old Bull's war stories. The adventures of his father as a *Garibaldino* were now hewn to the fibers of Enzo's very being. His father's tales of courage and sacrifice in the name of God and country pervaded Enzo's psyche, sometimes past the point of general restlessness. The fact that Enzo had survived thirty one years was not a testament to a cautious nature but rather an indication of the relative peace in the region at the time. Men of his passionate persuasion could usually be found at the bloody front lines of battle. But for all the patriotism and the swollen revolutionary pride, Enzo was a happy soul, quick with a grin and well loved by his men at the docks. All of Genoa, in fact, knew the handsome head of the longshoremen with the famous surname. Enzo had worked at the docks at the Port of Genoa unloading cargo since he was a boy, and he rose quickly as a natural leader and a man of impressive strength. He was an upright six foot with an extra twenty pounds of dockhand muscle that stretched over his neck and shoulders.

"Enzo!" A woman's booming voice came from behind him and snapped him out of this reflection. "Three days since I've seen you at my table. I worry. I worry about you, Enzo, you scoundrel." Greta Nonna, the Ferrando family housekeeper was studying Enzo with her hawkish eye. Her resonant voice played in direct opposition to her small, whip-like figure but not in opposition to her domestic authority at Casa Ferrando. She was only a decade junior to the Old Bull but still moved with a raw energy that she used to provide a maternal embrace to Casa Ferrando and fill a void left twelve years prior. Before her interrogation of Enzo could continue, Lucca and the Old Bull entered the kitchen through the garden door.

"We eat." Greta Nonna decreed.

The four sat down at Greta Nonna's table and ate. Lucca was not a talkative boy but did not even look up from his plate as his mind continued to contemplate his grandfather's story. He quickly excused himself and went to bed.

Shortly after, Greta Nonna retired to her quarters, and it was Enzo and the Old Bull who now sat silently at the table.

The stillness of the thick Ligurian night hung there above the table as each waited for the other to speak.

The Old Bull's unseeing eyes stared over Enzo's shoulder. The eyes were deep set under wild white eyebrows. The Old Bull had many of the same features as Enzo but without the light that happiness brings. Death and violence had snuffed out his inner child. He did not joke. And now he waited for his son to come forward with his admission.

Enzo shook his head, inhaled through flared nostrils, and began slowly. "It is obvious that you have been told. I can only assume it is our old friend the merchant Ligoria who has informed you." Enzo looked up at his father to see if this was true, but the Old Bull revealed nothing, so he continued.

"We received word that a munitions ship, billed as a merchant vessel, had come into port carrying twelve canon and thirty score rifles. The cargo belonged to Agostino Depretis's *Transformismo* thugs. It is widely known that our liberal friends, the last true bastion of *Garibaldismo*, are gaining traction inland of Genoa, and we suspected the munitions would be used to forcefully put down what should be free speech."

"What did you do with the guns?"

"I sank them," Enzo said with a touch of pride.

The Old Bull spoke plainly and without drama. "I am concerned for you, and I am concerned for Lucca. They will come to get what was taken from them. Sure as the tide, they'll come. Lucca has already lost a mother."

"They don't know who took their guns."

"A Ferrando with the keys to the docks is a good place to start. Do you see what have you done?"

"I have acted as my conscience—"

"A prank! And an insult to a powerful enemy. It does not further the cause. You and your rebel caprices. You have wandered into politics that you know nothing about. Depretis will take vengeance on our house." The Old Bull leaned forward in his chair as he hissed this to Enzo, bringing his face closer to Enzo and portraying anger for the first time in the conversation. The Old Bull's eyes widened as he settled back into his chair and said quietly but firmly, "You may have deprived Lucca of a normal life".

"Normal like my life?" Enzo, recovering from his shame, felt his own blood starting to heat as his mind reeled with his father's hypocrisy.

The Old Bull's eyes looked sadly quizzical as if Enzo did not understand. "Lucca is different than us, son. He is a good, caring boy. He has a sharp mind, and it will hunger for an education. Greta Nonna tells me he is a fine artist. She has found him in the Stagiliea cemetery sketching statues of the grievous angels. He is not meant for the docks, and he is not meant for some desperate battlefield where he is told to go kill other boys."

Enzo knew this to be true and felt a tightness in his throat as he thought of Lucca. The boy was gifted. He was not the rough and aggressive stock of soldiers and laborers. Lucca could swim with the best of the Genoese boys but would not climb the slippery rock walls and dive from dizzying heights like his peers. Or Enzo in his time. The shame returned to Enzo and chin was pulled to chest.

After a long while, the Old Bull spoke. "Tomorrow you will take Lucca to the merchant Ligoria. Lucca will take a position in Ligoria's company as a deckhand aboard the *Albatro* under Capitano Bartolo, which sets sail midmorning. Lucca will work for Ligoria under a false name until his eighteenth birthday and then will start his formal education with the help of Ligoria and the rest of my modest estate. As for you, you are bound for Eritrea. Do you know it?"

"Yes," a stupefied Enzo said quietly.

Without paying any mind to Enzo's response, the Old Bull continued. "Eritrea is Africa. On the coast of the Red Sea. You'll take a commission with the Italian army under Colonel Cristofori, and my name will protect you there. The orders are in, and anything short of you sailing for the dark continent will be desertion. You can help our good King Umberto with his delusions of Italian colonialism." He spat as he said these last words.

The Old Bull lurched up from his chair and felt his way to the doorway. Turning, he said to Enzo, "Gather Lucca at dawn and do this thing that you may be restored as a good father."

3

R ed pillars of smoke. Erupting into the sky like a metronomic geyser set to the beat of Lucca's own heart.

Lucca lurched up in bed and instantly awoke from his nightmare, wild-eyed and full of dread. His father was there and was now trying to comfort him. Lucca calmed himself and realized his father had spent the night in a rocking chair next to his bed.

"Bad dream?" Enzo asked. They were both waiting for their eyes to adjust to the darkness, searching for the other's features.

Lucca nodded.

"Was it like the fever dreams you had when you were younger?"

Lucca shook his head. "No. Those were scary because they did not feel like reality. This was terrible because it felt so real."

"It was just a dream, Lucca. It is almost dawn now, and we must get moving. We're heading to the docks, and I will explain more when we get there."

Lucca dressed by candlelight and packed a little bag as his

father had instructed. He sensed this was no ordinary day ahead of him, and his excitement started to build.

Lucca took a tacit cue from his father to remain silent until they were out of the house, but as they were entering the city, he could no longer help himself and started peppering his father with questions.

"Why do we leave for the docks before the sun? Why don't we take the main road, which is faster? Why are we being quiet and walking so fast?" Each question was met with a hiss for silence as Enzo navigated them through the winding alleys of Genoa to the back gate of the docks. It was not until they reached the low-ceilinged storehouse under the customs office that Enzo felt safe enough to speak.

Enzo turned his hunch into a crouch and started to explain how Lucca's life would change drastically over the next few hours. Lucca nodded dutifully and had only one question after Enzo concluded.

"When will I see you and Grandpa and Greta Nonna again?"

"You will see Grandpa and Greta Nonna whenever the *Albatro* berths in Genoa. It could be in six months, maybe a year, but not longer."

"And you?"

"You will see me again, Lucca, but I don't know when exactly. I will write to you, and you can write to me. I will give Captain Bartolo information for correspondence with my post, and you can send a letter every time you come into port." Lucca nodded, and Enzo pulled him in for an embrace.

Lucca concentrated on trying to remember this moment in his father's arms. He was told that his mother got to hold him before she died, but he could not remember that moment. Despite countless nights trying to call up her image from his deepest memories, he could not see her. He would remember this moment, though. This moment was his. This storehouse, damp and cramped, mildew and burlap, puddles lapping up drips donated from the creaky ceiling. He pulled it all in. His father's coarse beard against his cheek. The cold light of the morning tracing the storehouse door frame. He decided to memorialize this moment in his sketchbook before the memory faded.

Enzo released the boy and indicated it was time to see the merchant Ligoria. Enzo turned quickly, but Lucca noticed his eyes were wet.

4

The city of Genoa was only starting to stir, but Enzo was sure he would find the merchant Ligoria at the eponymous trading company's headquarters. It took only one soft knock on the door of Ligoria Trading Company for it to swing open, revealing Ligoria himself who beckoned them in quickly.

They followed Ligoria wordlessly across the marble-floored vestibule through a decorated hallway toward Ligoria's office at the back of the building. Ligoria was thin and tall. Age had bent his back but not his good nature, and he had a pair of blue-grey eyes that could crinkle and deploy a wry sense of humor. These same eyes could also set on you and make you believe you and he were alone amid a crowded room. Enzo knew Ligoria to be among the best of men. As an honest businessman and philanthropist, Ligoria was not only respected across the Mediterranean, he was loved.

They crossed the threshold into Ligoria's office, which was a natural extension of the man. Solid oak furnishings, sturdy but not extravagant, strewn with maps of far-off lands, exotic bills of lading, and contracts with kings and governments. Ligoria motioned for Enzo and Lucca to be seated in the two chairs in front of the desk as he settled behind it, donned a pair of spectacles, and sorted through a stack of documents.

Standing off to the side of the desk was a squat, bald man standing with feet spread wide and his hands clasped behind his back in a fashion that betrayed his naval pedigree. Scored onto his brow was an eternal frown that betrayed little of what was going on behind it. Enzo recognized this man as Bartolo, the captain of the *Albatro*.

Ligoria looked up quickly as if he had committed a faux pas "I'm sorry, have you met the good Capitano Bartolo?"

"I believe I have." Enzo nodded politely at Bartolo. Lucca glanced at the man furtively.

After a time, Ligoria removed the spectacles and gave a kindly look to Enzo and then to Lucca. "How old are you Lucca?" Ligoria asked softly.

"Twelve, Signore."

"A good age." Ligoria nodded sagely. "I was your age when I started working for my uncle aboard a packet ship. Some of my fondest memories. It was how I learned to love the sea. And I learned many more things too. Your grandfather Antoni tells me you do fine work with pencil and paper. Take a look at this. Tell me what you think."

Ligoria handed Lucca a small scroll and indicated that Lucca should open it up. Lucca carefully unfurled what was an ornate map of the Adriatic Sea and the surrounding territories. The map was bordered with inlaid gold paisley patterns. The shading on the Italian Alps in the northwest drew the mountains up from the surface to add another dimension to the scene. An intricate compass rose firing arrows in each cardinal direction set on the bottom left balanced a beautiful cursive legend on the opposite side. Lucca's finger traced trade routes arching from Venice to Bari to Dubrovnik to Athens.

"We are in need of good cartographers, navigators, and pilots, Lucca." Ligoria was smiling as he saw how intently Lucca focused on the map.

Ligoria shifted his gaze to Enzo. "Bartolo is the best captain in our fleet. Your boy will be well protected in his charge and can receive no better training. In fact, my own daughter, who is but a year ahead of Lucca here, is working as a deckhand on the *Albatro* under Bartolo."

Enzo had been nodding solemnly but paused upon mention of Ligoria's daughter. "Did you say your daughter, Signore?"

"Yes, I did Enzo. The future of my house and the light of my life."

This was curious, Enzo thought. He was sure that Ligoria had an elder son. He was also relieved that Ligoria was entrusting his own daughter to the crew of the *Albatro*. Bartolo seemed larger the next time Enzo glanced his way.

"The *Albatro* sets sail on the tide. I have here Lucca's employment contract and a ticket for your passage to Eritrea. You'll be sailing with the *Castelfidardo* under Capitano Al-Dapo."

At the mention of Al-Dapo, Enzo gritted his teeth.

Ligoria saw Enzo's jaw clench and thought Genoa's head longshoreman was darkly considering his own uncertain future. Ligoria spoke to Enzo but suspected his words would find themselves of more use to the boy. "Enzo, I have known you all my life as a man of energy and competence. You will succeed in rough environments where other strong men will fail. It is more than a name that has been passed to you. And about that Ferrando name ... you have done nothing to sully it. All courageous acts call for sacrifice. I think in some way, my old friend Antoni is proud."

5

Sure as the tide, they came.

The sun was high in the sky when four horsemen rode up on Casa Ferrando. The Old Bull was seated on the veranda. Laid across the blind man's lap was an Austrian M1849 long rifle. The beechwood stock of the old weapon had been brought to a polish that morning.

"We come to speak with Enzo Ferrando. He is not at the docks. We are told we can find him here."

The Old Bull's chair was situated in the shade of the veranda, but he stood now, and as he walked toward the veranda's edge, the sun revealed to the horseman an impressive sight. The Old Bull had drawn himself up to his full height, clothed in the scarlet cashmere blouse of the *Risorgimento*, his wild white hair adding a terrible intensity to his grizzled bearing.

Seeing the long rifle, the horsemen drew pistols. One of the men whispered to another that he knew Antoni Ferrando to be blind.

"Who are the armed visitors who wish to speak to my son?" the Old Bull asked without drama. He could tell from the efficient sound of steel sliding from leather holster that these men were experienced.

One of the four horsemen spoke. "I am Corrado Depretis. I have an uncle you may have heard of. My compatriots are private citizens, as I am, undertaking an investigation of our stolen cargo."

"You speak of a crime. Where then is the magistrate? Where then is the Polizia di Stato?"

Corrado was growing frustrated, and he had not expected an armed old man to obstruct him. "This is not a public matter, Signore. This is a private matter. But we do seek answers to our questions, and we seek justice. We are aware of your reputation, and I do not wish an old man harm. Give us what we need, and maybe House Ferrando survives by your grandchild."

"You say you are Depretis?" the Old Bull boomed.

"So your ears still work," Corrado snapped.

"I know Depretis. I know your uncle. I've heard him speak. He speaks as if he speaks for Italy. He recollects the triumphs of the unification for all to hear. How he pulled Italy out from the hold of the Bourbons. But he was not there."

Corrado's mouth started to form a snarl, but it was unease that gripped his three mounted compatriots. Their horses shifted anxiously beneath them.

"I know he was not there because I did not see him to my left or my right when I fixed my bayonet and ran uphill at Calatafimi. We liberated Sicily that day, and when it was time to dine, it was not Depretis that sat at Garibaldi's right." Antoni Ferrando said this as his unseeing eyes stared eerily over the heads of the horsemen.

The horsemen started to look to their leader and at each other. The realization that they were on the doorstep of a man melded with history was starting to erode their resolve. Even their horses were sensing their disquiet, and they started to bray.

"Corrado, let us leave this man," one of them whispered. "Enzo is not here."

But Corrado's blood was up. "We have no dispute with you old man." Corrado's voice got higher and more frantic, and cords surged from his neck. "We come for your mongrel dog son. He has taken from us. I will enter this house."

The blind man still had very sharp hearing, and he trained his focus on the frantic voice and slowed his breath. The Old Bull seemed to nod meditatively and then lifted his long rifle in one fluid motion, discharging the weapon at the top of its upward arch. His aim was true, and his bullet found the left eye of Corrado Depretis, viciously snapping the man's head back before the lifeless body slumped back in the saddle.

The horses reared up immediately, but it took three full seconds for realization of what just happened to register with the three men. When realization came, they emptied their rounds into the Old Bull before reigning up and fleeing.

6

Four *days hence.* Captain Geraldo Al-Dapo took a deep breath of the Red Sea air. He was not looking forward to his task. He was a short man, and he was not a young man. But this was his ship, and he had his orders.

Al-Dapo walked purposely from the helm of the *Castelfidardo* toward the bow, along the way nodding to several large deckhands to follow him. The ship was an old ironclad christened in the wars of Italian independence, two hundred and sixty feet long, and fifty feet at her broadest beam. When he got to the bow, he carefully cleared his throat and announced to the sleeping man that he had news.

Enzo, who was lounging peacefully, stirred and tilted his hat from his face. "What news 'Dapo?"

Al-Dapo cleared his throat again. "We received news about your father when we berthed in Suez yesterday."

Enzo yawned. "It was news yesterday, it's history today. Speak, man, what is it?" Captain Al-Dapo was an old friend of Antoni Ferrando, but Enzo never cared for him. He was too formal and stuffy and too prone to make long, winding soliloquies that, when combined with his paunch and quivering chin, turned him into a caricature of the aging *Risorgimento* guard. Enzo longed to get to Eritrea and off this ship so he could free himself of the old fool's gab.

"Your father is dead," said Al-Dapo. Enzo moved slowly from supine to seated. All the fog of his afternoon nap was gone, and he was now focused on Al-Dapo.

Al-Dapo continued. "He was killed. Gunned down on his veranda by four Depretis men on horseback. *Transformismo* mongrels."

Enzo slowly shifted his gaze to some far off spot on the Red Sea horizon.

Al-Dapo was watching Enzo carefully, as might a tamer watch his lion. "He killed one of the Depretis men. They say it was a nephew of Depretis himself. Your family maid found him an hour past the skirmish. He was still taking labored breaths. He did not want to be moved. She comforted him, and it is said he comforted her before his passing on."

"Did he say anything?"

"Not a word, Enzo. He died well. He was the best man I've known in my wayward life, and I have known many good men. He was a true son of Italia, a man of the *Risorgimento*. In life he helped Garibaldi unify our great nation. Now in death he has helped secure the liberal future of Italy. The *Transformismo* party is reeling, and Depretis may be deposed before the week is out! Think of it—a national hero gunned down in his own house by Depretis's own hand. Our friend Francesco Crispi and his party are already moving to take advantage. Your father, the great oxen, has fallen, but we and others will pick up the yoke and till this—"

"—And the three men?" Enzo interrupted.

"Fled. They have gone deep into hiding. We have names, but that will not be of much use currently. If it's vengeance on your mind, then you must let that thought simmer, Enzo, at least for the time being. These men will come up for air eventually, but it is not only you who want them brought to justice."

Enzo lurched to his feet. "Give us a bottle of whiskey, 'Dapo. And turn this boat. We sail for Genoa and for *vendetta*."

"Enzo ... my ship is bound for Eritrea. Firstly, this vessel carries supplies needed by the Italian garrison in Eritrea. Secondly, you have been given your army commission via conscription. If you do not report to Colonel Cristofori, you are a deserter and you will be hanged, no matter your surname." The little man tried to assume his full height as he said this.

Enzo focused a murderous gaze on Al-Dapo. "Sir. Do you stand between me and my father's killers?"

Al-Dapo gulped audibly and said, "Your father himself has given me orders, Enzo. He suspected that an event like this might occur and a conversation like this might transpire. He has instructed me to bring you to Eritrea and deliver you to Colonel Cristofori ... even if that means in irons. His exact words."

For the first time Enzo noticed the burly deckhands who had accompanied Al-Dapo to the bow.

Enzo grimaced, then threw his head back and barked with laughter. "Dead but still playing the marionette."

The crew of the *Castelfidardo* watched Enzo apprehensively. He leaned over the side and heaved. The crew all breathed a sigh of relief as if the release valve had been pulled and the situation's pressure had abated. But looking at Enzo they could tell from the man's facial contortions that his passion was not yet settling. Like a carnival wheel, emotions whirled through Enzo—grief, rage, shame, sorrow—and settled on ... rage. He clothed himself in the rage. It was easy, and it felt natural.

Enzo straightened up again and wiped his mouth with his sleeve. "Turn the damn boat, 'Dapo."

Al-Dapo took a full step back and cried, "Enzo, take care I do not hang you myself for mutiny."

Enzo dove for the bewildered Captain Al-Dapo and got his dock-hardened hands around the man's throat. He was immediately fell upon by the deckhands, who put him in a choke hold of their own. After a full minute, Al-Dapo was able to pull himself free of Enzo's grip and crawl desperately away from the surging mass of bodies struggling to restrain the man possessed.

Al-Dapo, still gasping for air, now understood the Old Bull's specific permission to use chains on his son as he heard the guttural howl coming from underneath the melee.

* * *

THREE HOURS later the sun had set, and Captain Al-Dapo and Enzo Ferrando were seated in the captain's quarters sharing a bottle of whiskey.

"I've never really liked you, 'Dapo," Enzo said as he stared at a spot on the cabin floor. Al-Dapo looked at him and smiled wryly as if he knew the true meaning of Enzo's words to be filled with nothing but love, respect, and an ancient bond only known to brothers in arms.

Enzo was holding his tumbler, carefully swirling the brown liquid around the glass. "And this liquor is shit ... and I am sorry for my earlier actions. Truly."

And he was.

Al-Dapo nodded his head solemnly. He then withdrew a thrice-folded envelope from his waistcoat and held it out to Enzo with formality. "Three names and suspected whereabouts."

Enzo reached out and made to take the paper, but Al-Dapo did not immediately let go. "I have your word that you will report to Colonel Cristofori on the morrow when we berth in Assab Bay?"

"You have my word," Enzo replied.

"And you will apologize to my man with the dislocated shoulder?"

"Yes. I will." Enzo narrowed his eyes at Al-Dapo and finally tugged the envelope free.

Al-Dapo seemed satisfied and relieved. "Goddamn crazy Ferrando."

Enzo scoffed. Maybe 'Dapo wasn't as bad as he remembered. He and Al-Dapo lifted their glasses again and again. He was not listening to Al-Dapo's toasts at all. His mind drifted to his father's final hours and to Lucca and to the realization that the boy never said goodbye to the old man. He hoped Bartolo was as good a man as Liguria claimed. He lifted his glass again and let the brown liquor burn his throat as it went down. He felt as if he were being tugged through life with an invisible lead that had him round the neck. Whoever controlled the lead was faster, and he could not match the pace. He would work like hell to catch up and produce slack in the line that he might stay put for a while, but inevitably the line would grow taught and jerk him forward, stumbling and tripping into strange places where the once familiar was turned foreign. This same feeling was strong when his wife died shortly after childbirth. He remembered being jerked back to reality when Greta Nonna snatched up the infant Lucca from his arms. She had come home to find Lucca wailing frightfully and Enzo staring into nothing, holding Lucca but unconscious of him. He did not cry when Anita left this world and left him alone. Even his father wept. He did not blame Lucca—how could a babe be anything but innocent?—but seeing Anita's features in his son's face never got easier for him. She was supposed to help him. She was not supposed to leave.

Al-Dapo was now snoring next to him. Enzo started to think about this Colonel Cristofori and what sort of man he was. Was he another harmless dinosaur like the snoring fool next to him, or would this Cristofori get in his way? He needed to deal with the men responsible for his father's death. He needed to get to them before someone else tried to avenge the Old Bull. He would not be surprised if Garibaldi himself, though sick and dying on the island of Caprera, would put out a bounty on these Depretis mongrels. Enzo found he was drunk enough to start speaking to the unconscious Al-Dapo.

"If we cannot avenge our own blood, then our line is doomed to cowardice. But now, if I pursue vengeance and shirk my responsibilities to the Italian army, I will be a deserter. Cowardice incarnate."

He slammed his hand onto the small wood table out of frustration. 'Dapo snored an octave higher but did not wake. Soon Enzo too drifted off to sleep.

7

T he *Castelfidardo* made the Bay of Assab the following day. Like all of the Eritrean coast, Assab would bake and sizzle in the unrelenting sun. As the crew made ready the longboats that would ferry them ashore, Enzo surveyed the place that would be his new home until he could figure a way out. The port of Assab looked well protected. It was nestled south of headlands that provided safe harbor against the tempests hurled down the northern Arabian Peninsula, and two looming rocky crags protected the army garrison from attacks coming from the interior.

Good, thought Enzo. Italy chose the entry point into this continent well, even if entering this continent was a brutal mistake.

Enzo could see most of the army garrison from the deck of the *Castelfidardo.* He strained his eyes to find a structure that looked like a headquarters building where he would find this Colonel Cristofori. Al-Dapo, still unsteady from the prior evening of drinking, had come up next to Enzo and was pointing out the Strait of Bab-El-Mandeb to the south, which opened generously to the Gulf of Aden, which politely presented the Arabian Sea, which warmly introduced the treasures of the Indias. The Indias reminded Al-Dapo of a half-Hindu, half-Portuguese girl he had met in Goa, and he proceeded to describe her smell to Enzo in great detail.

Al-Dapo's men were readying the longboats for the row to shore. Al-Dapo had now started talking about a witch doctor he had met in Africa without taking a breath.

"—and then this witch doctor proceeds to read me my fortune. He tells me I must not eat yams for seven days. Seven days? I said, 'Make it fourteen for all I care!'"

Al-Dapo's ardent work as interlocutor continued to increase Enzo's eagerness to debark from the *Castelfidardo* until Enzo had enough and decided to jump over the rail and onto the first longboat going ashore, surprising the crew that was making her ready. Enzo had been playing out his upcoming encounter with Colonel Cristofori over and over in his head, and he was now anxious to meet the man. He pictured an overfed, overzealous sabre rattler who would be eager to have a Ferrando at his side just as Garibaldi had. Let him believe I'm his white knight, Enzo thought. Let him believe I can help him make a colonial power out of Italy. Let him believe I can give him Africa. He could play to the man's ambitions and soon get permission to take leave and sail for home.

By the time the hull of the longboat was scraping the Eritrean sand, Enzo had already jumped from the boat and was making his way up the beach with a powerful stride. Al-Dapo was scurrying after him but could not match his pace. The garrison headquarters building was easy enough to pick out, a simple yet functional construction that flew the flag of Italy and the flag of the Galliano Battalion.

He took the three steps that led to the building's entrance in a single bound and thrust open the door. He immediately found himself in the middle of a somber room, face to face with two men standing stiffly in pressed white uniforms and jet black boots brought to a shine. The taller of the two men had an aquiline nose separating hawkish eyes that immediately fixed on Enzo. They had a map splayed out in front of them on a square table and were clearly in the midst of a serious conversation until Enzo's interruption. Enzo immediately regretted barging in without knocking or presenting himself. He was dressed as a sailor, desperately out of place.

Enzo cleared his throat to speak, but before he could say a word, the door swung open again, almost knocking Enzo over as Al-Dapo lurched inside, breathing heavily. The hawkish man looked to Captain Al-Dapo and immediately made the connection.

"You must be Enzo Ferrando," he said, turning back to Enzo.

"Yes I am," said Enzo, awkwardly adding "Sir" a moment after he realized he was probably addressing the colonel. The whole entrance had thrown him off, and now he felt foolish in front of these men with the jet black boots.

"I am Colonel Cristofori. We use rank and surname here and adhere to proper military decorum." He glanced at the red-faced Al-Dapo, still sucking wind, and the implication was clear. He then motioned to the dour man next to him, "This is my aide-de-camp, Major Betruscio."

Betruscio did not so much as nod.

"Capitano Al-Dapo," Cristofori said and turned once again to the small man.

"Sir," Al-Dapo said loudly.

"Find Sergeant Tencreto. He will instruct your crew where to unload and store the munitions and fortification materials."

Al-Dapo nodded and turned to leave, trying to catch Enzo's

attention for a good luck wink, but Enzo was preoccupied thinking about how he could recover some face.

The colonel then opened a drawer in a desk behind him and brought out a small stack of documents. He started to turn through them, then looked up suddenly.

"I am sorry to hear about your father. I am sure there will be a parade for him in Genoa."

Enzo nodded slightly, and Cristofori continued to sort his papers until he found what he was looking for. This colonel was not resembling the foppish idealist Enzo had hoped for.

"Here is your direct commission as a captain in the Galliano Battalion. As captain you will have under your charge a company of eighty-two men. Upon signing this document, you will be put in command of Fifth Company." Enzo thought he saw the aide-de-camp try to contain a smirk, but then Cristofori produced a pen with flourish and held it out to Enzo, who signed his name.

Cristofori continued. "Direct commissions to captain are rare, and normally this post is reserved for men with military education and training. Assigning you this responsibility was not my idea, and I profess that putting eighty-two souls in the hands of a dockworker seems to me dangerous and irresponsible. But this commission came down from the top, and I am a man that follows orders. Your father had powerful friends. It is not for me to debate my superiors on the decision to commission you as an officer in my battalion, but it is my right and my obligation to make sure your entitlement stops there."

Enzo bristled but tried to remain calm. "I did not ask for this, Sir."

"But yet here you are, and your name is now signed in blood." Cristofori was glaring at Enzo, lip curled, and Enzo averted his gaze toward the floor.

This act of submission seemed to calm Cristofori slightly,

and he said in a more measured tone, "You will find Sergeant Tassoni outside, and he will take you to your men and tour you around the garrison. But before you go, tell me how much you know about our little war in this nasty corner of uncivilization. Do you know who the enemy is, Captain Ferrando?"

Enzo blinked at the question. "The savages that have been raiding our settlements. The natives, sir."

"I'm afraid the correct answer is more subtle than that. We fight the Ethiopians, if you want to be simple about it, but nothing is simple here." Cristofori's tone made Enzo feel as though he were back in the schoolhouse.

Cristofori continued. "The Ethiopians may look primitive in their tribal garb, but their methods of war are advanced, and like us they carry rifles and utilize horse and cannon. At the present we are allied with the Askari tribe. You might call the Askaris native Eritreans. Of course, politics must be considered, and allegiances are subject to change." Cristofori then abruptly looked as his timepiece as if he'd been spending too much time with Enzo already.

"You are dismissed, Captain Ferrando."

Enzo did not even consider pleading his case for a leave of absence. This man Cristofori was going to be a problem. Enzo turned and walked outside, squinting in the sunlight. Al-Dapo was there waiting for him.

"How did it go, Enzo?" Al-Dapo asked cheerfully.

"Not well, 'Dapo," Enzo said flatly.

"Oh come now, Enzo, we are both *Capitanos* now, eh? I have a gift for you that should cheer you up." Al-Dapo produced a large leather holster with a belt wrapped around it. He gave it to Enzo, and Enzo was surprised at the weight of it. Enzo unwrapped the belt and withdrew the largest revolver he had ever seen.

"Colt Dragoon. For your adventures on the Dark Continent.

The Americans used that steel with some success over their own savages. I am glad I did not give it to you back there on the ship." He winked and rocked back on his heels. He wasn't sure Enzo got his reference to their recent dispute, so he made a choking motion with his hands, chuckling all the while.

"Thank you, 'Dapo" Enzo said, smiling. He realized he was looking at the only friend he had on this entire continent.

Al-Dapo was puffed up with pride, sensing Enzo's affection. "I took it off an American named Tatum with no teeth—"

"Captain Ferrando!" Al-Dapo was interrupted, and both men turned to see a skinny youth running toward them. The youth did not look a day over eighteen or an inch under six and a half feet. His gangly limbs and loose joints produced an effect on his stride that reminded Enzo of a newly birthed draft animal taking its first steps in the world. "I'm Sergeant Tassoni, Sir. Welcome to Assab, Sir."

The young sergeant gave a salute that appeared exaggerated due to his lanky assembly. Enzo looked at him and nodded.

"Now you say *at ease*," Al-Dapo informed him.

Enzo put him at ease and turned back to Al-Dapo, and the two men bade each other farewell.

"Now then, sergeant, help me get the lay of the land," said Enzo.

8

The Italian army garrison at Assab sat on 160 acres that stretched clumsily along the coast. The garrison's innards were hemmed in by a stockade of wooden stakes reinforced with iron stakes on its coastal flank and stonewall on its western flank. The western wall was high enough, but the parapets were low such that a man on guard duty atop the wall would have to crouch so as not to reveal his entire upper torso to enemy fire. No trenches had been dug, but the area immediately west of the wall was all rocky crag, which yielded nothing but ill footing and low cover for would-be invaders. Beyond the rocky crag was the start of the sandy hillocks of the desert interior where the heat created wavy distortions that could play tricks on the sun-addled mind.

There were ten structures that freckled the bird's view of the garrison: the headquarters (which doubled as the Colonel's quarters), the officer's mess, the artillery shed, the cavalry stables, the five barracks (one for each company of Galliano Battalion), and the latrine. The structures were built hurriedly from imperfect lumber by imperfect craftsmen, and through the cracks and imperfections crept the fine sand and dust of the Eritrean coast. The accumulation of sand was so rapid that the buildings had to be swept daily, and some men preferred to sleep with bandanas to thwart the uncomfortable morning ritual of purging their mouths and nasal passages of dust.

The 540 men of Galliano Battalion called the garrison many things but never called it home. When it was not oppression by dust, it could be oppression by fog. Even the fog was dry and hit the lungs more like smoke than vapor, and it rolled in like a sinister mist, sometimes pervading the garrison for days on end. But most days the garrison was just assailed with the unrelenting heat and oppressive sun of the low latitudes.

This day was like most days: oppression by dry heat. Enzo Ferrando and Sergeant Tassoni walked the walls and then trudged through the garrison toward the barracks.

"The men of Fifth Company are excited to meet you, Sir," Tassoni said and smiled encouragingly. "The Fifth has been without a captain for some time."

"What happened to the last one?" Enzo asked.

"He died, Sir," Tassoni replied without much emotion.

"In combat?"

"No, Sir. Dysentery. The Fifth Company does not see much combat. Our duty is generally focused on construction and maintenance of garrison defenses. We also tend the horses." Tassoni said this and cast his eyes downward under the glare of Enzo.

"Who does the fighting?" Enzo stopped walking and forced Tassoni to stop with him, compelling the boy to give his full attention to what was turning into an uncomfortable conversation.

"The raids are conducted by The First and Second. They are cavalry companies, and they have some Bashi-bazouks as well."

"Goddamn it all." Enzo turned and spat. "I'm in charge of a children's crusade of stable boys sentenced to dig ditches."

Enzo closed his eyes and shook his head. When he opened them moments later, Tassoni was still standing stock still, red faced and looking at this feet. Enzo Ferrando regretted showing his frustration in front of the boy. He took the boy by the arm and asked him to lead on.

"What is a Bashi-bazouk?" Enzo asked Tassoni.

"What?" Tassoni looked at him in confusion.

"What is a Bashi-bazouk? You said First and Second Companies had Bashi-bazouks."

"Oh, they are mercenaries, Sir." Sensing Enzo's confusion, Tassoni continued. "They are professional soldiers for hire and quite formidable in battle. I believe they come from the lands of the Turks. Very mean and seem to be devoid of the honor codes possessed by Western militaries. They are on our side, but I try to steer clear of them."

When the two reached Fifth Company barracks, Enzo was immediately hit with a stench that was almost suffocating. It was not long before he discovered the root cause: the latrine was situated not fifteen feet behind the Fifth Company barracks.

Each company's barracks had a canopy overhang where the men would try to escape the sun during downtime. About twenty of the eighty-two men of Fifth Company were stretched out under the canopy in a display of inactivity that could be likened to old, leathery crocodiles sunning on the banks of a meandering river.

As Enzo and Tassoni walked up to the canopy, Tassoni cleared his throat and announced Enzo's presence. The men, as if awakening from a long slumber, slowly and silently stood up and came to attention. They were a sorry bunch. To Enzo they looked lifeless and hopeless like dogs who have had their bark beaten out of them. Some were young and some were old. None looked particularly soldierly.

The score of men looked expectantly at their new captain, and then Enzo remembered. "At ease," he said, even though they looked well enough at ease already.

An awkward silence was followed by the younger men shuffling about to busy themselves with this or that. The older men continued to stare at Enzo furtively even as they made to resume their positions of wretched repose. Though these older men were not the generation of Antoni Ferrando, they had doubtless heard the tales of the Old Bull Ferrando. Enzo recognized this and realized he was not cutting a fine form in his sailor's garb while sweating like a plow animal, but he did not much care at the present moment.

Enzo sighed and turned to Tassoni. "Where can I find food and drink? By food and drink I mean a bottle of something brown."

9

The following months were a prosaic procession for Enzo Ferrando, and even as territorial tensions increased with the Ethiopian and Eritrean tribes, he continued to live in an anticlimax where the very thing that kept him going was the momentum of repetition.

Every morning he would wake with the dawn and haul himself miserably out of bed. He would stand in the same spot where his feet first touched the ground for a long minute while he waited for the abuses of the prior night to stop pounding in his head. He would then rouse his men with the handle of a shovel against the floorboards of the barracks, and Fifth Company would gather their tools and head to the western wall to resume the digging of the trench.

It was not long before rituals and traditions started to form around Enzo Ferrando. At the beginning of the day, the eighty-two men of Fifth Company, spade or pickaxe in hand, would stand silently and wait for their captain to strike the earth with his shovel. Sometimes Enzo would stare down at a spot on the rocky floor for a full five minutes. No one knew what the captain was thinking about during these times of silent contemplation before the day's toil began, but most of them wondered, and there were rumors aplenty about their dark-featured leader. Then their leader would infallibly strike rock with steel and begin his benediction. The men would follow suit, and the day of hard labor would begin.

Enzo Ferrando would begin his toil and not yield to fatigue until the day was done. The men would take breaks throughout the day, to drink coffee, to eat, to get out of the sun. But Enzo would continue striking rock with steel. His inhuman capacity for work was first interpreted as a childish fury, a tantrum that would soon burn down. Then they thought he was trying to prove superiority, maybe to prove that he deserved his rank, maybe to rail against a reputation tainted by entitlement. They thought he would tire of this high mindedness and settle into a more common routine. But as the days and weeks rolled on and his dogged labor did not relent, it became clear that it was something else driving the man to pour his soul into that damned trench every day. They could not figure what drove him, so they gave up and figured him for a different breed.

When the angry sun would start to nestle into the hills far out on the horizon, the men of Fifth Company would traipse wearily back into the garrison for supper. Enzo would leave them at the barracks and head to the artillery shed where he had constructed his own canopy. Back aching with the labor of the day, he would seat himself in the lee of the shed, and he would drink. He would grit his teeth and pour a glass and think of the sonsofbitches who had killed his father and pour a glass and rage internally and pour a glass. He would have one or two of the men from Fifth Company sit with him as he drank so he would not be seen drinking alone. Mostly it was the older guard who would sit by him. Sometimes he would have a set of twin brothers join him. The twins were Askari warriors, natives of Eritrea, sons of a tribal leader, and acting guides of the First and Second Company raiding teams. These twins did not speak a lick of Italian, one of their redeeming qualities in Enzo's eyes. He would never ask Tassoni to join him. Enzo did not want the boy to see him wallow in his self-loathing.

Despite the copious amounts of liquor consumed, not much talking would get done in the lee of the artillery shed. His honored guests might talk of home or the weather or of the damned Ethiopians, but Enzo was alone in his head, stewing and drinking. He would, in lighter moments, constantly amuse himself by flicking the ashes of his cigar behind him at the artillery shed and imagining the stored munitions igniting and engulfing half the garrison in a lovely fireball. His last thought of the day would always wander to the names written down in Al-Dapo's thrice-folded envelope, the identities of his father's killers and the focus of his hate. But night after liquor-soaked night he would never bring himself to open the envelope.

So Enzo Ferrando found himself in a Promethean cycle. Just as the god Prometheus, bound and tethered to a rocky cliff, would perpetually regrow his liver only to have it torn out by vultures, Enzo Ferrando would cleanse himself daily with honest labor only to wade back into the shallows of self-abuse.

Despite the painful stasis of Enzo Ferrando himself, a careful observer could see changes occurring at the Galliano garrison since the man's arrival. The changes were minor, but like cracks in the dike, they held promise for something more ferocious. The fervor of Enzo's daily toil and the fact that he seemed to be getting stronger and more fervent by the day was unusual. More unusual, however, was the fact that a commissioned officer was dirtying his uniform and lowering himself to manual labor usually reserved for the enlisted man.

The first small changes could be seen in the men of Fifth Company. They were easier to rouse in the morning and quicker to the western wall. When Enzo's inaugural shovel thrust would pierce that raw earth, they would take up his example without goading, and even the old guard would dig their shovels in a little deeper. Even Enzo, in his constant state of rabid industry, noticed his men were taking fewer breaks and the trench was progressing at a dizzying pace. He started to notice the individual men more, and what started with nods of encouragement grew to compliments, which the men relished in. He taught them songs that he had sung when he was back working on the Genoese docks, and the cadence of Fifth Company's shovel strikes formed the coordinated chugging sounds germane to a steam engine. The men started to stand up straighter.

They finished the trench in half the expected time, and Enzo decided the western wall needed reinforcement. They gathered stone and mixed mortar and added two feet on the top of the wall so men standing on the palisade would not have to crouch for cover. They started at the southern end of the wall and worked their way north. By the time they finished, the craftsmanship of the reinforcement had improved so much that Enzo decided to redo the southern part of the wall. Then they started on the coastal side. Slowly, the garrison was turning into a fort.

One morning, after stepping out of the barracks and getting hit again with the indomitable stench wafting from the latrine, Enzo gathered Fifth Company, and over the course of a foggy morning demolished and rebuilt the latrine one hundred yards away from the Fifth Company barracks.

10

Lieutenant Adolpho Tencreto of First Company was the battalion supply warden. All provisioning for the Italian Army at Assab Bay lay under his charge. His ledgers accounted for all orders of goods moving through the camp, legitimate and illegitimate. He was born the sixth son to a noble Sicilian family with an ignoble history. He had a face more reminiscent of a Slav than an Italian, with oversized, apathetic eyes drooping down into dark bags and impudent lips that could curl into a sneer practiced for generations.

Wherever possible, supply wardens in the Italian Army were appointed from noble stock because members of the aristocracy were thought less inclined to use their official capacity for personal enrichment. This was true in Adolpho Tencreto's case. He cared little for wealth accumulation, but he did like his sport, which had been known to foster a different type of corruption.

News of the new captain of Fifth Company and his quest to work himself to death had spread thoroughly through the garrison until Adolpho Tencreto's curiosity was piqued and he decided he would go meet this man and see if the rumors deserved credence. He was also curious about what opportunities this man with the famous name could present.

Despite the heat, he wore a long, black duster that twisted in the wind behind him like a cape as he walked to Fifth Company's new worksite located on the south side of the outer wall where they had established the beginnings of a moat. He spied the man named Enzo Ferrando quite easily. Indeed, no mistake could be made as to the identity of the new Fifth Company captain. Enzo Ferrando was waist-deep in the beginnings of the new moat, shirtless and hacking at rocky earth with a pickaxe swung so proficiently it looked like a natural extension of his own body.

Adolpho Tencreto crouched ten feet from Enzo, lurking in his blind spot and observing the man with an intense curiosity. Sergeant Tassoni, working with a shovel abreast of Enzo, noticed the crouching man and called to Enzo, "Signore, it looks like you have a visitor."

Enzo ceased his swinging, turned, and wiped his brow. He looked at Tencreto blankly as if coming out of a trance. Enzo was somewhat unnerved as it was apparent the man had been crouching there for some time. The two men stared at each other for a long moment, Tencreto with a slight smile on his face, Enzo with a look of impatience.

Tencreto smiled wider and said, "Buon giorno, Enzo Ferrando. My name is Lieutenant Adolpho Tencreto, supply warden of Galliano Battalion, at your service."

"Buon giorno," Enzo returned, squinting at the crouching man. "What can I do for you, Signore?"

"Not a thing, Signore," Tencreto replied, grinning. "I just wanted to come meet the one they are calling the Italian Paul Bunyan." Tencreto noticed the reference was lost on both Enzo and the young sergeant, and he could already sense their impatience.

"Say, Signore Ferrando." Tencreto shifted his weight from one side of his crouch to the other. "Maybe there is something you can do for the men of Galliano Battalion in the spirit of national pride. You seem like a man who knows something of king and country even though you are new to us."

Enzo remained expressionless and motionless apart from his breathing, which was still settling from his labor.

Tencreto smiled wide. "You see, we have a game we play here called La Bacchetta. It's a contest really—good for morale, good for a laugh. Lets the boys get a wager in. The trouble is, that damned Albanian mercenary Zagranos Pasha has come along and hasn't been bested in three months. We can't let a Bashi-bazouk scourge reign supreme over us Italians in our own game, in our own army. You see, it is a matter of national pride."

"You, sir, look like you would be up to the challenge," concluded Tencreto, nodding at Enzo whose powerful upper torso was now the subject of Tencreto's unsettling stare.

Sergeant Tassoni, who had been listening to Tencreto with a look of scorn spoke up. "Captain Ferrando, La Bacchetta is an uncivilized game where two men fight over a stick. It is a game for enlisted men or dogs, but not for officers and certainly not for company captains."

"Ah, but how many captains of Galliano Battalion have you seen dig ditches, Sergeant?" Tencreto waved a hand at Enzo. "Clearly this is a man of the people. He can transcend rank as he pleases."

The Ferrandos were not members of Italy's aristocracy but rather of humble birth. The Ferrando name was elevated from the exploits of Enzo's father, Antoni Ferrando, with his part in Garibaldi's *Risorgimento*. Humble birth notwithstanding, Enzo could tell a well-bred man from a man of low birth, and he could clearly identify this Tencreto as a member of the Italian nobility. Growing up in his father's household, Enzo had occasion to sup with many of the esteemed families of Italy, including members of House Savoy and House Piedmont. Even though Garibaldi's Italian revolution had dulled the luster of Italy's heredity titles, the impressions made on Enzo by these nobles and their dying elegance were scalded into memory. Enzo could also tell this man Tencreto had an understanding of manners and was choosing to dispense with them at the present moment.

Enzo had heard enough. "Not interested, Signore. If you have nothing else, I must get back to my responsibility here."

Tencreto stood up smoothly from his crouch, bowed, and walked off. After the man was out of earshot, Enzo asked Tassoni to explain La Bacchetta.

"It's just as I said, captain. Two men fight over a stick. Both men start with both hands on a wooden staff about three feet in length. To win, one man must pry the stick away from the other man and can use whatever means necessary. It's as simple as it is crude."

Tassoni nodded in the direction of Tencreto's exit. "That man is also the battalion bookie. He wants something to wager on because he is bored."

"Can't blame him for that," Enzo said and grunted as he resumed his clash with the rocky earth.

When the sun kissed the horizon line and the men of Fifth Company broke from the day's toil, they found Enzo in a more jolly mood than on most days. After walking back to camp and stowing the tools of their labor, the men of Fifth Company would have a moment to rest their aching backs before mealtime. Instead of stalking off to his artillery shed, Enzo lingered at the Fifth Company barracks. He asked one of the men about the subject of a letter the man was writing. The man, as startled as he was excited from receiving this unexpected attention from the captain, stammered that it was a letter to his brother's new widow. Enzo then inquired as to the cause of his brother's death. When cholera was given as the cause of death, Enzo nodded gravely and placed a hand on the man's shoulder.

As this interaction was taking place under the canopy of the Fifth Company barracks, many of the Fifth Company men were furtively observing their captain, wondering why the man had taken an interest in them and why he was not following his nightly protocol in the lee of the artillery shed.

One observer, an old Venetian with a shiny, bald head, did not sit and speculate about their captain's sudden deviation in routine but instead called up his courage and cleared his throat.

"Signore Ferrando," spoke the old Venetian softly. "Maybe, Signore, you could do us the honor of supping with us tonight."

Enzo turned to the man and raised his eyebrows. The whole of Fifth Company seemed to hush as they waited for his response. Officers rarely dined with enlisted men, and this would have been a bold request even if Enzo had been less of a mystery to the men.

"Well, what is for dinner?" Enzo asked pleasantly. This was joke, as the menu never changed from salted fish stew. The men laughed as much from mirth as from relief.

And so Enzo accompanied his elated band of misbegottens to supper that evening. Galliano Battalion's meal was hosted outside in the middle of the garrison with five long tables set up parallel to each other and perpendicular to the water's edge. Each table, consisting of many smaller tables, was claimed by one of the battalion's five companies. These tables were only for the enlisted men as the officers of Galliano Battalion dined in the officer's mess, a building Enzo had never seen the inside

of. First Company's table was located closest to the boiling cauldrons of fish stew and Fifth's table, the farthest. This hierarchy
determined the order of how the meals were doled out as well
as the pecking order for many other aspects of life at the garrison. First to the cauldrons meant more chunks of salted fish,
last to the cauldrons usually meant just broth and fish heads.

But the fish heads did not bother Enzo. The broth was hot,
and he felt good sitting among these men who treated him as a
guest of honor at their humble table. Enzo even joked with the
cook who was ladling out his stew by asking where he had
studied haute cuisine. It was a rare night in that it was a cool
night, a blessed reprieve from the oppressive heat. A man from
Fourth Company started strumming a new instrument from
Naples called the mandolin. Enzo felt himself breathing slower
and deeper than he had in a long time.

This moment of tranquility was not to last, however, as a
guttural shout reverberated above the din of dining soldiers.
The shout came from an ogre of a man standing on top of the
First Company table. The man's first shout could not be heard
clearly over the casual cacophony of Galliano's five companies
who were eating and talking, but once the men realized the
man was Zagranos Pasha, the chatter abated, and Pasha's
second shout could be heard as clear as a bell.

"*Ferrando!*"

All eyes of the enlisted men of Galliano Battalion turned
from the howling Albanian to the man sitting calmly at the
head of Fifth Company's table. Enzo was looking back at the
big Albanian as might a third party to a street quarrel, interested but not personally invested.

Now that he had the attention he wanted, Zagranos Pasha's
voice grew quieter but still carried the strange accent in his
broken Italian speech. "You have a hero name. Come prove
your mettle against me in La Bacchetta."

Zagranos Pasha was a soldier of fortune, a Bashi-bazouk mercenary who, along with several of his countrymen, had signed up to fight for Italy in exchange for gold. As soldiers, the Bashi-bazouks were the most experienced men in the battalion, but their contracts provided for military service as enlisted men. This challenge of Zagranos Pasha was exceedingly bold in that an enlisted man was challenging a high-ranking officer. Despite the audacious challenge and the scrutiny of the entire battalion, Enzo was sublimely unperturbed.

"No," Enzo said without emotion. "Thank you for the offer."

"You are a coward then?" Zagranos Pasha bellowed.

At this, a wave of shock rolled through the tables as the men could not believe the gall of the Albanian. The outraged men of Fifth Company yelled insults at Zagranos Pasha and told him to sit down.

But Enzo, still calm as a halcyon sea, raised his hand to silence his company and replied to Pasha with a smiling voice that could be heard by the entire battalion. "You have me mistaken, man. I am not your playmate."

Enzo considered the matter settled and went back to sipping his broth. The matter was not closed for Zagranos Pasha, however. He jumped down from his perch and started walking toward Fifth Company's table, shouting as he made his way closer.

"Look at how the dogs of Fifth Company bark for their master! You call yourselves soldiers and wear those uniforms, but you don't fight. You dig ditches, and that is all you're good for, you *mutts*! We fight, you dig. Cowards and mutts. Go build us another latrine!" These last words were roared when he was in spitting distance of Enzo himself.

During Pasha's rant, Enzo had been looking down his table at his men. At Pasha's words he had noticed the downcast eyes and the slouches that came along with resignation. Resignation, a vacuum that sucked meaning and hope out of a man's lungs, a slow suffocation of self-worth. When Enzo saw Tassoni bow his head in shame, he felt cold anger creeping up his back.

Enzo stood up very slowly, still calm from the outside. He looked at Zagranos Pasha and said flatly, "I accept the challenge. Let us get on with it."

And so the garrison turned into a gathering storm of excitement. Adolpho Tencreto seemed to appear out of thin air and started his bookmaking. His big eyes sparkled with excitement as he feverishly recorded wagers from the mobs of enlisted men who were waving fistfulls of copper coins at him, only looking up from his ledger to shout orders regarding the preparation of the makeshift arena for La Bacchetta.

The five long tables were shuffled to form a pentagon, and a ten-foot-diameter circle was drawn in the sand at the midpoint of the shape. The best vantage points for spectators would be the highly sought after spots around the circle, but standing on the tables could also offer a view into the action, as could the roofs of the nearby barracks. The mass of men in Galliano Battalion started to surge into the positions that would give them the best glimpses of what was about to unfold. The crowd of five hundred enlisted men was formidable and electric. It had been a long while since Zagranos Pasha had a challenger at La Bacchetta, and the revival of the game represented a lusty reprieve from the prosaic lifestyle of the garrison. La Bacchetta was revving them up into a dull roar.

The two combatants were pushed toward the middle of the pentagon, into the circle, where they stood less than ten feet apart. Enzo was expressionless, feet spread wide apart and head cocked to one side. The only movement he allowed was the occasional clenching and unclenching of his right hand. Zagranos Pasha was Enzo's antipode, goading the crowd of spectators, spitting, hurling insults, and gleefully yelling every

Italian cuss word he knew. He was like a caged bull working himself into a rage.

Even from the small movements Pasha displayed in his heckling of the crowd, Enzo noticed this man Pasha was quicker than his girth might suggest. At such a close distance, it was also impossible not to appreciate the Albanian's size. Whereas Enzo was large and powerfully built, he was still of a size that assigned him firmly into the human species. This man Pasha was something else. He had a full head of height over Enzo and was almost twice as broad, but it was the prehistoric brow and the mangled, twice-broken nose that seemed to make *humanoid* a more appropriate taxonomic classification for him. Pasha was about the age of Enzo but had seen a half hundred battles that were forever reenacted with the scar tissue spread over the man's body.

"Enzo!" Sergeant Tassoni was shouting in Enzo's ear to be heard above the din of the excited crowd. Tassoni, along with the two Askari warrior twins, had shouldered their way behind Enzo. "Signore, the key is to keep your feet! The longest anyone has lasted with Zagranos Pasha is two minutes, and it's because he kept his feet. Most people don't last ten seconds before La Bacchetta is ripped from their grasp by Pasha. He is incredibly strong. You've got to keep your feet, Enzo, and don't let him drive you into the ground!"

The two Askari warrior twins who had been Enzo's favorite drinking companions were trying to paint his face and chest with the colors of their warrior tribe, but Enzo kept pushing them away.

Having finished taking all bets, Adolpho Tencreto pushed and shouldered his way into the circle waving a revolver. He discharged the revolver twice into the air to get the silence of the crowd. He was as animated as he'd ever been, and it was as if he was feeding off the primal energy of the mob around him.

He switched the pistol into his left hand, and from inside his black duster coat he withdrew a gnarled oak staff about three feet long and held it above his head. Five hundred voices then started chanting, "*La-bah-chet-ta, La-bah-chet-ta, La-bah-chet-ta, La-bah-chet-ta.*" He then silenced them all with another discharge of the revolver and started to speak with a tone that was reminiscent of a carnival magician with an undertone of mockery.

"Who says we don't have any fun here in Galliano, eh? Eh?" Tencreto smiled like a maniac. "Gentlemen, we have for you tonight a duel of epic proportions. The Champion, the Beast from the Balkans—Zagranos Pasha ... *versus* ... The Challenger, an upjumped stevedore from the docks of Genoa—Capitano Ferrando!"

Tencreto sneered at Enzo as he roared this last barb, but Enzo only nodded since the *nom de guerre* was not far off from something he would have chosen for himself.

Under the roar of the crowd, the two combatants assembled shoulder to shoulder, each gripping the stick, La Bacchetta, with two hands. Starting from the top was Pasha's right hand, under which was Enzo's left, then Pasha's left, then Enzo's right. Once the men were set, they did not stand on ceremony. Tencreto fired again into the air and shouted "*Cominciamo!*" to begin the primal struggle of La Bacchetta.

As soon as the shot was fired, Zagranos Pasha issued an explosion of strength and power, twisting and lifting the stick over his head, with Enzo clamped on to it. With Enzo in the air, Pasha then twisted further and brought Enzo down savagely into the ground with all his own girth along with it. Enzo was driven hard into the earth by the momentum, and the large man came crashing down on top of him. The residual air in Enzo's lungs was driven out of him, and he gasped for breath, only to find Pasha had quickly regained his feet and was pulling Enzo up into the air again. Again, Enzo was thrown down brutally into the earth as the crowd groaned in sympathy or cheered in barbaric revelry.

This pulverizing continued, a third, a fourth, a fifth time until Pasha, finally winded, paused to catch his breath. The reprieve was short-lived, however, as Pasha ambled up and swung Enzo up even higher and brought him down with terrible force, driving his shoulder into Enzo's rib cage. The observers close to the circle could see Enzo starting to spit up blood, but still Enzo remained clamped on to La Bacchetta.

The display was akin to a sullen child playing with a rag doll. The cheers started to die out, and then silence pervaded the competition, only interrupted by the sound of Enzo's body repeatedly hitting the earth and the sympathetic groans. Some men found it too hard to watch and turned away. Still Enzo held.

An hour had passed since Tencreto's starter pistol fired. Both men's backs were slick with sweat, their breathing ragged. Enzo's face was slick with blood. Still Enzo held.

The two men had their heads no more than six inches away from each other when Zagranos Pasha whispered so only Enzo could hear. "Enzo, why don't you yield? You know I'm the stronger man."

He heard no answer. Finally through cracked lips, Enzo's broken voice returned, "It is not about strength."

Still in a horse whisper, Pasha replied, "You are doing this to yourself. I was put up to those insults by Tencreto, if that isn't obvious enough. He told me to call you a coward, and if that didn't work to go after your men. That doesn't change the fact that you will not beat me in this game. I'll kill you if that what it takes."

And the beating continued. Though Pasha was thoroughly tired, and the ferocity of the attacks was reduced, each and every time Enzo was thrown down, the ground seemed to shake. After another hour passed the once raucous crowd was now more of a candlelit vigil. The bloodlust of the crowd was beaten out of them. The competition had gone well into the night, and some the observers started to wonder if they were watching a death sentence.

Both men were now sufficiently exhausted and had had no water. Enzo was closing his eyes for long periods of time, but still his grip held. Pasha, having to work to get enough saliva into his mouth to speak, again tried to appeal to Enzo's reason. "You don't have to prove anything more, Enzo. Please ... yield before I kill you. You don't have to prove anything more."

A minute passed before Enzo responded to Pasha's whisper. Enzo had his eyes closed as he made his reply as if on the other side of a trance. "Don't I, though? I have lived all my life in the shade of a great oak, yearning for sunlight."

Enzo then opened his eyes and looked at Zagranos Pasha with a vitality that contrasted violently with Enzo's battered face. Pasha then knew that this fight was not yet over. Pasha decided to end it by breaking Enzo's arm. With Enzo on his left, Pasha rolled hard to his right, lifting Enzo up and over him so he would be able to pin Enzo's arm, continue his roll, and snap whatever limbs Enzo had left on the stick. At the top of movement, as Enzo was in the air, Enzo swept his leg around to dig his heel in and stop the roll. In the same movement, Enzo reared back away from Pasha as far as he could, and as Pasha used his strength to pull Enzo and La Bacchetta back in, Enzo used Pasha's own force to come back down on the man with a savage headbutt that connected Enzo's forehead with Pasha's twice-broken nose. A sickening crack was heard round the circle as Pasha's nose erupted in blood. With Pasha shocked and on his back, Enzo planted his right heel against Pasha's sternum, ducked his shoulder under La

Bacchetta, and surged upward with a fury not shown heretofore in the contest.

And the stick was pried loose from Zagranos Pasha's mighty grip. Enzo stood weakly holding the stick in middle of the circle as the crowd, dumbfounded, struggled to make sense of what had just happened. Cries went up. "He's done it!" The crowd was once again electrified and brought to a point of rapture. "He's beaten Pasha!" The ale was poured with gusto, firearms discharged wildly into the night sky.

Zagranos Pasha, blood pouring down his face and still sitting in the blood stained circle, was laughing maniacally and pointing at Enzo. "Hahaha! I see you for who you are, Enzo Ferrando! You are the Rebel Jove. You are the Thundermüchen! Hahahah! Let us beware the trickster Gods!"

Enzo limped away from the commotion. Helped by Tassoni and an Askari twin, they half led him, half carried him to the artillery shed. Through swollen eyes, Enzo thought he could make out Colonel Cristofori staring him down as he made his way out of the crowd.

11

Enzo woke the following morning feeling eighty years older. His face was still swollen, and he found that anything deeper than a shallow breath would cause him a sharp pain in his side. Getting to his feet was an ordeal, and he relied heavily on the post of his bed as his legs did not seem to want to work.

Just as he was starting to consider the appropriateness of asking Tassoni to come help him dress, a visitor appeared at his bedroom door. He immediately recognized the portly frame of Colonel Cristofori's aide-de-camp.

"Captain Ferrando," the aide-de-camp said with a formality that seemed out of place, considering Enzo was still naked. "The colonel requires all captains of Galliano Battalion to convene at HQ on the hour. That is all."

The man disappeared as suddenly as he had come, leaving Enzo to wonder what this was all about. He had never attended a captains' meeting during his time with Galliano. His memory flashed to the cold stare of Colonel Cristofori after his scrum with the big Albanian. He shook his head and bellowed, "Tassoni! I need you."

After Enzo was dressed and the dried blood was washed from his face, he and Tassoni made their way to the Battalion HQ. Enzo would have gladly accepted Tassoni's assistance with the walk across the garrison but chose to hobble on his own due to the crowd of soldiers watching him and speaking in hushed tones.

The three steps up the the door of the HQ were the hardest, and he winced in pain. He opened the door to find Colonel Cristofori, the aide-de-camp, and the four other captains of Galliano sitting at a long table. Enzo made his way to the open chair, which was unfortunately on the other side of the room, and did his best to hide his limp. Enzo winced again as he took his place at the table. There were no windows and thus no natural light in this room. All the light came from candles dispersed evenly along the table. Enzo's eyes took a moment to adjust to the darkness, and when they did, he noticed that the whole room was staring expectantly at him, save for one man with an imperial mustache who was looking dead forward, sitting straight as a ship's mast. This man was sitting to Colonel Cristofori's right.

"Thank you for joining us, Captain Ferrando," Colonel Cristofori said, ending the silence.

Enzo inclined his head slightly towards the colonel, an act that caused him a dull ache.

Colonel Cristofori continued to study Enzo and made a "tut tut" sound recognizable to a pupil who was sitting before a disappointed professor.

The colonel began to speak, all the while looking straight at Enzo. "I won't trample on the accomplishments of Garibaldi or your father, but from a military perspective, the *Garibaldinos* were little more than an impassioned rabble. They were disorganized buccaneers following a cult of personality. They were good for pilfering chicken coops and sniffing out the nearest brothel, but they were not good for professional soldiering. You will find professional soldiers here, Captain Ferrando. In a professional army, in *this* army, officers do not brawl with enlisted men."

"I apologize for my actions," said Enzo.

"Disgraceful behavior, but not surprising," concluded Colonel Cristofori.

The mustached man cleared his throat and spoke. "And what of the larger issue here, Colonel?"

"What larger issue do you speak of, Captain Vittori?" The colonel turned to the man at his right.

The mustached Captain Vittori spoke loudly in the terse, controlled manner that marked him as a man with many years of command. "I do not mind if a man defends his honor against another man. What I mind, what I mind very much, is when an enlisted man feels that he can challenge and insult an officer. Our system, our chain of command, is built on the deference of the enlisted man to the ranking officer. We cannot function if there is any ounce of doubt in that deference. Disrespect breeds rebellion."

Colonel Cristofori looked perturbed and made to interrupt Vittori. "Thank you, Captain Vittori. You—"

"Rebellion breeds mutiny," Vittori said, plowing ahead. "If an enlisted man, mercenary or not, made to call me a coward, I would have had him shot. Or I would have shot him where he stood. Seeing as the guilty party is an enlisted man in my own company, First Company, I request this man be subjected to firing squad. I will not suffer insubordination in my own company."

Colonel Cristofori considered this a minute. His eyes then glimmered with inspiration. "Seeing as we have the victim of this enlisted man's insult at our table, let us ask him. Captain Ferrando, should this man be shot?"

Vittori looked down the table at Enzo for the first time. Enzo immediately realized Cristofori's game. If Enzo allowed the man to be shot, he would have a death on his hands and possibly the ire of the battalion. If he waived the sentence, he would have an enemy in Captain Vittori for allowing a "mutineer" to persist in the man's company. He had heard of Vittori and knew this was not a man to trifle with. Vittori was known to be brutal in war and in disciplinary action. He was also the finest horseman in the battalion and came from a line of soldiers dating back generations.

"A firing squad will not be necessary," Enzo replied. "I will take this man into my company and discipline him my way." The answer seemed to satisfy Vittori and cause Cristofori's face to darken.

"Fine," Cristofori said curtly. "Let us be done with this nonsense so we can talk about why I brought you all here." Enzo was grateful that the conversation had shifted away from him and that the purpose of the meeting seemed to be separate from the events relating to La Bacchetta.

Cristofori stood up and placed his palms on the table, leaning forward. "We have negotiated an accord with Great Britain. Great Britain has ceded the city of Massawa to Italy."

Cristofori placed his index finger on a spot on the map three hundred miles northwest along the coast. No one, including Enzo, needed a map to understand the significance of what Cristofori had just said. Massawa was the largest city and trading port in Ethiopia[1].

"Massawa will be the new seat of the Italian empire in Africa. We will march to Massawa in two months time to assume control of the city and the region." The colonel withdrew his finger and sat back down calmly.

Captain Vittori was the first to speak. "Colonel. I am a soldier, not a politician, so my understanding of these matters is limited. With that said, why has Great Britain ceded us one of the greatest cities in East Africa when we are not at war with Great Britain?"

"Captain Vittori, the European powers are always at war with each other, even if they are not," replied Colonel Cristofori. "A treaty is simply a transference of hot war to cold war, of open aggression to subterfuge. Of course we are at war with Great Britain. Of course Great Britain is our ally."

Vittori was not to be put off. "That all may be Colonel, but what does Great Britain want in return for Massawa?" Enzo was asking himself precisely the same question and found himself starting to like this Vittori.

"This is a game of chess, captain, there are no discreet duels when it comes to global politics. Ceding Massawa to Italy is in Great Britain's interest because it achieves a balance of power against Britain's other foes. Her Majesty also has her hands full with the Mahdist War in the Sudan, and the British garrison in Massawa has been sucked in to support those efforts. We will fill this vacuum. You may not have the perspective to see the full board from your vantage point."

"It feels like at trap, colonel," said Vittori. "I urge caution."

Another man, Captain Merli of Third Company, spoke up, "Colonel, how do we know this is not a ploy to get us out of the garrison so we might be set upon by the Ethiopian hordes? We pick British weapons off their dead in our raids, and we know the British cannot be trusted."

The other two captains nodded in agreement. "Caution" they both echoed. Colonel Cristofori was massaging his temples. "Gentlemen. It is not a trap. There is a document, which I have seen with my own eyes, that contains the signatures of our King Emmanuel and Queen Victoria."

That fact should have been enough to silence the captains, but Cristofori continued. "And let me remind you all here and now that this is not a Socratic debate."

Cristofori slammed his fist on the table for emphasis, and even Vittori stiffened. "It is mine to command and yours to obey!"

All of a sudden, the colonel softened and almost looked tired. In a much quieter voice he said, "There is a condition related to this accord with Great Britain that we have agreed to. You will be informed when the time is right. Dismissed."

All five captains and the aide-de-camp got up to leave.

"Except you." The Colonel nodded at Enzo, who sat back down. After the others had left, the colonel walked over to the open chair across from Enzo and sat down. He looked suddenly disheveled and drained, as if the meeting had taken an immense amount of energy.

When it was just the two of them, Cristofori spoke up. "I need your loyalty."

"And you have it," said Enzo.

"Swear it."

"On my life."

Two beaten men stared at each other. One was physically beaten and wore the scars and bruises outwardly. The other was emotionally battered and preyed upon from within.

The colonel nodded slowly. "This Massawa business. This will not be pretty. I need you. You cannot go run off to avenge your father's death. Not now."

Enzo was taken aback. He did not expect this direct request, but then the colonel was a perceptive man. Enzo also sensed desperation from Cristofori. He could not decide if this was another game, another ploy of the colonel's.

"I'll stay until my work is done."

Cristofori seemed not to hear Enzo and had his mouth

open as if he was trying to decide whether to say what was truly on his mind.

"Italy is a mess," Cristofori said carefully. "King Emmanuel is just as unpopular as your Prime Minister Crispi. The factions churn and strain against the loosening ties that bind our nation together. The population is in decline. There is only one thing that can unite Tuscans and Venetians, Sicilians and Lombards, Neapolitans and Genoese. The only thing that can bind us is a vision of the former and storied greatness of our origins. I'm speaking of the Roman Empire. The path to a united, strong nation is the return to imperialism. That is what we are doing here. Do you know another way?"

Enzo was careful in his response. He was not prepared for this topic of conversation and was facing an intellectual superior.

"In the *Risorgimento*," Enzo replied, "Italy united under the ideals of liberty and civic virtue. Those ideals can sustain us now."

Cristofori rolled his eyes as if he were speaking with a child. "Spoken like a true *Garibaldino*. Those 'ideals' worked once when they were used to rabble-rouse. That's exactly what we don't want. We are experiencing the largest migration out of Italy in our history. Our population is hemorrhaging. The light is leaving our country's eyes. The only solution is to regain some semblance of national pride. That is why this is important."

Cristofori waved his hands around the room. "We have won our independence. Now we need to start operating like one of the great European powers. The key to power? Colonies. Colonies bring wealth. This may look like a sunburnt waste-land to you, but look closer and you will see this is the first step towards a new empire. The second coming of the Roman Empire."

"The Romans were conquerors and slavers," Enzo ventured. "We live in modern times, Colonel."

Cristofori shouted his retort. "The Romans brought civilization to the uncivilized. They brought fire to the dark wood. They established the greatest society the world has ever known!"

Cristofori then stood up wearily, motioning Enzo to leave him. Before Enzo's hand touched the latch of the door, Cristofori addressed him once more.

"It's not only me that needs your loyalty, Capitano Ferrando, it's Italy."

---

1. Massawa is part of present day Eritrea but during the time period of the novel Massawa was part of the Ethiopian domain.

12

In June of 1882, the architect of the Italian Unification, Giuseppe Garibaldi, drew his last breath on the Island of Caprera. Galliano Battalion, while in the midst of readying for the march to Massawa, held a feast in Garibaldi's honor, and thick-throated toasts went deep into the night.

Most of the men of Galliano Battalion had fathers whose lives intersected with Garibaldi in some form. In many cases, it was a parade or a march, which the passage of time and national pride had inflated and massaged into a rousing battle. In some cases, men had fathers with real stories to tell of the Wars of Italian Independence. They were all heard and toasted and cheered on, but all souls present were awaiting a toast by Enzo Ferrando. The camaraderie of Garibaldi and his most loyal lieutenant, Antoni Ferrando, was legendary, and they yearned for authenticity. Finally, Captain Vittori called for Enzo to toast to "his Uncle Giuseppe," and Enzo rose. All were quiet as they waited to hear gospel direct from the disciple's lips. Even the drunkest were hushed, swaying silently, trying to focus on him with one eye closed. The audience wanted to be taken away to the famous battlefields where Garibaldi and the Old Bull had smashed through Bourbon lines, fighting shoulder to shoulder. They wanted to feel the intrigue and suspense of the narrow escapes from assassins. They wanted to fix bayonets and charge along with the thousand red-shirted volunteers at Calatafimi. Most of all, they wanted to forget about their current exile but remember why they signed up for the Italian Army. But when Enzo spoke, he did not take them to a battlefield. The memory he invoked was of a small house on a hill in Genoa, and he spoke about a woman.

But first, Enzo started his speech with a wry smile. "To Garibaldi the War Lord! May he come again in glory to judge the living and the dead!"

The men laughed heartily at the superlative that only Enzo could have gotten away with, and someone shouted, "St. Garibaldi!" which was met with more laughter.

And then Enzo grew more somber. "Some of you know, Garibaldi had a wife. Her name, Anita. If you've heard her name, you've heard of her beauty. She taught him how to ride a proper horse. They were inseparable until her death. She died in a barn while they were being chased by the Neapolitans. They did not even have time to give her a proper burial. He loved her, and then he lost her."

He paused to take a draw from his wineskin and looked at the crowd. They were hanging gently on his words.

"I too had a wife. Her name, as it happens, was also Anita. Garibaldi was a simple sailor who rose up to cast down kings and emperors. He united the country I love, and for that I am grateful. He kept my father safe—well not safe, but alive— through countless battles, and for that I am also grateful. But I am most grateful to the man for his comfort in my season of sorrow after the passing of my Anita. He came to my simple house, dirt floors and all, and he squeezed my shoulder and talked to me as might a father.

"He told me that in order to love someone fully, you hack away a part of yourself—to make room for the other. If the other leaves, you are left with a gaping void. If you don't collapse into yourself, you at least list over to the left, like an old man walking with a limp. He told me that I would lean a little left of center for the rest of my life, and sure enough that is true. But he also told me that even a cripple can be of use. Even a cripple can lurch ahead."

The crowd was hushed for a long moment. Some of the men had their heads lowered. Then, breaking the spell, Enzo shouted in a booming voice, "To burying our dead!" As the crowd stood and whistled approval and echoed his last line, he added under his breath, "Lest they impede the living."

13

T*he Dunant Letters*

26 June, 1859

Dear Jean-Marc,

I write to you in a solemn state of stress. It has been two weeks since I have borne witness to one of the most tragic, heartbreaking, sorrowful episodes in human history—or at the very least, the modern history of civilized Europe—and I use the word "civilized" with high caution.

My dear friend, I have been in a condition of hollow disbelief and confusion, and of late I must strain to glimpse any evidence of God's love in this country of pitiless bloodshed. I attempt to put these letters to you as much to gather up my thoughts as to gather up my self.

Allow me to begin at the beginning. As you are aware, I have started a business venture that is now a going concern. Via capital raised from friends, family, and a few Geneva notables, I've secured a land concession in Algeria where I am engaged in the growing and milling and trading of maize. With the land concession, I acquired water rights, but with the water rights, I also acquired some trouble. I won't bore you with the ugly details, but let us say that my agrarian neighbors have been less than neighborly, and I have proof of foul play. In the dry climes of Algeria, water is critical, and I wasn't getting my share.

With Algeria being part of the French protectorate, I thought it perfectly natural and appropriate to bring my cause up with the Emperor Napoleon III. It's amazing what a little perspective can do, and now I shake my head at such a pompous, self-aggrandizing scheme. Why would Napoleon deign to meddle in my humble affairs? What would the emperor care for an irrigation dispute in Algeria, particularly when he had a war to wage with Austria? But that is what I did, in all my retrospective shame. I set off from Algeria to seek out Napoleon in Solferino, where he had made camp, and register a plea for him to intervene on my behalf.

When I got to Solferino, I immediately requested an audience with the emperor but was told to wait and that his highness was engaged on the field of battle. When I inquired as to when his highness might be done, restating of course that I had important matters to discuss with him, I was dismissed rather curtly. So I resolved to wait in a hotel across the street from the headquarters. How long would a battle take? I did not know. I had never been close to a real battle before. The hotel had a decent bar on the first floor with a window that opened to the street—and thank god, as the heat was oppressive. I sat myself down with a julep while keeping a vigilant eye on the emperor's HQ.

I must have dozed off for a decent interval because when I awoke, still seated at the bar by the window, the street had transformed from quiet to chaotic. Shouting and wailing was to be heard, and injured men on stretchers were jostling by my window. More men were being unloaded from ambulance carts, and a handful of medical men, nurses, and persons from a religious order were struggling to maintain order against the rush of wounded soldiers.

Now I have been self-centered in my life, as I have in this letter demonstrated, but when it comes to helping a fellow in need, I lend hands—yes, both of them—without compunction.

So I got to work. I must have seemed quite an oddity in my white linen suit, but I threw myself into the work as it was clear the doctors and nurses were losing this war of numbers. Support a stretcher here, tighten a tourniquet there; pretty soon I was on first-name basis with the nurses, and they were running me like a rabbit! We were using the church as our field hospital, and I soon came to the conclusion that the arrangement of the beds would soon impede our ability to access each patient. I instructed my compatriots to start loading the infirmed into the pews to keep the aisles free, and that worked for a while. When the church overflowed, I conscripted my hotel to provide space for the injured and dying. The proprietor was less than eager until I provided him the monetary courage needed to do the right thing.

Still, the wounded warriors flowed into town. I was scurrying around on some errand when a rough man who I would later identify as an army medic grabbed my arm and volunteered me to accompany him to the battlefield to procure fresh wounded. Even if this was a voluntary mission that I could decline, my curiosity would have gotten the better of me. I jumped up to the cart, and the horses were cajoled into movement. Up until that point, I had only been seeing the output of battle, you understand. I had been seeing what comes off the battlefield, but I had not yet glimpsed the field itself. This sight shook me to my core.

I had in my youth traveled to Munich for Oktoberfest. After the singing and dancing and—more importantly—drinking, hundreds of men in leather chaps would exit their tent and find a cozy spot on the fields of Theresienwiese for a midday slumber. When we reached the hillcrest overlooking the Battle of Solferino, this silly memory of Oktoberfest was the first thing that filled my head. Only here there were no happy dreams of busty barmaids playing in the heads of slumbering celebrants. I was gazing at over five thousand dead or dying men littered about an otherwise beautiful countryside. It is, in short, the stuff of nightmares. My stomach turned, and I felt that if God looked upon this place, he would see us men as an embarrassment to creation. I felt the guilt of my species on that hillcrest. What have we done?

Where there is horror, there is also hope. In my time at Solferino, I saw many acts of courage large and small and met many inspiring people. There was the Selve de Sarran, a young second lieutenant of the horse artillery that had lost his arm but not his spirit. I met many heroes of the Crimean War who knew the stakes and sallied forward anyway. But there was one fellow I shall remember until my final moments. I came across him on the rotting battlefield, one half league east of the Chiese river, north of Gaffredo. This poor fellow was sitting upright, back against the remains of an upturned Austrian weapons caisson. I approached the man, and as I came closer I saw his breathing was labored, and he wore a ghastly wound below his left breast. In spite of his current condition, his voice was calm and he addressed me in Italian, of which I am familiar. I crouched beside him as his voice was calm but very weak, and he informed me that he believed he was dying of thirst. He also informed me that he had wet himself (not out of fear, mind you, but because he could not stand up) and that his boots had been stolen a few hours ago by pillaging, no good, Lombard peasants. He did not blame the peasants as they were fine boots. He also admitted to me that his feet were swelling anyway, and the boots were getting tight, so it was just as well. Sure enough, the poor man's feet were swollen to high heaven and had a greenish, bluish hue. After giving the man a drink of water, for which he was most grateful, I set about getting a horse and cart to transport this man to medical care; after all, he was a large man and was unable to ambulate himself.

As surreal as this interaction may seem, it was not the battlefield acquaintance that holds to my memory so tight but rather a second acquaintance with the same man three days hence. I was walking through the Madonna Della Pieve convent. We had set it up as one of many other battlefield hospitals and packed it to the gunnels with make-shift gurneys, surgeon's tables, and sick beds. I was walking down a crowded corridor in the covenant when I felt a hand on my wrist and turned to find my shoeless friend, looking now half alive as opposed to half dead, which given the circumstances was a remarkable improvement. He then said to me a series of words that in any other context could have been as mundane as bidding the postman a good morning or a transaction with a local clerk. He said simply, "Grazie per l'acqua" (Thank you for the water). But behind these words I saw the man's face change, and though I did not know this man, I knew him in that instant for forty years and then some. With great difficulty and just for a brief moment, the man pulled down the inscrutable visage of the war-worn soldier and showed me an innocent. A child grown old. It was like a beautiful admission that came from somewhere deep in the earth below the bloodstained fields of Solferino. I won't forget that face. "Grazie per l'acqua." There is innocence betwixt the chaos, Jean-Marc. He then offered me a gift in the form of a small parcel that contained a neatly folded flag of his home city. I have the standard hanging above my desk, and I look upon it now as I write to you. It is a simple standard, a red cross on a white field. It is striking as it is the inverse of our Swiss flag, and perhaps I am drawn to the idea of opposing yet binded forces, like the yin and the yang of the Orientals.

Yours Faithfully,
Henri Dunant

* * *

5 May, 1860

Dear Jean-Marc,

It has not yet been a year since my impassioned and protracted letter found its way to your study (and I hope to your prayers), but I am happy to report that I am doing well, mended of mind and body, though I confess my spirit still pains for those wretched souls at Solferino.

I have resolved to record my experiences in a memoir of sorts. In fact, I have taken up the activity of this memoir just yesterday, and upon commencing the activity of writing, a great weight has been lifted from my neck. The relief is not unlike the original comfort I found in writing you on that solemn day not one year ago. I will say I much prefer this medium to the spoken word as I find myself a rather tepid conversationalist, and when I am driven to socialize, I imagine the victims of my chin-wag growing wearisome of the sound of my voice almost as quickly as I.

In addition to the emotional relief that a chronicle of

Solferino is bringing me, I also feel the slow burn of purpose coming back after many years of dormancy. Jean-Marc, I want to lay this history bare for all to see, and if I cannot stir something compassionate in the high castles of the European powers, then maybe, just maybe, I can dissuade a young man from a barbaric turn. My friend, I swear that my account of the Battle of Solferino will be as vivid and as unsterilized as my recurring nightmares, and while I do wish to honor the misguided bravery that surged and swayed on that battlefield, I shall not create heroes to perpetuate the idealized evil that is war.

Yours Faithfully,
Henri Dunant

* * *

23 FEBRUARY, 1863

DEAR JEAN-MARC,

I hope you are well, my friend. It has been a long time. I am happy to report that my memoir has been published, though I will admit I had to finance the publishing out of my own savings. Still, the feedback has been marvelous and well beyond anything that I could have anticipated.

Kings and queens, princes and prime ministers, and even Pope Pius can be counted among the readership.

The book has made me somewhat of a *célébrité du jour,* a passing phenomenon I assure you, but if I can somehow transition this momentum and continental attention into a more permanent promotion of humanism, then maybe there could be some larger purpose for the souls of Solferino.

I have been in discussions with several gentlemen who I

feel share my sentiments, and we have formed a five-person committee to push forward the agenda of humanism, especially as it relates to warfare, and to mitigate the dastardly effects of combat. The committee is yours truly, two doctors named Appia and Maunoir, a military man named Dufour, and a gentleman named Gustave Moynier, whose ambition I hope will serve our noble purpose.

What is our noble purpose, you ask? Well, why not reach for the stars? We intend to hold a convention this fall with all the European nations in attendance. The goal of the convention will be to set out bold new terms for how wars are waged. If the great nations of Europe can agree on more humane procedures on the battlefield, then maybe our humble race can inch forward and become more deserving of God's love.

Yours Faithfully,
Henri Dunant

* * *

29 August, 1864

Dear Jean-Marc,

I suppose I should be happy—elated even. From many perspectives it would seem that our noble plan came to fruition.

Fourteen European nations attended our conference last October to discuss the treatment of wounded soldiers. As a direct result, the Swiss Parliament called the sovereign nations back for the Geneva Convention, which occurred last week. In what will no doubt be considered an historic accord, twelve nations pledged their support for "the Amelioration of the Condition of the Wounded in Armies in the Field."

I am happy, Jean-Marc, but I daresay I would have come away from this success a great deal more satisfied if I had not been shunted into a trivial role through all of these proceedings. I had seen the gentleman Moynier as a man of ambition from the outset, but now I fear that ambition has me in its sights. Moynier has positioned himself as the practical progressive and has me playing the radical idealist. My suggestions are cast down, only to be picked up by Moynier, dusted off, and submitted with resounding appeal.

I strive to remind myself that any success, any progress toward our noble cause, is my true success, and personal recognition is a base aspiration. My function was relegated to the charge of catering and hotel accommodations for the delegates of the Geneva Convention. I've transgressed from savior to steward!

Yours,

Henri Dunant

* * *

15 September, 1868

Jean-Marc,

I am starting to see Moynier's predatory eyes in the faces of strangers. I expect to see him around every corner of Geneva. I had to leave the butcher's shop the other day because every meat-cleaving villain behind the counter was Gustave Moynier.

Mother has been dead nine months. My businesses are in bankruptcy proceedings. The coup-de-grace was my expulsion from the committee I helped found. Of course, it was Moynier who managed it. As he was committee president, I actually pleaded with him to allow me to stay on the committee. I pleaded to stay on if not as secretary than perhaps in a less dignified function. Then I just asked for emeritus status. This was my life's work, I told him, my life's purpose. The answer was no. On account of my bankruptcies. That was the official reason, anyway.

I plan to tuck my tail and leave Geneva. Maybe I will be left alone. Maybe I can free myself from his terrible leer.

Goodbye,

H.

14

———

L ucca sat cross-legged with his back to the foremast of the *Albatro*. His eyes would close and then open and then close again. In the dark intervals, he would try to envision the subject of his art work. In the lighted intervals he would steadily sketch the line or accent that he had been focusing on. It was dawn, and though the seas were calm, it took a practiced hand to account for the pitch and sway of the merchant vessel in the Mediterranean. The subject of his sketch was a young woman, about his age. He had drawn her face a thousand times but could never get her perfect. Sometimes it would be her smile that gave him trouble, and he could not capture the mischievous flare at the corner of her mouth. Sometimes he could not quite translate the hairline scar that traced her chin, delicate yet common and proof of a roguish nature. Some artists might have skirted over the scar in an apparent kindness to the subject, but to Lucca it was the imperfection that injected humanity and created the masterpiece. The scar allowed her beauty to be accessed by the mortal world. He loved it and he would sometimes trace it with his thumb when they were making love. He could always get her eyebrows right—dark and highly contrasted against her sandy blonde hair enlivened with sun and salt.

Lucca yawned, stretched, and put the sketch back in his leather folio. The folio was thick with paper, the buckled straps almost bursting against portraits of friends and strangers, detailed landscapes, and hurried croquis. Five years of memories on the *Albatro* and then some from his childhood in Genoa. Lucca was seventeen.

He turned the folio over and opened randomly to his prior work from earlier years. His lines were less confident then; he used many when only a few would have sufficed. His discerning eye saw many lost opportunities to use more of the negative space. But the sketches did bring him back to a long ago place.

His fingers traced the edges of a sketch of a compass rose hastily drawn on his first day aboard the *Albatro*. He remembered it well. It was the day he last saw his father. And the day he met Grace.

* * *

Twelve-year-old Lucca had just finished stowing his belongings in his locker beneath his bunk when he felt the ship start to heel. He hadn't spent much time at sea, but he understood that this meant the *Albatro* had left the Port of Genoa and picked up the morning southerly breeze of the Ligurian Sea. Captain Bartolo had instructed him to deposit his things and then report to him immediately in the captain's cabin where he would start his first navigation lesson.

Lucca did not know where the captain's cabin was and decided to ask someone. The first two men he came across seemed too occupied to pause from their duties, and the third seemed too scary on account of having no visible teeth. As he climbed up out of the ship's hold and onto the main deck, he firmly told himself he would ask the next man he saw. The next man he saw was pulling on a line Lucca later learned was a halyard, which was having an effect on something high above, which Lucca later learned was the main topsail. Lucca tugged on the man's sleeve to get his attention and asked him where he might find the captain's cabin. The man looked around and then down and then pointed toward what Lucca would come to know as the stern of the ship.

Lucca walked toward the back of the boat, trying not to look like he was struggling to keep his balance. He found a door at the end of the main deck that he supposed could provide entry to a captain's cabin.

"Enter!" came the voice of Captain Bartolo from inside.

Lucca walked into a spacious but simply decorated room with a large table dominating the center. Behind the table was Bartolo, hands clasped behind his back. To his right was a girl of Lucca's age. She stood in a similar fashion to the captain, feet spread slightly apart, hands clasped behind her back. She stood straight but not stiff. Her blonde hair was pulled back into a bun, and her hunter-green eyes, alert and intelligent, followed him as he approached the table. She had trousers on. Lucca nodded to them both, unsure of what else to do.

Captain Bartolo cleared his throat and began a rather awkward and seemingly rehearsed speech. "We are Italians, but more importantly we are Genoese. Genoa has produced the finest sailors, navigators, and merchants the world has ever known. We sail in their wake, and we learn their craft. What we learn here is not just a means to go from one place to another; it is an art. The art of navigation. Master the art of navigation, and you will never be lost."

The girl was listening politely, and when Bartolo finished his remarks, she raised her hand.

"Yes?"

"Uncle Bartolo, who is he?" She pointed directly at Lucca, who immediately felt embarrassment tickling his neck.

"Grace, remember, you must call me *Captain* while on board this ship." Bartolo, clearly frustrated with himself that he had not introduced the two children straight away, cleared his throat again and said, "This is Lucca. He is joining our ship as a deckhand and will be joining in on your lessons."

"What's his last name?"

Lucca made to answer, but Bartolo cut in. "We won't be using his last name onboard."

Grace was looking at him so suspiciously that Bartolo felt obliged to answer. "Lucca's last name is quite well known. We must keep Lucca's identity secret for his protection. He will be using a different last name."

"And what will his new name be?" Grace asked.

"Well, that's for him to decide." Both Bartolo and Grace turned to Lucca.

Grace seemed to light up with excitement at the idea of a christening right here, right now. Lucca, to his shame, felt tongue-tied. He couldn't think of a new name on the spot. Could he use his mother's maiden name? Would that be safe?

Before Lucca could put forth a suggestion, Grace blurted, "Topolino!"

Lucca frowned. He was only about an inch shorter than her, so why did she think "mouse" would be a fitting last name for him? Bartolo hushed Grace's giggling and looked expectantly at Lucca for his choice.

"Nonna," Lucca declared. He was already excited to tell Greta Nonna he had taken her name, even if it was just for pretend. Grace's giggling began again.

Bartolo cut in. "How about Pani. Lucca Pani. If anyone asks, you're an orphan. Now let's get started. Take these and we'll go up on deck."

Bartolo handed various instruments to Grace and handed what looked like a spool of thick fishing line to Lucca. He himself took a rolled chart and they exited the Captain's cabin onto the main deck. The trio continued up a flight of steps to the quarterdeck. Grace was ahead of him. She seemed to glide rather than walk, and even in simple movements she displayed an animal-like coordination, like a jungle cat. Lucca felt clumsy and out of place by comparison. This girl looked like she was born on this ship; the seasoned way she scampered up the shallow stairs amid the tilt produced by the ship's heel and the pitch from the ocean's roll seemed to magnify Lucca's growing feeling of inferiority.

All of that self-doubt was quickly forgotten as he climbed the final stair and onto the quarterdeck. Standing on the highest deck of the ship, Lucca felt like he had stepped into the very essence of the Mediterranean. The salty wind pushed fresh air into his lungs, quickening his heart. Up there he had a view of the entire ship stretched out before him. It was an exhilarating feeling, especially with the ship running at a good clip.

Also on the quarterdeck was a young man of about twenty casually leaning on the ship's helm. The man gave them a friendly nod, and Bartolo nodded back, saying, "Lucca, say hello to Mr. DiSesa, the *Albatro's* pilot."

Bartolo then gathered them to the area behind the helm. "Now pay attention, Lucca. First we will get a fix of our position. Grace, use the compass you have there, and tell me which way is north."

Grace cupped the compass and brought it to her belly. She then rotated herself until she found north and extended her arm straight to show Bartolo and Lucca. It looked to Lucca like she had done this many times before. Bartolo then spread his chart out, angling it so that the chart's north was in accordance with Grace's arm.

"Lucca, look out over the port side and find a reference point," Bartolo instructed.

Lucca didn't know port from starboard, but there was only open water on the right-hand side of the ship, so he looked over the left-hand side where land was visible. He also didn't know what made for a good reference point, but he squinted his eyes and caught sight of a lighthouse.

"That lighthouse there?" Lucca asked.

"That will work. Grace, give me a bearing on the lighthouse please."

Grace rotated her body clockwise and then called out, "One-hundred-twelve degrees, Captain."

"What is one-hundred-eighty less one-hundred-twelve?"

"Sixty-eight," said Grace, instantaneously.

Bartolo found the lighthouse on his chart and took out a flat, semicircular piece of metal with markings on the curve. He placed the middle of the flat part of the tool directly on the lighthouse and aligned the flat side with north. He then made a mark with his pencil where sixty eight degrees showed up on the curved side. He then used the flat part of the tool to draw a line from the lighthouse to his mark and then extended the line well beyond it.

"Now, Lucca, I used a shortcut here since I only have one-hundred-and-eighty degrees at my disposal," Bartolo explained, holding up his semicircular tool. "This is called a protractor. If Grace was looking at our ship from the light-house, do you know what her bearing would be?"

Lucca had no idea. After a few moments of awkward silence, Lucca shook his head. Grace handed him the compass helpfully.

"Pretend you're on the lighthouse," she said encouragingly. She had already slipped into the roll of Lucca's teacher, it seemed.

Lucca accepted the compass, walked over to the rail and looked over his shoulder to try to align his back with the lighthouse, as if he were standing on the top of it and looking at the ship. He then looked directly at Bartolo, who was waiting patiently, and then looked down at the compass.

"Two-hundred-ninety?" Lucca guessed.

"Very close," Bartolo said and nodded. "It is difficult to get a good bearing when you're so close to the reference point. The correct answer is two-hundred-ninety-two degrees, which happens to be three-hundred-and-sixty degrees less sixty-eight. You can now see why my shortcut works."

Bartolo then turned their attention back to the line he had drawn on the chart. "Now, we know we are somewhere along this line. But that is not very helpful, is it? What shall we do?"

"Find another reference point," Grace said cheerfully.

This time Grace picked a mountain peak as a reference, and Lucca called out the bearing. Bartolo drew another line, starting from the mountain peak and intersecting his prior line.

Bartolo placed a finger at the intersection of the lines. "This is our fix. This is where we are on the map. Now go eat your breakfast and meet me back here in a half hour. We will learn dead reckoning."

Breakfast was biscuits and black coffee. Lucca rather liked the biscuits, but the coffee was terribly bitter, and he couldn't help contorting his face on the first sip. Another young deckhand with the adolescent beginnings of a beard was happy to relieve him of his coffee, though he did not wait for Lucca to offer.

Lucca made his way back to the quarterdeck where Bartolo and Grace were already waiting.

"Alright, dead reckoning—" Bartolo began.

"Why do they call it dead reckoning, Captain?" Grace interjected.

"I don't know, that's just what it's called," Bartolo answered mechanically, as if he was well acquainted with Grace's inquisitiveness. "Dead reckoning is the method we use to figure out our position if we do not have any reference points. Of course we need a starting fix, which we got a half hour ago."

Bartolo, as if to head Grace off at the pass, said, "Pretend we cannot see land over the port side. Pretend we have no reference points available."

He continued, "To dead reckon we need to know our heading, we need to know time since our last fix, and we need to know speed. Grace, what is our heading?"

Grace rotated her body and her compass toward the bow of the ship and obediently called out their heading. "One-hundred-ninety degrees, Captain. South."

Bartolo drew a third line on his chart, starting from the intersection of the first two lines and continuing south at a heading of one-hundred-and-ninety degrees. "Good. Now let's assume Mr. DiSesa is a competent helmsman and we have kept this constant heading. We now know we are somewhere on this line. We must now find time and speed to know how far we are along it. How do we find time, Lucca?"

Lucca was unsure if this was a trick question or if they thought he was a dullard. "A pocket watch?"

"Sure—any time-keeping device. We have a chronometer aboard this ship. But what is it that we measure specifically?"

Lucca was not quite sure what the captain was asking and started to feel embarrassment coming on, compounded by the fact a girl his age seemed far superior to him in this whole navigation thing. When Bartolo provided the answer, it seemed so simple that it shook Lucca's confidence even more. "We measure the amount of time that has elapsed since our last fix. In this case, thirty minutes. Now we know our heading, we know time elapsed, but we need speed. How do we get speed?"

Lucca had no idea how to measure speed and saw Grace fidgeting. Clearly she knew the answer and was holding it in, ready to burst.

"How do we measure speed, Grace?" Bartolo finally asked.

"Chip log!" Grace shouted happily.

"Right! Lucca, hand me the spool you brought up here. Now this is a chip log. On the end of the line, we see there is a weight and a small cloth canopy. When thrown into the water, this acts as a miniature version of a drogue or sea anchor. It is meant to stay stationary while the boat advances. Lucca, cast it down into the water and let the line slide through your hand. Don't grip it tightly. Don't provide any resistance. Good. Did you feel anything just there?"

Lucca nodded and said, "It was a knot."

"Exactly. A knot indeed. The line has knots tied into it at equal intervals of fifty feet. Each knot that you feel passing through your hand represents a *knot*, which is a rate of speed equaling one nautical mile per hour. Hence the name. Now pull it back in and we'll try it again."

Bartolo produced a small sandglass from his pocket. "Now let the line out again and count how many knots you feel in thirty seconds."

Lucca let out the line once more as Bartolo started his timer. Lucca concentrated very hard, focusing his entire being on the thin line slide through his fingers. *One knot, two, three, four, five.*

"And ... stop! How many knots did you feel Lucca?" Bartolo asked.

"Five, Captain," Lucca answered.

Bartolo made a practiced glance at the spool. "Good. let's say five and a half. So we are going five and a half knots. That's our speed. Assuming we've been traveling at that speed for the last thirty minutes, how far along my chart line have we gone?"

"Two and three quarter nautical miles," reported Grace.

Bartolo took out a tool that looked like a large pair of pincers. He explained that they were called dividers and turned a dial on the dividers to match the distance between the two pincer points with a legend on the map that displayed the scale for a nautical mile. He then placed one of the points on their original fix and walked the dividers two nautical miles up his line. He then dialed the dividers tighter and matched the gap between the pincers to measure three quarters of a nautical mile as prescribed by the map's legend. Finally, he made a mark along their heading line that was two and a quarter nautical miles from their original fix.

"This is our new position, and now you know how to dead reckon," he said.

"Why is it fifty feet between each knot, Captain?" Lucca ventured.

"Very good question, Lucca!" Bartolo said approvingly. Lucca felt a touch of pride swell in his breast, though it was to be very short lived.

Grace answered as if she didn't think it was such a good question at all. "Because if you're sailing at a speed of one knot, you travel fifty feet in thirty seconds."

Lucca must have looked at her in a very unenlightened way because she sighed and continued with her explanation.

"A speed of one knot is one nautical mile per hour. Six thousand feet in a nautical mile, and three thousand six hundred seconds in an hour. We are talking about traveling at that rate for thirty seconds, remember? Six thousand divided by three thousand, six hundred multiplied by thirty ..."

Lucca was still speechless. He was quite intimidated by this girl of arresting beauty, who seemed to live in a world where youth was no boundary to the world of grown-ups, to the world of men. The hunter-green eyes combined with the dizzying numbers created in Lucca a full-body paralysis.

"Let's simplify it," Grace said and pressed him. "How many times does thirty-six go into sixty then?"

"Once ...?" Lucca said hesitantly, and he could feel his face grow hot.

Grace rolled her eyes and was about to dumb it down further for Lucca when Bartolo cut in. "That's enough, Grace."

But Lucca could tell Bartolo was not angry at Grace. On the contrary, he seemed to be quietly relishing in her display. He wanted her to continue but not at Lucca's expense.

"OK, Miss Smart Aleck. Here is a question for you. The English ships all use a 28.8 second sandglass for their chip logs. How many feet between their knots?"

For added pressure, Bartolo flipped his sandglass and started the timer. Grace immediately scrunched up her face in deep concentration. Her eyes were open but fixed on a point on the deck. Lucca could not even grasp the type of mathematical magic she was performing in her head, but he was sure that he had never seen a more beautiful creature in all his life.

Before even half the sand had fallen, Grace raised her eyebrows and said hopefully, "48?"

Bartolo broke into a slight grin for the first time that day. "Exactly right."

Bartolo then bent over and put his hands on his knees to be eye level with the children. "Now we have our position. Or do we? Whenever we make an observation of any kind, we must also think about how that observation could lead us astray. Remember, we are trying to figure out our position by how much distance we've traveled, and we used our speed versus the water we are sailing through. Can you think of a way that speed could mislead us? Grace, don't answer. Let Lucca have a try."

Lucca, who was now slightly recovered from Grace's arithmetic inquisition, gave it some thought. For some reason a memory fought its way up from the depths and replayed itself in Lucca's mind's eye. He tried to push the memory back down and focus on the captain's question, but it kept forcing its way up. He had been swimming off the coast of Cinque Terra. His father had taken him there when he was eight or nine. He was far from shore and tired of swimming, so he flipped onto his back, filled his lungs, and floated for a time. He could float for hours. The warm sun and the water lazily licking at his ears felt good and lulled him into a state of tranquility. It was some time before he decided to swim back to shore. But when he reached the beach, everything was unfamiliar. He started to walk south along the beach until a rocky outcropping barred his way, and then he doubled back. It was an hour before he found his father, and when he did, he got a stern talking to. Why did this memory surface? When he was floating, his speed was zero, but he sure traveled a distance.

Lucca looked up. "What about current?"

Bartolo grinned for the second time that day, and Lucca, beaming, saw that he had answered correctly.

"Good first day! Tomorrow we will begin trigonometry."

LUCCA QUICKLY LEARNED to love his daily lessons with Captain Bartolo and Grace, and while he could not match Grace's aptitude with any maritime subject, he made steady progress. He also learned that the lessons represented a time separate and distinct from life on the *Albatro*. During lessons, Bartolo could be the most gentle, encouraging of teachers, patiently going over the steps involved in tying a half-hitch. But as Lucca would come to find out, if Lucca tied that half-hitch incorrectly outside the lessons, and a fishing net were to be lost on account of his incompetence, Lucca would feel the wrath of Bartolo just like any other sailor. The wrath of Bartolo usually meant hugging the mast and receiving a number of lashes that would befit the respective infraction. The loss of the fishing net cost Lucca three lashes across his bare back. But Lucca learned this well, and the lessons were a safe place, a place where it was OK to make mistakes. Outside of that, mistakes on the *Albatro* were answered harshly, and Bartolo was not a man to cross. The incident showed Lucca the two sides of Bartolo. Like the Mediterranean, he could be calm, transparent, and inviting, but when the weather vane spun, he could turn steel gray and serious as the storm. In short, he was a good captain and a fair leader once you learned the rules.

The rules were simple: *work hard and don't make mistakes.* Lucca would lay in his bunk practicing his half-hitch, eight-knot, sheet-bend, and bowline until he could tie them in the dark. He would rise with the dawn and force down coffee and biscuits before going topside to swab the decks. Then he would lend hands to the rigging if needed. On days when they made port, he would unload cargo onto the piers or lighters. He would help the clerks treble check inventory and treble check their sums. At night, when the deck hands would lay about the forecastle, looking up at the stars, Lucca would lay among them and listen as they took turns telling sailors' tales. They also took turns at the rum, and with the smell of the tobacco, it was easy to drift along with the tale and believe every fantastic word of it as the stars got closer and closer. He enjoyed these nights and he felt part of the crew but anonymous, together but alone, which suited him.

The apex of Lucca's day, however, would be his lessons. He

and Grace would take their lessons from Captain Bartolo every day. Lucca relished in the education he was getting, and even at his young age understood how lucky he was. They learned how to read charts, chart courses, and course correct. They learned celestial navigation and how to rig for the different points of sail. They learned how to read signal flags and memorized the hulls and rigging of competing merchant vessels.

Lucca knew he was receiving a first-rate education, and so did other members of the crew, but they did not know why. Lucca, sensitive as he was, felt a feeling of resentment come from some members of the crew, particularly deck hands close to his age. One boy by the name of Mateo was especially unfriendly to him despite Lucca's overtures of peace. Mateo was two years older than Lucca and had the size benefit of puberty. He was the same boy who relieved Lucca of his coffee on his first day about the *Albatro*. Mateo had a cruel streak, and Lucca believed Mateo had it in his mind to hate him. What started as sneer and insult gave way to shoving and tripping. Lucca could not understand the malice this boy was showing him, and after several sleepless nights, he came up with a plan to befriend Mateo. During one evening of storytelling and stargazing, Lucca sought out Mateo and shared his ration of rum with him. Mateo accepted cautiously and Lucca asked him where he was from.

"Roma," Mateo replied, drinking down Lucca's rum without breaking his eye contact with Lucca.

Lucca nodded. He was in a crouch and now decided to sit. "What does your father do?"

"Orphan," Mateo replied.

Lucca viewed this as a slight setback in getting Mateo to open up but then remembered the identity created by Bartolo and saw an opening for common ground. "I'm an orphan as well."

This did not seem to have the effect that Lucca had hoped for, and Mateo only curled his lip in disgust and spat. "What is it you want, little boy."

"I, I just ... I don't know. Why do you hate me?"

"Do I need a reason?" Mateo laid back on the deck and stretched his arms behind his head, essentially dismissing Lucca.

Lucca crawled back to his original stargazing position, feeling more unsettled than ever. Over the next few weeks, he tried giving Mateo a wide berth, but the bullying continued. Lucca was also aware that his reputation with the crew was suffering on account of not fighting back. He was not scared of getting clobbered, but he could not bring himself to strike back at this boy Mateo even though he could not figure out why the boy hated him so. Lucca's tentative reasoning was that there must be some wrong that he himself perpetrated because how else could such unfairness exist? Lucca believed he deserved this bullying and therefore could not raise a fist in response.

Then one day, while Lucca was on his hands and knees scrubbing the deck, Mateo walked by and with a heavy fire bucket, viciously smashed it into the back of Lucca's head. The blow rendered Lucca unconscious for a full ten seconds while he was face down in soapy water. Only the helmsman, DiSesa, witnessed this and came down from the quarterdeck to help Lucca to his feet. He peered into Lucca's eyes, which were trying to refocus.

"You alright there?"

Lucca seemed to ponder the question a long time while blinking his eyes slowly.

DiSesa brought Lucca up to the quarterdeck with him and sat him down. DiSesa waited for a few minutes until it looked like Lucca once again had his bearings.

"He hit you on the back of the head with a fire bucket,

unawares. That's dirty. You have to show him you ain't gonna take that kind of abuse, man!" DiSesa had his hand on the helm and was looking forward but turned back to Lucca who was seated behind him. "You hearing me, Lucca?"

"Yes," Lucca groaned.

"Well, what are we going to do about this Mateo villain?"

"I don't know. I don't know why he picked me to hate." Lucca was pressing both of his palms against his forehead, trying in vain to alleviate some of his headache.

"Who gives a shit about *why*? He's just a Goddman asshole. You need to punch him in his Goddamn mouth."

"Why do I have to fight him?"

"Well you know you can't go to the captain. The crew won't tolerate a rat."

"I know."

DiSesa looked back at Lucca. "You think you have a headache now? Wait until Bartolo finds out you put a dent in the fire bucket!"

Lucca had to laugh in spite of himself, and DiSesa delighted at Lucca's reaction. "You can come up here whenever you like, Lucca. Maybe I'll teach you how to drive this great bitch."

15

Lucca found a boon companion in DiSesa and started spending more and more free time on the quarter-deck. Though DiSesa was only nineteen, he was already a talented pilot and had started with the *Albatro* around Lucca's age. DiSesa's mixture of European heritage could be seen in the meld of his beard, scruffs of red, blond, and black. He had a casual confidence about him and was deliberate about all his movements, nothing wasted, nothing wanting. He cussed enough to make up for all the polite sailors of the Mediterranean.

Without Lucca touching the helm, DiSesa taught Lucca how to hold a heading and read the telltales to keep the sails from luffing. No one was allowed to touch the helm apart from DiSesa and Bartolo. DiSesa also taught Lucca about all the superstitions of a life at sea.

"Sharks are bad luck, dolphins are good luck, if that wasn't obvious enough. Steer clear of redheads, and make sure you don't have deadbeats in your crew—all debts should be paid before shoving off. No bananas, and be careful what you whistle for. Don't say the d-word, and definitely don't kill an albatross."

"What's the d-word?"

"*Drown*," DiSesa whispered.

Lucca nodded and took a mental note. This was good information. "Why are bananas bad luck?"

"They just are. And you never, never, wish any one good luck. That's one of the all-time-best ways to give someone bad luck."

"OK. Any other ways to get bad luck?"

"Well, there is one other big thing ..." DiSesa seemed to be uncharacteristically hesitant to expound.

"What is it?" Lucca asked earnestly. "I'd like to know. I could be giving myself bad luck right now!"

"Nah, not right to say." DiSesa was now looking straight forward.

"Oh come on, man!" Lucca pleaded.

"It's bad luck to have a woman on the boat," a voice came from behind them. Both Lucca and DiSesa swiveled to find Grace perched coolly on the back rail. She had seemed to apparate out of thin air.

"Isn't that what you were going to say, Mr. DiSesa?"

"I wasn't going to say it, Miss Grace," DiSesa managed. Lucca thought DiSesa's Adam's apple was going to break free of his neck.

"Were you thinking it then?" Grace asked, hopping off the rail and walking slowly over to the squirming helmsman. She wore the beginnings of her mischievous grin.

"No, Miss Grace—well yes, I suppose I was thinking of it, but I don't believe in that superstition."

Grace was now less than a foot away from the suffering helmsman. She slowly reached up her hand and took off DiSesa's hat, placing it jauntily on her own head. She then spoke softly, looking DiSesa squarely in the eye. "I'd like a turn at this bitch."

DiSesa, cowed but still frightfully aware of his duties, scanned the deck for Bartolo. DiSesa knew it would be at least ten lashes if Bartolo caught him shirking his responsibility. Finding no sign of the captain, he vacated his place at the helm to the thirteen-year-old girl. Grace grasped the wheel firmly and seemed to relish the feel of the mahogany. Her hunter-green eyes danced from the telltales to the helm's compass to the horizon. Lucca knew enough to see she was holding her course perfectly. They were running at a speed of ten knots, and any course deviation or change in tack would be felt by the whole crew. DiSesa was just as impressed as Lucca, albeit nervous as hell that Bartolo would come storming out of his cabin.

When she had enough fun at the expense of the poor DiSesa, she returned him his helm and stuffed his hat back on his head. It was only after Grace descended the quarterdeck that Lucca started to laugh. It took DiSesa a full five minutes before he shook his head in relief and laughed in spite of himself.

Slowly Lucca grew to be less nervous around Grace, though he was still in awe of her. Suffice it to say, she was not in awe of him. She tolerated him and even made an effort to help him in his lessons, which at times was helpful and other times demeaning. To his chagrin, Lucca felt himself sliding into the role of her little brother.

Later that day, when Lucca was sitting with his sketchbook, back to the foremast, as he was like to do, Grace snuck up behind him and yanked his work from his grasp. He tried to snatch it back, but she was too quick and danced from him at a safe distance, studying the sketch. His efforts futile, he stopped chasing her and waited impatiently for her to begin her teasing, but the teasing did not begin.

She finally took her eyes off the sketch and looked at Lucca. "This is the *Albatro*."

"Yeah," said Lucca irritably.

"You did this all today?"

"Yes," Lucca sighed.

"But this is the side of the *Albatro*. How can you draw the side of the *Albatro* if you're *on* the *Albatro*."

"I don't know, I guess I remembered how it looked when we were at port. Can you give it back now?"

"It's very good, Lucca," said Grace, continuing to study the page. "You even got the windows of the captain's cabin right."

The praise made Lucca shift uncomfortably.

Grace's green eyes fixed back on Lucca. "I have an idea. Come to my cabin tonight at eleven o'clock and bring your sketchbook."

"What? If Bartolo found out, he—"

"Or don't," Grace cut in, shrugging. She handed Lucca back his sketch and strode away.

Lucca's mind and his pulse were racing for the rest of the evening hours as the ship's chronometer cautiously made its way to eleven o'clock. Lucca was sitting on his bunk with his sketchbook in his lap trying to coax his thoughts back down to their normal pace. What if this was another one of Grace's practical jokes? Worse, what if Bartolo caught him in Grace's cabin? What if Bartolo accused him of attempting something devious? Sure, he was only thirteen, but that may not place him above suspicion. The fact that Grace's honor was perfectly safe among a crew of hardened sailors was a testament to Bartolo's iron hand. The fact that she was the daughter of the owner of the Albatro may have also contributed to her safety, but it was fear of Bartolo that kept the crew chaste and civil. The wrong look would get you lashed, the wrong words would get you marooned on the nearest loneliest island, and the wrong action —well, the wrong action would get you gutted and dumped lifeless in the coldest waters the Mediterranean had to offer.

At five of eleven, Lucca willed himself to stand up. He decided to ascend to the deck through the fore hatch where he could get a view of the deck, and by leaning over the rail, catch a glimpse of any light coming from the captain's cabin, which was adjacent to Grace's. There were sailors on watch, smoking and chatting softly at the forecastle, but if they saw Lucca, they paid him no mind. It was Bartolo he was afraid of. He nearly fell over the rail straining to see any indication of whether Bartolo was awake. The ship's beam was broadest in the middle, so he could not get a good look and decided to creep aft.

As he crept past the main mast's shroud, he reached out to steady himself, and his hand found a rope—a halyard actually —and he got a crazy idea in his head. He put down his sketchbook and untied one end of the halyard and wrapped it around his arm. He yanked it twice to make sure it was secure and then swung out, off the side of the ship over open water in an arc. At the apex of the arc, when he was farthest from the ship, he was able to get a look at the captain's cabin—all dark! He stumbled back onto the boat, and emboldened by his little ploy, scooped up his sketchbook and darted over to Grace's cabin.

Grace opened the door quietly after his gentle tap and beckoned him in. She looked at him quizzically because he was breathing rather rapidly. He had never been inside her cabin before. It was simple, about a fourth of the size of Bartolo's, with a small bed and a table and single stool whose legs could be set into divots in the floorboards. Illumination came from a lantern on the table, which cast a soft light around the room and especially on a family portrait behind the table. The painting featured a man, who Lucca recognized to be the Merchant Ligoria, and two children. One could have been a younger version of Grace, and next to her was a blond adolescent. Lucca could only assume it was her brother.

Grace was sitting on her bed, so Lucca went for the stool. Grace shook her head. "The stool creaks loudly. Bartolo used to listen for that and tell me to go to bed."

So Lucca took the floor. Then Grace knelt down and reached for something under her bed. She carefully took out a small chest. She opened the chest and handled its contents as one might handle fine china. The contents were wrapped in some kind of cloth. Grace informed him it was to protect against the salty air. Lucca craned his neck to see what had been so carefully stored. From the wrapped cloth, Grace produced a small stack of books. Lucca thought the books an anticlimactic treasure, but the way Grace handled them kept him keenly interested.

"Let's start with this one," she said, selecting one of the books. It was a brown volume, and it looked crisp and brand-new. The gold lettering on the spine said *Treasure Island*.

"It's a new one," she informed him. "I'll read and you draw."

She cleared her throat softly, and maybe a little nervously, Lucca thought. He opened his sketchbook and lay prone on the floor. Grace's voice slowly picked up confidence, and she read beautifully. Her intonation and pitch breathed excitement and suspense into the story. She did voices for the characters and even softly sung the pirate ditties. Most of all, the timbre of her voice was intoxicating. It was unlike her normal speech, which could be choppy and curt. When she was reading her voice resonated generously like flowing silk. It put Lucca into a tingly state of relaxation. After about thirty minutes, Grace paused and knelt down next to Lucca to look at Lucca's drawing. He had produced a likeness of the pirate Billy Bones, big and dark and tattooed, dragging a treasure chest. Grace was absolutely delighted to see her characters come to life in Lucca's sketches. Lucca was absolutely delighted in her delight.

Over the coming evenings, Lucca would sneak back into her cabin, and the portraits of young Jim Hawkins, the upright Dr. Livesey, and the peg-legged Long John Silver were added to their collection. Between the daily lessons, the idle time spent with the helmsman DiSesa and now the late-night readings with Grace, Lucca was in a state of bliss. Even the tortuous teasing endured from Mateo could not pry him off his cloud. As the days and weeks washed over them, Grace had to get new titles to read, and when all books were read, they both yearned for the next port where Grace could replenish their supply. They marched gallantly through *The Three Musketeers*, they skulked mischievously into *The Adventures of Tom Sawyer*, and they even pushed their way through the solitude of *Robinson Crusoe*.

When it seemed to Lucca that his level of bliss couldn't get any higher, he was proven wrong. He and Grace were making their way through *The Count of Monte Cristo*. A picture of the Chateau d'If was hanging on the wall of Grace's cabin, and Lucca had put the finishing touches on Sinbad the Sailor. Grace was reading of the harsh reunion of Mercedes and Dantes, then Monte Cristo, when she got down off her bed and lay down on the floor with Lucca. She laid her head down on the small of Lucca's back and continued reading. It was then, at the ripe old age of thirteen, when Lucca decided he was in love.

16

I n mid-1884, the *Albatro* received news that the Merchant Ligoria had taken ill, and an immediate course was set for Genoa. The *Albatro* was berthed in the Port of Genoa for four days, and when it set sail to resume its trade route, Grace was not on board. To Lucca's despair she stayed in Genoa with her father, who was bedridden and holding weakly to life.

Five long months passed like the doldrums, and Mateo was finally succeeding in making Lucca's life miserable. Lucca also noticed he had lost the respect of the crew with his perceived inability to fight back against his tormentor. Even his daily lessons lost their excitement without Grace's presence. Lucca was nowhere near Grace as a pupil, and Bartolo, despite his dogged persistence, could not produce the same epiphanies and flashes of brilliance in Lucca that he saw in her.

This is not to say Lucca and Bartolo did not grow closer. They both missed Grace, and it became an unspoken pain they shared. As with any vacuum, the space was filled with the objects nearest. One day, as Bartolo was teaching Lucca how to read tide tables, he asked Lucca about his grandfather.

"What was he like? I grew up on stories of Garibaldi and the Old Bull Ferrando. But what was he like as a man, as a grandfather?"

This was an unusual question from Bartolo. If Bartolo ever asked Lucca a question, it was either rhetorical or asked with the intention to teach. This was a new layer of the captain that Lucca had not yet encountered. It seemed Bartolo was genuinely interested, and Lucca struggled to put words to an answer.

"He was intense but loving." As soon as the words left his mouth, Lucca winced at his own inability to give a proper description of his grandfather, but Bartolo only nodded politely, sagely. They then returned their attention to the tide tables, but the question lingered with Lucca for a long time.

One month later, the *Albatro* got word that Ligoria had made a full recovery, and Grace would be returning to the ship. Lucca could not tell who was more excited, he or Bartolo. Lucca saw the captain personally cleaning Grace's cabin in anticipation of her arrival.

Finally the day came when they berthed in Genoa, and Grace strode up the gangplank of the *Albatro*. Everything about her was the same, but everything was different. Lucca saw it immediately but could not tell what "it" was. When she saw him, she hugged him, and he presented her with a newly published copy of the *Adventures of Huckleberry Finn*. She thanked him politely, but there was no mischievous smile. No allusion to secret readings. She also seemed taller. Perhaps it was her boots.

A few days went by, and Grace did not invite him to her cabin. Summoning up courage after a lesson, Lucca touched Grace at the elbow and asked if she wanted to read *Huckleberry Finn*.

"I can't exist as a child anymore, Lucca." Then she walked

away. Lucca stood rooted to the spot and all of a sudden felt very silly and very young.

He decided to talk to DiSesa about his feelings for Grace and get some advice from the older youth. Lucca waited a full week until he and DiSesa were on shore and he was sure that neither Grace or Bartolo were in earshot.

Lucca started to carefully present his situation, but DiSesa cut him off. "Lucca, it's obvious you have affections for young Miss Ligoria, so I don't need to hear you stammer about and flounder as you explain it to me." DiSesa was on his back, resting in a dingy that was tied to the dock. He was cracking open pistachios, throwing them high into the air and attempting to catch them in his mouth.

Lucca was taken aback and a little nervous. "Why is it so obvious? Do you think Bartolo knows?"

"Ha! Bartolo has the perception of a walrus!" Lucca did not know if walruses were imperceptive but assumed he was in the clear.

"She wants nothing to do with me now, and I don't know why." Lucca was sitting on the dock above DiSesa and occasionally intercepting a pistachio nut.

"She's becoming a woman, Lucca, and you're still a boy. You haven't noticed her growing up?" DiSesa looked at Lucca with a sly grin that made him uncomfortable.

Lucca tried to shift the conversation away from a discussion of Grace's maturing body and asked, "Why do you say I'm still a boy?"

"You're scrawny, and your face lacks fuzz," DiSesa said simply. Lucca had enough of stupid DiSesa and started walking away down the dock after angrily swatting a pistachio into the sea.

Lucca could not help sulking and even thought about asking for his book back. If she wasn't going to read *The Adven-*

tures of Huckleberry Finn, then she should give it back to him. He then kicked himself for wanting to read what was, according to Grace, a children's book and told himself to grow up. Over the coming months, he threw himself into his lessons with Grace and Bartolo and even started doing extra preparation. He freely admitted to himself that he was only doing this as a way to stir the attention of Grace. It didn't much matter. She was always polite to him, which Lucca decided was even worse than being totally ignored. He was back to being the little brother.

17

One morning Lucca arrived to the daily lesson with Grace and Bartolo sporting a grisly black eye. It was purple and angry-looking and was of course complements of Mateo. His eye matched his lip, which was fat and discolored. Upon seeing Lucca's face, Grace showed a look of deep concern, but Lucca, in no mood to be pitied, did not meet her gaze. Bartolo said nothing and showed no interest.

"Today we begin meteorology, the study of weather." Bartolo always began his lessons loudly and with an address that would be better suited for a lecture hall than an audience of two. "Integral to the study of weather is the measurement and analysis of atmospheric pressure. Here on the table we have a barometer."

Just then, Bartolo froze and had the terrified look of someone that's been caught unawares by a stealthy enemy.

"What is it, captain?" inquired Grace, who noticed the same change come over Bartolo.

Bartolo's stare was fixed on the barometer. He lifted it, adjusted it, and set it back down again. He then rummaged through chest under the table and produced another, similar looking device that Lucca could only assume was another barometer. In the next moment, Bartolo had ceased being the patient professor and donned the mantle of captain.

"Gale," barked Bartolo. "A big one. Stay here. Make fast this whole room." He left the cabin. Lucca and Grace could hear him shouting, "Down the cloth! Up the trysail!"

Lucca and Grace scrambled to stow all the papers and devices and make fast anything that could move. They then left the cabin to find the eerie beginnings of a ten-year storm. Bartolo had taken the helm from DiSesa and had the crew scurrying around to make the *Albatro* ready for what was to come. The swells had started, and the *Albatro* was already surging up and down on giant rolling seas. The most disquieting thing was the quiet. Lucca would later learn that it was the low pressure causing this sinister silence. It was a soundless blanket that made the hairs of his neck stand up. Something deep and instinctual told him trouble was bearing down on them.

Lucca made out the voices of Bartolo and DiSesa, who were shouting above the silence.

"Take the helm, run her before the wind," Bartolo ordered.

"Captain, a beam reach would point us toward the coast where we might find a cove." DiSesa's voice calm but intoned an understanding of the dire situation.

"A beam reach capsizes us in eighty knots, which is what we're looking at. Besides, there's no time, it's already upon us." Poseidon seemed to hear Bartolo's words, and a great spray shot up over the bow as the Albatro came down one swell and into the back of another. The winds were picking up now, and Bartolo left the quarterdeck and resumed his shouting, which now competed with wailing winds from the west.

"*No cloth on the foremast! Trysail to the main mast! Batten her down there, man! You there, help me with the drogues.*"

After the wind came the rain and then the darkness. The rain came in great horizontal sheets, attacking them from the stern. Tremendous sprays of seawater rose high above the deck before pummeling them from the bow. DiSesa was putting in a heroic effort to keep the swells, now cresting and crashing, at the *Albatro's* stern, for any wave that hit her port or starboard would surely roll her.

Lucca was holding fast to the rail on the *Albatro's* port side when he heard a sickening crack and saw the foremast break and crash over the bow. A moment later, Bartolo and half a dozen of the old salts were attacking the felled mast with hatchets and the tangled lines with knives, trying to free the *Albatro* of this danger that threatened to destroy the main mast.

Lucca moved to help the effort at the bow but stopped cold when DiSesa, from the helm, screamed over the storm, "*Rogue wave starboard!*"

DiSesa steered the ship hard to port to keep the wave at their stern, and it might have prevented the capsize of the *Alabtro* but an ocean of seawater smashed over the deck, scattering the choking sailors and causing chaotic confusion. In the chaos, Lucca thought he saw the body of a man washed over the port side into the sea. Lucca, choking on seawater, scanned the black, frothy water for anything that looked like a man. Just then, a bolt a lightning illuminated the maelstrom.

And as if frozen in time, he locked eyes with Mateo, buoyed up high by a swell.

Without hesitation Lucca grabbed the nearest line and fixed one end to the rail. He then worked to tie the other around his waist. He needed a knot that wouldn't cinch on him. His hands deftly tied a bowline as he had done thousands of times in the dark. Lucca scrambled up on the rail and dove out into space, out into the storm. No sooner did his feet leave the rail did he feel the rope around his waist grow taught, and then he was hauled mightily back into the ship, where he landed in a heap of confusion. He looked up to see Bartolo standing over him, holding the other end of his line. Bartolo was as angry as the storm itself.

"*Goddamn you, sailor, stay in the goddamn boat!*"

Bartolo strode off, back toward the broken mast, shouting orders as he went. Lucca looked over the port side but never saw Mateo again.

The *Albatro* rode out the rest of the storm and limped into the Port of Tripoli a day and a half later.

18

Mateo, the only man lost in the storm, received a burial at sea. A ceremonial coffin was constructed and cast empty over the side and into the depths. Lucca received ten lashes from Bartolo for endangering the life of a sailor (himself), but Lucca could tell Bartolo was not putting his back into it, and the bullwhip did not even break skin. Bartolo was not the only one to witness Lucca's selfless rescue attempt. Indeed, the entire crew of the *Albatro* was aware Lucca would have thrown himself into the storm to save his tormentor, the very source of his emotional and bodily pain. The crew had read this boy wrong.

After the burial at sea, one of the old salts came up to Lucca, gripping his hat. This was a man Lucca knew to have rounded Cape Horn on multiple occasions. The weathered face looked at Lucca and spoke plainly. "I'm sorry I thought you a coward." He then shuffled away before Lucca could respond.

The *Albatro* spent several weeks at Al-Mina, the harbor city of Tripoli, undergoing repairs. Most of the crew holed up in the taverns and brothels while the *Albatro* was dry-docked. Lucca spent his days in the old city of Tripoli itself, wandering the narrow streets. He could not banish the final, ghostly image of Mateo from his mind. Mateo's life and death did not make sense to Lucca. Why had God breathed life into Mateo? What was the point? An orphan grows up in the gutters of Rome and struggles against a harsh existence at sea just so he can inflict cruelty on others and then die senselessly without redemption. Lucca was not religious, and in fact much of Italy had become secular in the wake of the *Risorgimento* and the Italian independence. Still, Lucca had found comfort in the philosophy that life had purpose. Existence had purpose. It was more than a philosophy; it was a promise that was made to him over and over again throughout his life. Good prevailed over evil. Parents loved their children. Fathers protected their families. These were the natural truths of Lucca's world. Lucca knew there was evil in this world, but despite its momentary triumphs, good must ultimately prevail. Where was the ultimate triumph of good in Mateo's life? It was all so unsettling. The only good that came of these unsettling thoughts was that they crowded out thoughts of Grace. Her ambivalence and lack of attention had only strengthened his feelings toward her.

His meandering and philosophizing led him to the citadel, the ancient fortress brooding on the hilltop above Tripoli. He could see for miles and had the full view of the Al-Mina crescent, the protective spit of coast line that provided safe harbor for so many ships. He sat himself on a damaged part of the fortress wall that had not been restored after a long-ago battle. After a time, he saw a figure walking up the hill toward him. The easy gait of the figure made it possible to identify Grace at a distance. It was a long hike up to the hilltop, and when she arrived she was flushed but not winded. She gave Lucca a nod and sat next to him. Silence sounded like the whoosh of the wind and far-off seagulls. Grace was first to break it.

"When I was home, in Genoa, I spent a lot of time with my father. I believe you've met him. He has always been a giant in my eyes—not physically, you understand, but in the way of a king. It was very hard to see him so sick, so weak, so frail. He is better now, but his mortality shows. It shows in his movements and his words. Some day he will ..."

Grace cleared her throat, and her voice hardened. "I have a brother, Lucca. A brother I don't much like. I believe him to be miserly, vindictive, and cruel. He is my elder and a natural successor to my father's company given the inheritance laws that favor male progeny. If he takes control of my father's company, he will twist and distort my father's legacy and good name until it is unidentifiable. Lost. I know this to be true with my head and my heart. My father also knows this, and upon finishing my minority, he will sign the company over to me. My claim will be tenuous though, even if he is alive and of clear mind. There will be a lawsuit, there will be fighting, and I imagine there will be some underhanded schemes to subvert my rights. They will call my competence into question. They will call my abilities into question. I must finish my minority in the best possible position I can so I may demonstrate a fitness for the task that is beyond question, beyond reproach."

For the first time, she looked at Lucca, who was looking at her, his eyes full of sympathy and understanding.

Grace hesitated before continuing. "I'm telling you this so you know my priorities. I know the way you look at me. What you want must not be."

Lucca did not recoil or show any sign of defensiveness. He had expected this was coming, and if anything he felt relief. Words had been finally assigned to unspoken frustrations. The mental anguish he had been shouldering was acknowledged; it existed outside his own head. He was saddened but relieved, and he appreciated the tenderness that she was showing him.

Her explanation was also a confession of her deepest desires, and she favored Lucca enough to be truly honest with him.

"I understand," said Lucca. Then he added, "However I can, I'll help you win what's rightfully yours."

Grace hugged him then, and Lucca reaffirmed his positive philosophy. All was right in the world. Grace nodded goodbye and started back down the hill. After about five paces, she turned and said, "Lucca, that was a very brave thing you did during the storm."

Lucca lingered on that wall a while. Strangely, Grace's rejection had actually freed him. Loving Grace was no longer an option, and that iron truth freed him from the tiring, gut-wrenching sickness of love that he had been suffering from. He looked out across the sea, and he was filled with hope. Some new thought was taking shape in him. Deep within his mind, an amorphous cloud of gray whispers was working itself into a clean, bright formation known as purpose. Grace would need good helmsmen. He would be the best goddamn helmsman in the Mediterranean.

19

When the Tripoli shipwrights finished with her, the *Albatro* was as proud a schooner as ever was. Bartolo had taken the opportunity to make some improvements, and as soon as the *Albatro* had departed Tripoli and was on a downwind run, he gathered DiSesa, Grace, Lucca, and Otto, the first mate of the *Albatro*, together at the bow.

"We now have a new sail in our arsenal." Bartolo placed his foot on a large wooden spar lashed onto the foredeck. "This is an extendable bowsprit that will support a spinnaker. It slides through this hole here and will extend out some ten feet, allowing the spinnaker to get out of the shadow of our foremast sails even though the halyard will be run up the foremast."

"Sir, beg pardon," Otto said and scrunched up his weathered face in confusion. "If the sail's tack is fastened to this here spar, how will clew become tack after a jibe? And no pole to hold the clew to windward?"

"Mr. Otto, this is an asymmetric spinnaker. Think of it as a large genoa sail, with more camber. It must be shifted as would a genoa." Bartolo was getting excited. "But speculation won't get us as far as spectation. Let us see for ourselves. Mr. Otto, set the chute and let us see how she flies! Those shipwrights promised me three more knots of speed on a downwind run!"

Otto set about barking orders to the crew, and they hastened to comply. Bartolo and DiSesa took the quarterdeck, and Grace and Lucca stationed themselves at the leeward rail so they could work the sheet when this asymmetrical spinnaker was hoisted. The *Albatro* was foaming along at nine knots, a good clip for the double-masted schooner in a fair breeze. Lucca had the spinnaker sheet through a series of new blocks set into the rail purposely for the new sail. He remarked to himself how sturdy they were. Two men cranked on the spinnaker halyard, and the sail came up in a hurry. The sail was of off-white color and looked to Lucca like a finer, lighter fabric than the robust canvas that made up the mainsail. As soon as the head of the sail made the top of the foremast, it billowed out and then snapped full, generating a sound like the crack of a bullwhip. The power coming through the sheet that Lucca held was immense, and with the help of Grace, it was all he could do to get it cleated off.

Lucca felt the boat surge forward, driven faster and faster by the added sail area. The bow was bravely cutting through the sea, converting dark blue into foaming whiteness. DiSesa was hooting and hollering from the helm, as were the old salts.

"We must be over fifteen knots!" Grace breathed excitedly.

"Lucca, Grace," Bartolo called down from the quarterdeck. "Give me a few feet more of trim on that sheet. Let's see what she can do."

Lucca and Grace strained with all their might against the sail. Finally, with the help of the new blocks that worked like a pulley system to add mechanical leverage, they succeeded in trimming the spinnaker. As they did this, Bartolo nodded to DiSesa, who put the ship's wheel down a few spokes to head them from a downwind run to a broad reach. The *Albatro* was positively flying. Though they were still running downwind, the leeward rail was now gliding just above the sea; such was her heel. The speed was exhilarating, and Lucca felt himself become almost giddy. He looked back over his shoulder at Grace, who was equally enthralled, green eyes flashing with excitement.

* * *

THE *ALBATRO* CHURNED west through the Levantine Sea, passing Cyprus in a day and making up lost time and trade. The breeze was stiff, the weather fair, and the morale high for the next half year. From Lisbon to Tangier, and from Tangier to Murcia, Valencia, and Barcelona. Then to Marseille and a brief layover in Genoa.

On these rare stops in Genoa, Lucca would stop in on Greta Nonna, who had taken up residence with another family to help with the household. She had little, but what she had she shared with Lucca who was still her child in her heart. She would not accept money from Lucca. Sometimes Lucca would walk up the hill to their old house, which was standing vacant and slowly dilapidating. Greta had been keeping it clean for the first few years, but now to walk up the hill was getting to be too much for her.

"Enzo refuses to sell it or even rent it," Greta told Lucca. "He thinks he can put all things back in their place when he returns from Africa."

But time in Genoa was always brief, and before the earth could finish a full pirouette, the *Albatro* would be back at sea, running down the coast to Napoli, then to Siracusa, rounding the boot and up the Adriatic to Firenze, Venezia, and Ragusa. Every port was an exchange, and every exchange was negotiated, validated, and consummated. Indigo for iron, leather for linen, flour for flax, copper for cotton. The Adriatic would become Ionian, and if weather were fair, the *Albatro* would cut up to the Aegean, then pass through the Bosporus and into the Black Sea, where accents were strange and the goods exotic.

The Mediterranean, along with all its small seas and tributaries, had a rhythm to it, and Lucca could feel himself fall in time with that rhythm. His lessons continued, and what's more, he was receiving another entire education from the old salts, who had taken a liking to him. From the old salts he learned how to listen for and hear the whispers of the *Albatro*. The creaks and groans of the hull told more than a dozen navigation tools ever could. He learned how to feel the weather and read a sunset like a book; the barometer was demoted from leading indicator to sanity check.

From the old salts he was also receiving a primer on the fairer sex, a subject that Lucca was becoming infinitely more curious about as puberty started to come on strong. Lucca had noticed his body changing simply from his ability to lift more cargo, but he downright startled himself when he caught a glimpse of his reflection in a barber shop window in Alexandria. He ducked into the shop and borrowed a hand mirror to study his discovery. The face looking back at him now had a distinct jaw, and his eyebrows seemed darker. The most shocking part was that he thought he looked more like Enzo Ferrando than Lucca Ferrando. The thought of his father made his heart pang, and he told himself he would write a letter that evening.

Lucca had also been noticing steady differences in his height. He was now looking down on Grace and eye to eye with Bartolo, and he was catching up with the lanky DiSesa. It was a dizzyingly fast growth spurt and resulted in an awkwardness that produced constant entertainment for the crew. Low-hanging booms and doorframes became his worst enemy, and he no longer trusted his voice not to embarrass him. But as the months passed, so too did the awkwardness. Muscle caught up with bone. Lucca's chest broadened, and he found he could trust his grip in the most trying situations a life at sea offered up. He did not have the august build of his father, much less the Old Bull Antoni Ferrando, but he could no longer be mistaken for a boy. Though generations had slenderized the Ferrandos, Lucca stood a near six foot, larger than most of his countrymen.

During the same time, Grace had emerged from childhood as well, but her progression had no time for awkwardness. In her womanhood she had retained all her athleticism and then some, still prowling the *Albatro* like a jungle cat. What's more she had become the second captain of the ship, and Bartolo encouraged her to assume command whenever possible. She had put her vast intellect to work and could now claim mastery over the subjects put to her by Bartolo. Lucca had progressed as well and was now allowed to spell DiSesa at the helm, but it was Grace's terrific progress that Bartolo could relish in. With six months left until Grace's eighteenth birthday and the end of her minority, Bartolo had thus far done his job masterfully. Through care and diligent tutelage, he had produced the makings of a sea captain that would make her father proud.

20

Lucca's seventeenth birthday started off as any other day on the *Albatro*. After wolfing down his breakfast and completing his chores, he made his way to the captain's cabin for the daily lesson. He knew the lesson would be a continuation of bookkeeping, a subject he was less than enthusiastic about, and even though these lessons with Bartolo and Grace were still a highlight of his day, he found himself dragging his feet. As he traversed the deck to Bartolo's cabin, he noticed the boat was eerily quiet, even for early morning. In fact, the only sailor in sight was an old salt lazily manning the helm. He nodded at Lucca with a glimmer in his eye, and Lucca nodded back.

Lucca finally reached the cabin door and opened it, expecting to find Bartolo and Grace, but to his surprise the cabin was packed to the gills with the entire crew of the *Albatro*. Upon his entry they let out a loud cry of "Happy Birthday!" and before he knew it, they were slapping his back, and DiSesa was trying to force rum down his throat. Lucca must have pulled an amusing face because many of the crew were doubled over with laughter.

Rum was poured and toasts to Lucca Pani and his ascent to manhood were made. Then Grace came forward and presented Lucca with a package wrapped nicely in brown paper. She urged him to open it while the crew stood around watching, rum in hand. Lucca unwrapped the packaging to find a wooden box, which he carefully opened to find a beautiful scrimshaw straight razor.

After he held the razor up for the crew to see, Grace piped up. "It is a newfangled contraption called a razor, Lucca. It's to be used for shaving one's whiskers."

Lucca's fuzzy face reddened as the crew doubled over with laughter once more at Grace's jest. Grace came forward and hugged him and wished him a happy birthday into the whorls of his ear. Bartolo ordered everyone out of his cabin and told Lucca he was excused from today's lesson and chores.

Lucca spent the rest of the day lounging luxuriously on the forecastle. It was a day of boundless blue sky, and the shimmering Aegean Sea stretched out before Lucca like a hundred thousand pieces of silver. He was propped on his elbows, head buzzing slightly from the rum, gazing at nothing. He was thinking about Grace. He was ashamed to admit to himself that after the hug and breathy whisper, he had become aroused, and now he couldn't get her out of his head. Just then DiSesa provided a welcome interruption from his daydreams.

"What's on your mind, you old scoundrel? Seventeen and no chores. You know what they say about idle hands. I dare not ask where those hands have been, but I know where they will be."

Lucca sat up and looked at DiSesa apprehensively. "What do you mean by that?"

DiSesa slugged him in the arm. "The *Albatro* is berthing in

Skopelos tonight. Most beautiful women in the Aegean! I know a whorehouse that will blow your immortal soul out your ears and back up your asshole. What say you?"

Lucca was relieved DiSesa was not reading his thoughts about Grace and had to laugh at his way with words. He had never been to a brothel before, but it seemed like just the thing to get his mind off Grace. He agreed to accompany DiSesa to the brothel under the condition DiSesa teach him how to shave first. The pair shook on it.

The *Albatro* made the island of Skopelos by dusk and was able to secure a slip on a deep-water dock. Lucca was clean-shaven with only a few nicks, despite the fact he and DiSesa had been drinking at a courageous pace since the early afternoon. The night was hot but not humid, and a million insects seemed to hum all at once in a melody that complemented the lazy rolling of the ship on the dock. The two started down the gangway of the ship to venture into the town when Captain Bartolo called to Lucca. Lucca turned and Barolo, standing in the doorway of his cabin, beckoned him over. Lucca told DiSesa he would catch up with him and doubled back to see what Bartolo needed. When he stood in the cabin door, Bartolo beckoned him in impatiently with an informal wave of his hand as if Lucca was standing on ceremony unnecessarily. He motioned for Lucca to sit down at his table.

Lucca walked over to the table and sat, doing the best he could to disguise how drunk he was. He soon noticed, as Bartolo was pulling a cork from a bottle with his teeth, that he had not been the only one drinking. Bartolo poured a generous amount of rum into two glasses and held one up. Lucca picked up the other, and they clinked together.

"Happy birthday, Lucca Ferrando," Bartolo said, looking Lucca directly in the eye. "I wanted you to at least hear your real name today. I confess it hurts me that the crew still only knows you as Lucca Pani, and on this day, the day of your manhood, you should hear your real name. It's a good name. A heroic name that has earned its place in Italian history."

They gulped down the rum, and Bartolo poured another, even stiffer than the first. Lucca could not remember even seeing Bartolo drink before, and he sure had never seen the man inebriated. It was out of character for the man who was the epitome of control and discipline.

"Your father would be proud of the man you have become. I'm sure he is proud, but when he sees you, well, that will be something grand."

"Thank you, sir."

"To see a child thrive is perhaps the greatest gift in the world."

Lucca did not know what to say and was concerned he would slur his speech, so he only nodded respectfully. Bartolo was speaking slower than usual, more deliberately, perhaps to hide his intoxication. It seemed his tongue was lazier than usual, and it gave his voice a sandpaper quality.

"Have you ever heard of Skopelos before, Lucca?"

Lucca shook his head. He had not before the *Albatro* docked at Skopelos today.

"It is an interesting society. It is a matrilineal society. Wealth is passed down via the female line. Our society could learn a lot from Skopelos. Do you have any idea what I'm talking about?"

"Yes." Lucca believed he did.

"What am I talking about then, just so I'm sure."

"I believe, sir, we are talking about the end of Grace Ligoria's minority and her claim to Ligoria Trading Company."

"Good man," said Bartolo, and they downed their glasses, which Bartolo refilled as soon as they were set back on the table. Bartolo continued with his sandpaper voice.

"Alexander the Great. Why was he so great?"

"Because he never lost a battle, sir," Lucca replied after puzzling over the question.

"No, that's a result of being great. I'm talking about a cause. The answer is Aristotle. Why were the Ptolemies great? They had the Academy of Alexandria, Archimedes, Eratosthenes, and other thoughtful, loyal men at their side. Do you know what I'm talking about, Lucca?"

"I think so," Lucca replied slowly.

"What then am I talking about?"

Lucca took a deep breath. He was getting increasingly uncomfortable, and Bartolo's direct stare was upon him. "Maybe that you are the Aristotle to Grace's Alexander?"

"Absolutely not." Bartolo leaned slowly back in his chair. "I'm talking about you, Lucca. I'm a dinosaur. I will do whatever is in my power to help Grace, but I'll die off while she is approaching her prime. You are her peer. She needs good people around her whom she can trust. If she has you, she will stand before kings."

Lucca nodded, and after Bartolo finished, he opened his mouth to assure Bartolo he would sail to the edges of the earth with her, but Bartolo silenced him with a wave of his hand. He then grabbed Lucca's wrist, stuffed a few coins in his hand, and said, "Happy birthday, Lucca Ferrando. Now get out of here and don't be afraid to spend that all in one place."

A rare smile played on Bartolo's lips as Lucca got up and walked to the cabin door, but before he even grabbed the door handle, Bartolo called to him again.

"Lucca!" The soft, sandpaper voice was replaced by the steady timbre of a ship's captain. "A few years ago I was cleaning out Grace's room, and I found many sketches under her bed. Many beautiful sketches. There's only one man aboard the *Albatro* who can draw like that. You're now a man, and she is a woman. If there is any hijinks aboard my ship, you will have crossed me, and my general fondness for you will not save you."

Lucca nodded, mumbled something that had the word "sir" in it, and extricated himself from the captain's cabin as fast as possible. Heart beating like a bass drum, Lucca walked briskly down the gangway and down the docks in search of DiSesa and something that could take his mind off Grace.

21

Lucca woke in his bunk the next morning with a splitting headache. He groaned and rolled over, shirking from the light penetrating the boards above. What had happened last night? He had trouble remembering anything at all. Slowly, flashes of the prior night came to him. He remembered meeting DiSesa and a few of the old salts at a tavern. He remembered the cheer that had gone up when he had entered the tavern and some of the songs that had been sung. He remembered a bar fight, though he could not recall the winner, loser, or any of the participants. He remembered following DiSesa through dark alleys and up windy steps. He remembered a woman, an older woman with painted eyes. He remembered DiSesa laughing in the next room. He remembered stumbling back to the *Albatro*, supported by DiSesa. He remembered tripping over the gangway and thinking it the funniest thing in the world. He remembered finding Grace on the deck of the *Albatro*, smoking a cigarette. She was asking him questions, frowning, asking about brothels. He remembered taking her by the waist and kissing her. He remembered her pushing him away, disgusted. The last thing he remembered was vomiting over the rail.

As the broken memories surged back into Lucca's mind, he sat up and felt the need to vomit again. Not from alcohol but from shame. He wanted to wrap his legs in iron chain and throw himself in the deepest part of the Mediterranean. DiSesa was now coming down the companionway holding hot coffee. He extended a cup to Lucca, who accepted without looking up.

"Now that was what I call some serious bloody merrymaking." DiSesa sat on the bunk opposite Lucca.

"DiSesa?" Lucca asked slowly.

"Mmmmm?"

"Do you remember getting back to the ship last night?"

"Mate. I don't remember a Goddamn thing." DiSesa chuckled to himself as he sipped his coffee.

"So you don't remember seeing Grace when we got back to the ship?"

DiSesa's face turned thoughtful for a moment and then determined like he was trying to dust away cobwebs from an old attic. Then his face brightened and he said, "Nope. No memory whatsoever."

Lucca groaned again. Despite the splitting headache and his aversion to daylight, he knew he must go seek out Grace and apologize immediately. He must grovel if that is what it would take.

Lucca made his way up out of his bunk and up the companionway, shouting back at DiSesa, "I hold you responsible for the pounding in my head."

"Your head is on you, my friend," DiSesa called back at him. "But I will take partial credit for your virginity, or lack thereof."

Lucca stepped up on the deck and immediately shielded his eyes from the unforgiving light of the morning. Once he adjusted, he immediately saw Grace. Her back was to him and she was sitting on sail cloth she had spread over the deck. As he walked closer, he saw she was working with palm and awl, mending the sail cloth. He crouched near her but not too near.

"I'm sorry about last night. I don't know how that happened."

Grace did not look up from her sail mending. "You can apologize to me when you don't stink of alcohol ... and other things."

Grace was barefoot and had her trousers rolled to her knees. Lucca found he could not stop staring at her ankles. He wanted to smack himself but decided that would not improve his standing in this moment.

"I could have Mr. Otto douse you with a bucket of seawater," Grace suggested. "It's effective on drunks."

Lucca leaned toward her. "Grace, I—"

"I'm not kidding, Lucca, you stink. Clean yourself up." As Grace said this, she finally looked up at him. Her brow was creased, and there was no amusement in her eyes.

Lucca stood up from his crouch, took a few steps to the rail, and dove off the side of the *Albatro* into the harbor. The *Albatro* was still tied to the dock at Skopelos, but the ship was not yet laden with cargo, so it was a decent descent. When Lucca resurfaced, he saw Grace leaning on the rail, watching him and shaking her head.

"I'm sorry," he said.

She nodded and went back to her work.

22

The following day, the *Albatro* was running before the northerly wind on its way to the island of Crete. Lucca, supervised by DiSesa, piloted the ship himself and was glad to do it as the concentration required by the helm consumed all physical and mental faculties that could have been otherwise spent.

The *Albatro* foamed into the Port of Chania at midday. They had made excellent time skirting through the Greek isles and were five days ahead of schedule. Chania was a port city on the northwest end of the island of Crete and one of the main centers for trade. It was fortified by large walls and bulwarks built during the rule of the Venetians, now crumbling during the rule of the Ottomans. As the *Albatro* approached the harbor, a small lighter hailed them. Bartolo instructed Lucca to heave to, and Lucca guided the ship up to luff so the lighter could pull alongside.

Bartolo made his way down from the quarterdeck to the main deck so he could speak to the lighter. The lighter was a small craft, bucking in the throbbing seas, but she got near enough so Lucca could clearly see her crew. They were dark, mustached men in naval garb armed with carbine rifles. Lucca could easily identify them as Turks, members of the regular Ottoman navy.

"The port is closed off," one of the Turks called. He said it in Greek and then in English.

"Why?" Bartolo called back in English.

"Another uprising from the Christians," came the response.

"When will the port reopen for trade?" Bartolo called out, hands cupped around his mouth to be heard above the wind.

Lucca saw the Turk shrug. "Who can say? I see you're an Italian merchant vessel. What do you carry?"

"That business is mine and my broker's, sir," Bartolo returned.

"In that case, we need to come aboard. We cannot let munitions slip through to the rebels." The Turk turned to his skipper, and the man started working the boat closer to the Albatro.

Bartolo decided to head this off. "We carry farming implements of English manufacture. We trade this port often to exchange for Cypress timber. We are not licensed to carry munitions, as you know, Signore."

Lucca knew this to be only half true. They did carry farming implements, but they were also carrying ample tonnage of dynamite, the blasting powder invented two decades ago that was now stable enough to transport via ship. It was also true that the *Albatro* was not licensed to carry munitions, but dynamite was being brokered as a construction material. Bartolo turned to Lucca and gave him the silent orders to bear off and start putting Chania and the Turkish lighter behind them. Lucca made a passing glance at the Turks. They looked confused and started speaking hastily to each other in a foreign tongue. The *Albatro* was far faster than the little lighter, and the Turk's only recourse would be to fire on them.

However, Bartolo was artful in that he did not defy an order; as the Turks had expressed themselves, the boarding of the *Albatro* was a conditional. More importantly, firing upon the merchant vessel of another sovereign nation was not a thing to be done hastily. All this was the topic of the Turkish discussion as the *Albatro* sailed east and slowly out of range.

As the Turkish lighter grew smaller and smaller, Lucca looked at Bartolo for guidance. He still held the wheel. He could practically hear Bartolo grinding his teeth. The captain hated when anything was out of his direct control, and Lucca could tell the man's brain was churning through scenarios by which he could reinstate his natural order. Lucca also knew why this trading port was critical to the success of the voyage. They had loaded farming implements specifically for Crete, which was so hungry for good steel plows that she would pay double what a steel plow would fetch on the continent. If they could not trade at Crete, they would take a write-down on the value of that inventory and sell it off at a fraction to make way for higher-value cargo. They also needed the Cypress timber for their coming haul to the Levant.

Finally Bartolo spoke. "Take us due east. Keep the coast visible from the masthead no closer than fifteen miles. We'll go to the Port of Herkalion."

At the mention of Herkalion, he saw both Grace and DiSesa turn their heads to Bartolo. DiSesa was confused, and Grace looked intrigued.

"Isn't that harbor silted over, sir?" DiSesa asked.

"Yes, it is," replied Bartolo. "Not much activity there, which will be to our benefit."

"How will be make contact with our broker?" DiSesa asked slowly. "Besides, if there is a civil war going on, or uprising or whatever, don't you think it best to clear out?"

"I know the cove we'll berth in. I'll go to shore and make

contact with our broker." Bartolo patted DiSesa on the shoulder and walked over to his cabin.

They reached a solitary cove just east of the city of Heraklion, and Bartolo rowed himself to shore with one of the *Albatro's* small skiffs. The orders were clear. The crew was to stay aboard the ship until the captain returned.

Boredom ensued aboard the *Albatro*. Grace had taken to lying way up on the topsail boom, legs wrapped around the mast, smoking cigarettes. DiSesa was engaged in a methodical game of cards with some of the old salts. Lucca had his sketchbook open but was uninspired. The hours slithered by. Normally he would relish any relief from chores, but with the ship moored just off the coast and instructions to stay put for an indefinite period, he could not help but feel restless. He needed to do something, to put his body or mind or both to some outlet before he went mad with boredom.

Grace appeared at his shoulder and said, "Remember your birthday fiasco? I know what you can do to make it up to me."

He replied instantaneously. "Anything."

Grace's mischievous smile was back, and she asked for his help lowering a skiff to water.

"You're going ashore?" Lucca asked, eyebrows raised.

"We are going ashore," she informed him. "I've already told Otto that you and I are going to check in on the captain."

Lucca had the distinct feeling that this was bad news, but his eagerness to assist Grace and thereby alleviate his guilt combined with his eagerness to do something, anything, was overpowering, and he found himself lowering a skiff, climbing in, and rowing toward the shore. Grace sat at the stern. She had her legs crossed, a pencil in her mouth, and was studying an old map.

"Grace?" Lucca asked between strokes of the oars.

"Mmmm?" came the answer without looking up.

"What's with the map? I thought we are just going to Herkalion. It's just a mile down the beach."

"No, actually we are going a little farther inland."

"You said we were checking on Bartolo. He's in Herkalion."

"Believe me, Bartolo can handle himself. If you want, we can check in on him on the way back."

"So where are we going, Grace?"

"Knossos." Grace looked up, eyes glittering with mischief. Lucca stopped rowing and crossed his arms.

"Where is that? What is that?"

"Oh, keep rowing, will you, I'll explain. According to this map, it's only a two-hour hike from the coast. We can be back aboard the ship by sundown."

"Why do you want to go there? You know there's an uprising going on. We could get caught in the middle. Then there's the possibility that Bartolo beats us back to the ship, which might even be worse than being caught in the middle of an uprising."

"It's just an uprising. If it was serious, they would call it a rebellion or a revolt. I doubt we'll happen upon any troublemakers. Knossos is the site of a palace from thousands of years ago. That's where the kings lived who ruled an ancient race of people called the Minoans. One of those kings was King Minos —the one with the Minotaur and the maze and all that. They say the palace had running water and flushing toilets. From thousands of years ago!" Grace's eyes were afire with excitement.

Lucca sighed and resumed rowing. They felt the bottom of the skiff start to slide over sand a few minutes later, and Lucca got out and pulled the boat up the beach. Grace was again studying the map and was rotating her body around a compass she had brought. He also noted she had brought a rucksack. She turned and smiled at him.

"Ready?" she asked. He nodded. Her eyes lingered on his a moment longer before she turned and started into the woods at the edge of the beach. Grace set a good pace, and most of the first hour was spent working up a gently sloping hill. When the vegetation got thicker, she withdrew a machete from her pack and gave it to Lucca to hack out a path for them. It took them another hour to reach a river that Grace was sure would lead them to Knossos.

"This river runs from the ruins of the palace to the harbor. Look how silty it is—that's why the Port of Herkalion is silted up. We can follow this back if we want to check in on Bartolo."

Lucca kept looking up at the sun. It seemed to be sinking rapidly, and they were not making the speed that had been advertised. They worked their way up the river, which proved to be only slightly faster than hacking through the thick vegetation because the river banks were few and far between. The sun continued to slink away from them, and Lucca started to think of ways to convince Grace to give up the hunt and turn back when all of a sudden Grace stopped abruptly. Lucca looked ahead. He couldn't see anything past the bend in the river. He looked at Grace, whose eyes were narrowed and staring at a point in the distance. Then she broke into a run through the shallow water of the river's edge. Lucca followed, and soon, as the river bend gave way, he saw what she saw. A large hill with a clearing rose up regally from the earth like a waking lion. Atop the hill was a large corner section remnant of a massive stone structure. The palace had been drubbed and battered by the grinding millennia, but enough of the skeleton remained that he could appreciate the former majesty. The setting sun smeared the backdrop with reds and golds, adding to the awesome scene. Grace was now running along the top of the wall leading to the highest remaining portion of the palace.

"Isn't this amazing, Lucca? Thousands of years old, straight from the legends!"

It was amazing, and Grace's exuberance delighted him. Lucca took a step forward, and his foot crunched on something that was not quite stone. He looked down and picked up the object he had just broken into two. It was some type of ceramic. He wiped eons of dirt off what he guessed to be a fragment of a clay vase. It was clearly a display of an octopus, and an artful one at that. When he connected the other piece, he saw the full picture. It was an octopus with its tentacles wrapped around a seabird.

On account of the dying light, they decided to head back. Grace reasoned that they should just follow the river all the way back to Heraklion. That way they wouldn't have to navigate through the jungle in the dark, and they could check in on Bartolo. Lucca was relieved to get going, and he set the pace down river. They had trekked for about an hour and a half when the river started to widen out and get stronger. They heard the waterfall before they saw it. It was a big one. Lucca held onto a sapling and looked over. Thirty feet he estimated, cursing.

Grace spoke up. "If we go around, it could cost us a few hours."

Lucca snorted in amusement. "Are you suggesting we jump?"

Grace grabbed the sapling and took a turn looking over the fall. "Looks deep enough. I'll go first."

"It's not safe. If you break a leg out here, we're in deep trouble."

Grace was not listening. She took off the rucksack she was carrying and tossed it down so that it landed, dry, on the river-bank. Lucca noticed that after she had tossed it, she clamped her hands to her ears for some reason. The bag landed in the sand without bouncing. Then she turned to Lucca, and with a startling quickness, she kissed him on the lips and jumped into space.

Lucca heard a splash and a moment later he was looking wide-eyed over the falls as Grace floated happily, waving at him to jump. He jumped. What else could he do? He plunged deep into the water. He had expected a jolt that came with the colder water of the Mediterranean, but this was warm and smooth. Grace was laughing, and he broke into a smile as well. He made his way to the riverbank and sat himself down in the sand. Grace was still enjoying herself, floating on her back. He felt himself trying not to lock eyes with her and failing. She came up the river bank and took off her trousers and her waistcoat. Her white work shirt was wet and clung to her. Then she took that off.

Lucca found that he was having trouble processing what was going on. He knew that his throat was dry, and he probably looked very silly sitting there and not saying anything. Then the thought struck him that he was being very rude with his clothes still on while she was standing before him naked in all her vulnerability. He hurriedly took off his clothes. She watched him patiently.

After he struggled through the final article of clothing, she got down beside him, and he felt her warmth against him as a generous energy. Her body was as tight as his but smoother and drawn in by subtle feminine curves. She put one hand against his cheek and then ran her fingers through his dark hair, and with the other hand sought him out below. It was a forward, immediate maneuver, and Lucca found himself unable to respond. She felt his lack of response and grew shy. She removed her hand from him and put her head on his chest. They were still for a time. Her shyness allowed Lucca space for his own confidence to ascend, and he found he was now responding. She noticed and kissed his neck happily.

He steadied her while she mounted him, and the awkwardness of their first encounter was subdued by breathy giggles. Her hips started cautiously and worked to a slow cadence. The young lovers never retreated into their own individual ecstasy; they stayed together, present in the shared moment of pleasure, and when the singular climax occurred, each was breathing into the other's ear with love on their lips.

After a time, they got up and dressed silently, occasionally exchanging happy glances. Without words, the pair continued down the river. Lucca felt his legs moving without effort, like he was floating rather than walking. Grace was splashing ahead of him, and he had the frightful thought that this was just a dream. To be sure of reality, he caught up to her and turned her and kissed her. She did not shy away and smiled up at him.

It was dark by the time they got to Heraklion. Neither Lucca nor Grace had ever been to this city, but they both instinctively walked toward the wharf where they might catch a glimpse of their captain.

"Do you think he'll be angry that we left the ship?" Lucca asked.

"Yes, I do. I was thinking if we see him and he looks OK, we just head back."

Lucca agreed with that concept. As they walked through the dimly lit streets, they noted a stillness that was more than a little unnerving. Lucca guessed that the city had been partially abandoned once the port became unusable. As they were passing by the customs house, Grace held up her hand. They heard voices speaking in English from within and crouched below a window sill so they could make out what was being said.

"I told you. I don't know where my ship is. They mutinied

and sailed off. I've been left stranded." The voice sounded like Bartolo's.

Then another voice, gruffer and with a thick accent, could be heard. "Yes. The likely story you told to my sergeant when we caught you. Mutiny is what brings you here? Why then, captain, were you caught seeking out a broker?"

"He is the only man I know on the island. I need assistance booking passage back to Genoa." answered the voice that sounded like Bartolo.

Lucca slowly peered over the sill into a well-lit room. Sure enough, Bartolo was there, sitting behind a table. Standing over the table with two hairy fists planted on it was a big Ottoman navy man. Lucca could not tell if it was the same man who had come alongside the *Albatro* in the Port of Chania earlier in the day. Lucca also noticed two other Turks in the room with carbines close at hand.

"He's chained to the table," whispered Grace, who was peering into the room alongside Lucca. Sure enough, Bartolo had an iron cuff around his wrist that linked him to the leg of the table.

The gruff Turk started up again. "I think you are lying, captain. I think you are trying to circumvent our embargo. I think your ship is close at hand, and I'm fairly certain we will find it in the daylight tomorrow."

"Your men will be wasting their time," Bartolo spat. "My ship is long gone. It's probably halfway to Calcutta by now. You are the law here, you should be helping me enforce my rights rather than stalling me like this."

The Turk continued as if he had not heard Bartolo at all, leaning closer to his captive. "When we find your ship tomorrow, we will board it and do a complete survey. If we find anything that can be considered a munition or a weapon, we will have to assume you are aiding and abetting the Christian rebels. A capital punishment befits a capital crime. You and your men will be put up against the wall and shot."

Grace tugged on Lucca's arm, and they got back down into a crouch below the sill. "I have a plan. When those three men run out of the customs house, go inside and use the machete to free him. I'll be back in a bit."

Before Lucca could respond, Grace went bounding off with her rucksack. The men inside continued to argue, and Bartolo's voice got increasingly louder and more strained. Lucca's mind was reeling. They were sure to discover the *Albatro* with the morning light; it was only a mile down the beach. If he and Grace were caught trying to free Bartolo, they would be dooming the crew of the *Albatro* who would not be warned. With dynamite in the holds, they'd be put before the firing squad.

Just then an incredible boom tore through the city, and a column of fire and smoke erupted a few blocks away. The explosion was so powerful Lucca felt the wall he was leaning against shake. A moment later all three Turks were sprinting out of the customs house, their prisoner forgotten. Lucca got up and scurried through the open door, closing it behind him. He turned and walked across the room to Bartolo. Bartolo, who had already been busy trying to break the leg of the wooden table he was chained to, looked up in incredulity.

"Lucca? I thought I told you to stay on the ship. What are you doing here?"

Lucca didn't know what to say. "Here to save you, sir."

Bartolo nodded at the machete in Lucca's hand. "Well then, you should get on with it."

Lucca proceeded to hack the leg of the table to splinters, allowing Bartolo to work the cuff free. Just as Bartolo stood up, the door started to move open. Lucca gripped the machete tightly. One of the Ottomans must have doubled back to guard the captain. Lucca immediately felt sick to his stomach as he raised his machete, ready to strike a killing blow to whatever was coming through that door. The door flew open revealing a wild-eyed Grace. Lucca breathed a sigh of relief and let the machete clatter to the floor.

"Come on," she said. "We have to get back to the ship!" She turned and started running. Lucca and Bartolo followed, and the three darted over the wharf and down to the beach. They didn't stop their dead sprint until a mile later when they got to the skiff that Lucca had dragged up the beach.

Once they had the skiff in the water and started sculling out to the *Albatro,* Bartolo broke their winded silence. "Do not speak of this to other members of the crew."

Both Grace and Lucca nodded solemnly. Bartolo then raised his arm to show the iron cuffs that had been detached from the wooden table but not from his wrist. "I'm going to my cabin to saw this off my wrist. You two will wake the crew, raise anchor, and hoist the main and jib. We're leaving this place immediately."

When they reached the *Albatro* Bartolo made for his cabin before the crew could see the shackles and ask questions. Lucca was working with Grace to hoist the skiff back aboard the *Albatro* when a thought occurred to him.

"Grace? Why did you bring dynamite ashore with us?"

"There's an uprising going on, Lucca," breathed Grace as she smiled her mischievous smile.

23

Over the next few months, the Mediterranean became a playground of passion for Lucca and Grace. The grottos of Rosh HaNikra echoed with their cries of delight. They sneaked ashore at Algiers, and she found them a rooftop, a blanket, and a bottle of French wine. They made love under the stars. The stars were bright, and their bodies breathed together. Such was their ecstasy that Lucca felt that up would become down and they might fall into space and join that celestial swirl of stipples against the scrim of ultramarine. When the star-crossed stargazers slowly panted their way back down from rapturous revelry, a state of utter contentment accompanied their even breathing. The state of contentment held within it the rare bedfellows wonder and assurance. Even as they wondered at the weightless magic of it all, the universe assured them that this was how the world worked, that the Mediterranean was small and simple, and that this would last forever. In the stillness that followed, they whispered whatever non sequiturs came into their minds. The lovers were completely transparent, open, and free. For the second time in his life, and for a span of several months, Lucca was in a state of waking bliss.

He was still wary of Bartolo, but Lucca believed that saving the captain from the Ottoman captors had bought him some leeway. Also, Bartolo had commanded that there be no hijinks *aboard his ship.* So far, he and Grace had kept to that covenant, and none of their sensual symphonies were orchestrated on the *Albatro.* Their lovemaking was hidden from Bartolo. It was not fear that kept him from a more overt display but rather respect for the captain who had donned the mantle of father figure for both Lucca and Grace.

Of course Lucca would not welcome the inevitable lashings that would accompany Bartolo's discovery, but fear no longer held sway over his conduct with Grace. How could fear be made to interfere with that which was so divinely intertwined with love.

24

Seventeen-year-old Lucca, back against the foremast, closed his sketchbook and decided that he had done enough recollecting for one morning. He hefted his sketchbook; it was thick and heavy. *Full of memories, full of life,* he thought. The next moment, he sprang to his feet and walked lightly to the companionway, traversing down the stairs in two bounds. He stowed his prized sketchbook under his bunk and began his chores. On this day, he had a spring in his step. This was to be the first night that the *Albatro* would be making port in a three-day stretch. This night would mark the first time in three days that Lucca and Grace could see each other privately, and Lucca could think of nothing else. The day bobbed by at a torturous tempo.

During supper he stole a glance at her and was rewarded with a sly smile. After supper he was constantly scanning the horizon for the sight of land, sight of port. An old salt high up in the crow's nest saw it first, and when he cried out, Lucca felt the excitement build inside him. It was just then that Grace brushed by him, and he felt like he might lose control.

Steadying himself on the rail, he fought to regain his composure as the *Albatro* sliced toward the harbor where they would weigh anchor for the evening.

This would be a new harbor for Lucca as the *Albatro's* Cretan blunder had necessitated a new trade route to new markets. The quest for new markets had brought them down through the Suez Canal deep into the Red Sea. The port was called Al Mutaha. It was well north of the busy, Ottoman-controlled port of Al Lith. It was the farthest from the Mediterranean that Lucca had ever sailed.

As they approached the harbor, Lucca realized this port was little more than a cove with a few haphazardly constructed buildings. These buildings held no evidence of the severe symmetry of the Hejaz region, nor the layered stone and mud styles of the 'Asir region, though both domains laid claim to this port. This seemed to be a port on the outskirts. The most distinguishing feature was a pier, large and long, that thrust crookedly from the shore to halfway across the harbor. Piers were ideal for the rapid loading and unloading of cargo and allowed crews to handle their own cargo without the help of lighters or barges. The port was empty of ships with the exception of a colossal screw steamer that was docked to the pier with thick lines, several hinged ramps swaying and creaking with the roll of the sea.

They doused all cloth but the fore jib, and DiSesa navigated them through the harbor as they made to dock directly with the pier. As they got closer, Lucca could see that the giant screw steamer had four guns on its starboard side but still flew under merchant colors. It was common for naval vessels to be decommissioned and converted into cargo liners, but usually the guns were removed, especially if they were weighty wrought-iron nine-foot, sixty-four-pounders. Although he could readily identify most country flags, he could not recognize the country of origin for this steamer. It had the Union Jack in the upper left but a strange coat of arms displayed on the navy blue field. He asked Grace, who had come up alongside him. She was also intrigued by the massive ship.

"It's from the Cape Colony in the South of Africa," Grace replied matter of factly. "Self-governing, but still subjects of the English Queen. It seems like it has some sort of Scandinavian name, though."

Hafgufa was the name of the large screw steamer, stamped in red lettering on the stern. Lucca had an uneasy feeling about this ship, and it was not ameliorated when he caught sight of a few members of the *Hafgufa* crew. Decorum would call on these men to lend hands to the *Albatro* as it approached the pier and tried to dock, but all these men did was smoke and stare.

Once the *Albatro* was made fast to the pier, a customs man approached, and the unloading of the cargo began. Lucca, knowing what lay on the other side of this labor, worked like a Trojan and encouraged others to step lively. When the unloading was done, the reloading began. Between the toil and thoughts of an upcoming romantic adventure, Lucca forgot all about the strange screw steamer even though the sinking sun now put the *Albatro* into its massive shadow.

It was dark by the time the last crates were hauled onto the *Albatro*. Lucca's muscles ached, but he was anything but tired. Some of the crew journeyed into the shanty harbor town to find a drink or a diversion while others staggered to their beds, eager to rest. Lucca shared cigarettes with DiSesa and talked quietly about what the future held. Lucca loved jawing with DiSesa, but on this night he was eager for the man to head to bed or to the taverns so he could rendezvous with Grace. DiSesa showed no signs of doing either, however, as he slowly pulled the cigarette and watched the embers glow brighter. Lucca could tell he was in a philosophical mood.

"It will all be different," DiSesa said, "once we berth at Genoa next month. Grace will get her own ship. Well, she'll have her own damned fleet of ships. What will you do, Lucca?"

"I've told you. I want your job, DiSesa."

"You can have it. Bartolo's a damned fine captain, but I want a ship of my own. Maybe you pilot for me?"

"Maybe."

"Maybe you pilot for Grace?"

"Maybe."

"Maybe you take up as *land lubber* when your father finishes his tour in the Italian Army later this year."

Lucca was startled. He never told DiSesa about his father. As far as he knew, everyone aboard the *Albatro* still knew him to be an orphan. DiSesa pulled again at his cigarette and then passed it to Lucca.

"Take it easy, Lucca. Secret's safe with me. I caught that damned sneaky cook Brando reading your letters. I smacked him in his damned ear but then decided I might read the letter myself, haha."

Lucca shook his head. He would have to have a word with Brando the cook.

"How long since you've seen your father, Lucca?"

Lucca thought quietly then answered. "It must be more than five years."

DiSesa whistled. "Well, that'll be a nice reunion. I'm sure you both have stories to tell. I'm heading to the tavern. You probably have another reunion tonight you have to attend to."

Lucca was startled for the second time, but seeing DiSesa's easy smile, he relaxed and passed the cigarette back to DiSesa.

"You are a bastard, DiSesa."

"Yes. I am a bastard. And you are a lucky bastard." DiSesa winked at him, put out the cigarette on his shoe, and proceeded to walk down the gangway. Lucca watched him go. He wanted to do something meaningful for DiSesa, his friend, his teacher, and now his confidante. Maybe he could sketch him looking heroic at the helm. However, it wasn't long until Grace's image swam back into the front of his mind. He worked his way back to her cabin. He was about to rap the door softly when he heard a low whistle. He turned to see Grace standing on the pier, beckoning him.

They walked along the pier, but before they got to the lighted end that led to the main streets of town, they slid down onto the sand and crept under the pier. There on the beach, under the pier, they made love like spirits who had been separated for centuries. Afterward they held each other closely, savoring the forbidden intimacy like a worn traveler to a feather bed. Lucca noticed the rise and fall of her chest was in perfect harmony with the gentle waves lapping at their feet.

She turned to him slowly. "Lucca?"

"Yes?"

"Do you think having a woman onboard is bad luck?" Grace asked softly. Lucca knew that it was only in these times of intimacy when Grace showed any vulnerability, and he cherished it.

"Oh, absolutely," he replied with mock sincerity. "But they say having bananas on board is also bad luck, and that is so wrong it calls all superstitions into question. There you have it, a canonical proof. Call it the Bananical Proof it you like. Also, I happen to like bananas."

Grace giggled and punched him softly. "So I'm not bad luck because you like bananas. Lucca, you know what I mean. Do you think that superstition is still believed?"

Lucca could tell she was asking a serious question. He knew that she was thinking more and more about managing a shipping business and being herself a captain. He propped himself up on his elbow and gave her a serious answer.

"It's 1887. Those superstitions were developed centuries ago when people believed in sea monsters and mermaids."

"DiSesa still believes in mermaids," she said.

"Yes, well, what I'm saying is superstition is used when logic and science don't offer an explanation. We now live in a time where we can explain natural phenomena."

Lucca was proud of how he answered, but Grace made him want to eat his words. "But what natural phenomenon was explained by the female-bad-luck superstition?"

Lucca learned long ago that arguing with Grace was a losing proposition, so he decided to change his tack and get to the heart of the matter. "People follow good leaders. When you can see the best parts of yourself in a leader, that's a good leader. They don't have to look like you to see those parts."

Grace pressed herself up to a crouch and used her fingers to comb the sand out of Lucca's hair.

"We should be getting back," she said. They climbed back up onto the pier and made their way toward the *Albatro* docked at the other end. As they were walking past the big steamship, Grace stopped in her tracks.

"What is it?" Lucca whispered.

"Shhhh. Listen."

They both stood stock still and listened. A voice, a song, was emanating from somewhere deep within the hull of the *Hafgufa*. It was a low baritone and seemed to reverberate with a tremendous loneliness. They stood and listened. It was a beautiful song. The tongue was foreign, but Lucca heard the universal sound of sorrow and could guess at the meaning.

"It sounds like someone is trapped in there," Grace whispered.

"None of our business. I don't like the looks of this ship."

"Aren't you curious?"

"If someone is chained up in there I'm sure he's chained up for the right reasons."

"How are you so sure?" she demanded.

Lucca did not answer. Grace started walking back and forth, surveying the massive ship from the pier.

"I went aboard loads of screw steamers when I was a little girl. A ship this size probably has three cargo holds, not including the stoke hold in the engine room. The third hold would be aft of the engine room, so my guess is the voice came from the second hold, which is usually the biggest cargo hold. There will be multiple hatches, but I'll bet you a month's pay we'd find a hatch right here before the fore deck starts." She had lined herself up with her anticipated point of insertion, and now Lucca could tell she was thinking about ways to get up to the deck of the *Hafgufa*.

"You can't board this ship without permission, Grace. They could legally shoot you."

"They have no guards posted, Lucca. They put little value on whatever they are hauling." Without looking back to Lucca, she started to climb up a rope that descended from the deck of the *Hafgufa* to the pier. Before he could physically restrain her, she was halfway up, and his only choice was to follow her, cursing her in his head. When he got to the top of the rope, she offered a hand and silently pulled him over the rail. Without saying a word, she pointed to a hatch not five feet from them as if it vindicated her. They shifted over to the hatch but found it to be secured with a large, rusty padlock. She studied the lock for a moment and then took a pin from her hair and went to work on it. Lucca had to admit that watching her work on that lock with her golden hair flowing down to her shoulders was getting him excited once more despite the setting of this high-anxiety trespassing.

Chunk. The lock grated open. She motioned for Lucca to

help her lift the heavy hatch. They lifted slowly to avoid any creaks and groans of the rusted hinges and heavy wood. They both looked at each other, paused, then stuck their heads down through the hatch.

They did not see anything but the perfection of pitch black, but slowly, as their eyes adjusted and the light of the moon entered through the hatch, they started to make out shapes. Just then a pair of white orbs floating in the darkness sprang into existence. Then another pair of orbs apparated into being. Then another. Then tens and then hundreds of floating eyeballs where staring back at them.

Grace stifled a scream as Lucca tore her from the hatch. They scrambled back down the rope to the pier. Lucca's heart was practically beating out of this chest as they dashed another fifty feet to the Albatro and went straight into Bartolo's cabin. They entered without knocking and startled Bartolo to a degree to which he groped for his revolver. Once Grace started speaking, he relaxed and lit a lantern, then demanded to know what the devil was going on.

"Slave ship," Grace blurted out. "That big steamer docked next to us is a slave ship."

"What?" Bartolo demanded, still shaking off the last remnants of a profound sleep. He was sitting on his bed in his pajamas, trying to get his bearings.

"We saw hundreds, hundreds, of slaves in the hold of that ship." Grace was still breathing heavily.

"Slave trade has been outlawed since before I was born. And how the devil do you know they have slaves in their hold?"

"Does it matter?" she said, speaking rapidly. "We heard a voice and climbed aboard."

"You what!?"

"Captain, we should get out of here now," Lucca interjected. "We can use the ebb tide."

"What the devil are you doing in here, Lucca?" Bartolo seemed to notice him for the first time. Before Lucca had time to answer, Bartolo looked back at Grace. "Are you absolutely certain?"

She nodded, and Bartolo looked down at the floorboards. It seemed that he was still trying to decide if he had woken up or was still engaged in a bad dream. It seemed like an eternity before he spoke.

"Lucca, go around to the bunks and take a census of who is aboard this ship. Then go to Mr. Otto and give him the names of the men he has to round up at the taverns. Neither of you are to set foot on the pier. You stay on the ship. Grace, did any of their crew see you?"

"No. I don't think so."

Within one half of one hour, the whole crew of the Albatro, in varying states of sobriety, were aboard and readying to make way. The crew was instructed to go about their work soundlessly, but this was impossible, especially for the ones who had been in their cups, and soon Bartolo ordered all inebriated members of the crew to their bunks. Lucca kept scanning the pier and the decks of the *Hafgufa* for signs of life, but he saw nothing. Then just as they had shoved off, he saw a solitary figure on the pier smoking a pipe and watching them slip away. It was too dark and too far to make out a face, but nonetheless Lucca shuddered.

25

They sailed west through the night, though the wind was barely a whisper. All progress was due to the ebb tide, and when that subsided, they were all but drifting. Lucca and Bartolo both had their eyes set to the east. They had lost sight of land, so all they surveyed was a haunting horizon. Grace came up alongside him and pulled his arm to get his attention. He turned to her, and she was white with fear.

"Lucca. We didn't replace the lock."

Her words produced an ulcerous twist deep inside Lucca. He looked back at the easterly horizon and tried to breathe. The sun was starting to stab its way up through the horizon and produced a red glow of a remarkable intensity. Just then Bartolo ordered Grace to fetch his spyglass. When the spyglass was produced, he raised it to the horizon. Then Bartolo lowered it and passed it to Lucca. Bartolo's face was twisted into an unnamable expression. Lucca raised the glass to his own eye, and there on the horizon he saw a pillar of smoke, red like blood against the rising sun.

"Gather the crew to the deck," Bartolo told Lucca. When the crew was gathered on the deck, he bellowed at them from the quarterdeck. "Men. We are being hunted by a gunship of black-birding pirates." The crew of the *Albatro* was not stupid, and the hasty midnight getaway had clued them into their dire straits. Bartolo continued with a voice that held no fear, only the cold facts of the day.

"They can steam at six knots—seven if they burn down those engines. We have a lead of twelve miles, and we can outrun them if we catch a fair breeze. But we shall not sit quietly and pray for a lucky breeze. We make our own damned luck today. Today we put our backs into this and row! Clean the cargo out of the rowing galley and install the oars. Half the crew will be rowing, the other half will be dumping weighty cargo to lighten us. Then we switch on the half hour. Mr. Otto will take the helm and call out the distance every quarter of an hour. Make no mistake, men, we are rowing for our lives."

The rowing galley of the Albatro had not been used in decades, but with the ferocious effort of the crew, the benches were cleaned and oars were installed in the oar locks. The galley was down in the hull of the ship, and the ceiling height was too short for a man to stand but fine for a man to row. There were four benches to a side, and each bench held a pair of rowers. The crew started off clumsily, and oars were getting tangled. Then Lucca, seated in the first bench, decided to shout out a cadence, and slowly the rowers meshed into rhythm.

"Stroke ... Stroke ... Stroke."

Within the first half of an hour, Lucca was already feeling the ache of his back and was very glad to switch out. The weighty cargo that could be dumped had already been dumped, so Lucca staggered up to the top deck to rest. His half-hour respite flew by, and by the time he was hobbling back down to the rowing galley, Mr. Otto was calling down to Bartolo. "She is nine miles astern of us, captain."

Lucca realized they had closed three miles within an hour, and the *Albatro* was not going more than three knots. As he sat on his bench and resumed his toil, another grim thought came over him: the steamship did not tire.

"Stroke ... Stroke ... Stroke."

Every pull of the oar was pain. His hands had started bleeding from the blisters that bubbled up from his first shift. He looked over his left shoulder and saw Grace straining at the oars with a face full of agony, and he decided to row harder.

"Stroke ... Stroke ... Stroke."

The grueling cycles ground by in an intermittency of pain and rest, all the while Otto called out distances that were rapidly shrinking. Lucca heard men praying as he rowed, praying for wind, praying for salvation. Lucca felt his forearms and fingers starting to betray him; they were shaking and stalling, but he willed them into gripping that oar and pulling. Just once more, once more, once more, he muttered to himself. Every stroke was a work of tremendous effort, a mini miracle. Just when he felt he could go no longer, the call came to switch, and he collapsed in a grateful heap. His gratitude evaporated, however, when he heard Otto's call.

"One mile, captain!"

"Trim the sails!" Bartolo called up between grunts at the oar. "We'll get a breeze now or we never will."

Lucca picked himself up and climbed the ladder through the hatch and onto the deck to help trim the sails. As he was willing his beaten hands to yank on the sheet, he felt a soft breeze graze his cheek. Like a desert reservoir or a warm hearth in midwinter, the breeze brought with it hope of a tomorrow. It pumped new life into Lucca's veins, and he decided there was still some fight in this old bitch of a ship. He finished with the sail and looked east. There, in all its grotesque glory, was the *Hafgufa*, bearing down on them at no less than a half mile off the *Albatro's* stern.

Lucca shimmied down the ladder to the rowing galley and surveyed the exhausted crew. He picked the weariest looking old salt and swapped himself in behind the oars shouting, "Breeze is incoming! Hold her off a bit more and we'll outrun her. Breeze is incoming!"

He could feel his words electrify the nearly depleted crew; their strokes stiffened, and the cadence increased.

"Stroke ... Stroke ... Stroke!"

DiSesa, on a rest cycle, came down and relieved another weary rower. Then Otto, getting an old salt to replace him at the helm, came down and took to the oars as well. They were all rowing like fiends, and Lucca noticed the man to his right was at the same time crying and frothing at the mouth. Lucca no longer felt his hands or his back, and the oar seemed to glide through the waters with less resistance.

"Stroke. Stroke. Stroke!"

The rowers were in such a state of flowing focus that they almost missed the beautiful, uplifting sensation of the boat lurching forward under the power of sail. The breeze had come.

The triumph was short-lived, and in the next instant a deafening roar was heard, immediately followed by an impact that caused the whole vessel to yaw and roll. Dust rained down from the ceiling, covering the coughing, bewildered rowers.

Someone shouted down from the hatch. "Captain, they've shot our sails full of grapeshot and felled both masts. They are upon us, sir."

Bartolo, who had been rowing on the first bench, got up and pried open several wooden crates with a crowbar.

The voice called down again. "Captain, they are asking for

our surrender. They are preparing to board us, and they are saying that if they meet any resistance, they'll sink us here and now."

26

"They shall meet some resistance," Bartolo said loudly as he took shotguns and rifles from the crates and passed them around. The first went to DiSesa, the second to Otto. As Bartolo was loading the third, he heard double-barrel hammers cock, and the hairs on his neck stood.

"What are you doing, Otto?" DiSesa asked slowly. Otto had his shotgun pointed at the back of Bartolo's head.

"You—you mutinous sonofabitch," Bartolo said, turning slowly to face Otto, who was only a few yards from him. Bartolo was in a state of disbelief.

"We're outmatched, captain," Otto said as he was trying to grasp hold of his nerves. "We must surrender. Maybe we can pay them off." His voice sounded raspy and beat up, like it had been involved in a brutal struggle and only barely managed to escape Otto's lungs. He was shaking violently, but he kept his weapon level.

"What do you intend to do?" Bartolo said flatly. "Take control of the ship? Pull the trigger. You'll die shortly after." Lucca could see Bartolo trying to stay calm, but the captain could not hide the pulsing vein that had appeared at his temple. Lucca was standing stock still, as were Grace and a few of the old salts who came to realize what was unfolding. DiSesa had his shotgun trained on the trembling Otto.

"I don't want to kill you, sir!," Otto said. "I'm trying to get you to wake up! I'm trying to stir your wits! I've sailed with you for half my life. Never known you take risks. Never known you to act stupid. I saw you come aboard when we was anchored off Crete. I woke up when I heard an explosion. You had shackles on! Never known you to break the law, even if it was a Turk law. I don't know what's the matter with you, but you aren't acting like the captain I know. I know you as a captain to protect his crew. That ship coming after us is a gunship, and we will be blown to hell if we fight, and you know it."

"We are witnesses to their blackbirding," Bartolo growled. "We can identify them as slavers. What do you think they'll do to us?" He was getting impatient. Lucca started to slowly move out of Otto's periphery and inch closer to his back until he was within six feet.

"Please, Captain. I'd die for you, but not like this. We are not soldiers." As Otto whispered, his voice broke, and Lucca could see he was trying to stifle sobs that caused his whole body to convulse. The man was suffering under the weight of his own betrayal.

"As long as I'm captain, they shall meet some resistance. Pull the damn trigger or stand down. Enough of this." Bartolo stepped toward quivering Otto.

Otto managed to look even more wretched as he heard Bartolo's response. He played his final card and pointed his shotgun at Grace, who was not three yards from him.

"Think of her, Captain," Otto managed to say between unfettered sobs. Then everything changed. Lucca saw all the fight leave Bartolo, and the captain raised his palms.

"Stop," Bartolo said quietly. He looked sad. He moved to his left and put his hand on the barrels of DiSesa's shotgun, lowering it to the deck. He gave Lucca the slightest shake of his head, calling him off. "OK. Otto. We will try to reason with them."

"Swear it!" Otto barked.

"I swear."

"Swear on her!" Otto yelled again, thrusting his weapon in the direction of Grace.

"I swear on Grace's life, we will try to reason with them."

This seemed to be enough for Otto, and he dropped the shotgun, crumpling into a weeping heap of human. Lucca could not help but feel for the pathetic first mate. The man threw away his loyalty to a man he had served faithfully for half his life for what he thought was the good of the crew. Bartolo seemed to have had the same feeling of sympathy, and he walked over to Otto and placed a hand on the man's trembling head. Bartolo then hugged Grace and slowly climbed the ladder up to the deck.

"We are in God's hands now," he said quietly. The entire crew followed him up.

* * *

WHEN LUCCA DREW himself up through the hatch and onto the deck, he was immediately hit with the smell of gunpowder. Scattered around the deck lay splintered pieces of the *Albatro's* masts still clinging to tattered bits of sailcloth flapping in the belated breeze. The massive steamship was once again casting a shadow over them, this time its deck lined with three score armed men.

The *Hafgufa's* captain was first to step onto the *Albatro* and he was followed by his heavily armed crew of rough-looking men. The *Albatro* had rough men as well, but their roughness came from the work and salt of a seafaring life. These men of the *Hafgufa* had the additional agent of violence in their seafaring lives. They were runaway whalers and mutineers, men who shirked from civilized society as a vampire bat from daylight. They were also missing things; eyes, digits, remorse.

The *Hafgufa* captain's vulturine visage was swiveling to and fro, sizing up the crew of the *Albatro* with fiendish diligence. Lucca knew this man was dangerous. Firstly he knew it with his eyes as he saw the man's British naval coat, clearly pilfered, with bullet holes visible on the right breast. He watched the man move across the deck. His legs moved with a jerky swagger, but his upper body seemed of a different nature, more like a cobra, smooth and mesmerizing and ready to lash out without warning. Secondly, Lucca knew this man was dangerous as an animal knows, he felt the primal response that precedes a primal threat; the drying of the mouth, the pounding of the heart. Lastly, Lucca knew it in his soul. This man sailed for Judgement Day with an apocalyptic wake. Lucca had seen the man's steamship with its columns of smoke in his nightmares. Lucca knew him to be the terror that took, the destroyer of dreams, the oppressor opposed to life. Like Icarus, Lucca had flown from the Palace of Knossos to dizzying heights, and this man was the savage, burning sun that would pull Lucca to his reckoning.

"Hallo. My name is Lyle Jameson, Cap'n of *Hafgufa*. Yewer all under my command now. I am annexing all property aboard thus ship. My crew will be binding yewer hands. I've given them license to kill any man that resists." He had a choppy way of speaking. Lucca could only tell he originally hailed from somewhere in the English isles but may not have been there for a long time.

The crew of the *Hafgufa* lurched forward as a unit and

tightly bound the hands of the *Albatro* crew with rough twine. They led or hauled the *Albatro* crew up to the deck of the *Hafgufa* and made them stand in a cluster along the starboard rail, watching as the *Hafgufa* crew loaded cargo and anything else of value from the *Albatro* to the *Hafgufa*. Lucca noticed Lyle Jameson going in and out of Bartolo's cabin, instructing men to bring various items into his own cabin. Bartolo had remained expressionless since their hands were bound. The rest of the *Albatro* crew looked nervous, too nervous even to talk in hushed whispers. The only one to speak was Otto, and his only words were apologies offered to Bartolo, who stood in front of him, still as stone. The day remained irritably perfect; there was not a cloud to be seen, and the sea was calm. Lucca hated the incongruity of the perfect weather and the dark injustice being done. It was as if God was present but apathetic.

The men of the *Hafgufa* were industrious in their pillaging, but the task took the entirety of the day all the same. There was only one member of the *Hafgufa* not stirring. Lucca observed him sleeping in a hammock made of black sailcloth. The black hammock was lashed between two spars on a higher deck, the weather deck, so Lucca could not see into the hammock. Under it were empty wine bottles.

Over the course of the beautiful, terrible day, the crew of the *Albatro* were made to stand in their huddle. Neither food nor water were offered. All they could do was watch. They watched as the fruit of their ambitions was plucked and devoured. They watched as their home was dismantled so unceremoniously. They watched as the *Albatro* was set alight and cast off from the *Hafgufa*, drifting and burning away. Both crews watched the fire, but only one felt the heat of it. Occasionally Lyle Jameson would break his gaze from the flaming ship to grin smugly at Bartolo. When the fire was quenched with the sinking of the *Albatro* the spell broke and the attention fell on her crew. Quick as a cobra, Lyle grabbed

Grace from the *Albatro's* huddle and dragged her to the middle of the deck before anyone understood what was happening. He gripped her tightly and held her close to him. She tried to get her face as far away from his stinking breath as she could.

Lyle was looking closely at Grace but spoke to the *Albatro* crew. "It is no wonder to me why you men have had such foul luck. You 'ave a woman aboard! Well, I won't 'ave my crew suffer the same fate as you lot. The sharks will be lucky to 'ave her, though."

This was the second time that day Grace's life had been threatened, and it was too much for Bartolo to bear.

"Get away from her!" Bartolo bellowed as he started across the deck of the *Hafgufa* toward Lyle Jameson. A big dark-skinned man intercepted Bartolo and hit him hard in the mouth with the butt of a rifle. Bartolo, unable to block the blow while his hands were still bound behind his back, fell backward hard, landing on the deck with a groan. Turning on his side, he started to spit out bloody teeth. Grace struggled against Lyle's grip as a blade appeared in his hands.

Lucca spoke loudly. "You want her alive and unharmed." Both Lyle and Grace turned to Lucca. He could see true terror in Grace's eyes. Lucca spoke with all the composure he could muster. "She is the daughter of Ligoria. Ligoria of Ligoria Trading Company, one of the largest merchant fleets in the Mediterranean. If she is unharmed, unmolested, you can ransom her back to her father in Genoa for many times the value of your ship."

There was an intense pause in all action about the ship as Lyle's wild eyes studied Lucca. Lyle broke the silence. "Even if tha t'were true. Genoa is a long ways away. Yes, a long ways away. Much chance for foul luck." As Lyle finished speaking, the *Hafgufa's* bosun, a lumpy, bulbous man, walked over to

Lucca and delivered a fat fist to Lucca's unprotected stomach, doubling him over.

Lyle Jameson slowly turned back to Grace as her eyes widened in fear. Just as Lyle adjusted his grip on his dagger, a voice rang out and stayed the coiled cobra.

"Hold there a moment, Lyle." A hand protruded from the black sailcloth hammock above the deck. The man in the black hammock had spoken.

Lyle pointed his dirk up at the black hammock and cried, "Don't you interfere now, yewer a guest on my ship. My ship."

"I know the man Ligoria." The voice from the shadows of the hammock was lazy and unconcerned. "Let us not be too hasty killing off his daughter. If done correctly, we may come into riches, as the boy says."

"I decide who lives and who dies aboard this ship." Lyle's voice was hard, but his body language seemed to waiver. He started to fuss with his knife, and then his head, like a reptile's, darted toward the crew of the *Albatro* and fixed on Lucca. Lyle's cold smile produced a sinister chill that slithered up Lucca's spine. The fat bosun seemed to read Lyle's intentions and produced his own cruel-looking blade.

Bartolo, still lying on the deck, also saw these dark intentions and cried out amid more blood and teeth. "Wait. Wait. That boy there is the grandson of Antoni Ferrando."

The bosun paused and looked at Lyle for direction; he had his blade almost to Lucca's throat. Lyle's smile still held, and he looked rather amused.

Bartolo continued. "Antoni Ferrando was—"

"Yes, yes, I've heard of 'im. What is this game? Does ev'ry member of your crew get a famous relative when a noose is about their neck? Next you'll tell me this fellow here is the son of the Duke of Burgundy!" Lyle pointed his dirk at DiSesa. The crew erupted with barbed laughter, but Lyle soon silenced them and turned back to Lucca.

"And how is the Old Bull these days?" Lyle inquired with a sarcastic politeness.

"He's dead," Lucca announced with defiance in his voice. The crew of the *Albatro*, who had only just learned of Lucca's heritage, could not help a feeling of pride rise up inside them to challenge the pervasive feeling of fear that had dominated them only moments before. The upwelling of pride was not because their Lucca was a Ferrando and not a Pani but because their Lucca was not cowering before this maniac. Lucca was not even looking at Lyle. Grace was the only soul he saw. His eyes were locked on her. Her eyes were locked on him. He knew what was coming. She refused to believe what was coming.

"Well, you'll have to give 'im my regards." With that Lyle nodded to the bosun, and all motion aboard the *Hafgufa* slowed to a torturous crawl. The bosun brought his knife up and raked it savagely across Lucca's exposed throat. He then drove his shoulder into Lucca's sternum, causing Lucca to stagger backward until the back of his legs hit the rail and momentum drove him over the side. As Lucca fell into space, he didn't take his eyes off Grace. He fell from her then and into the deep waters of the Red Sea.

Then things started happening exponentially faster, tilting, then spinning, then whirling, then plunging the environment into irrevocable chaos and slaughter.

Amid the chaos, Grace had an out-of-body experience. After she watched the bosun's knife rake across Lucca's throat, she started to calmly float twelve feet above the deck of the *Hafgufa*. From her vantage point, she saw all. She saw Bartolo, hands still bound behind his back, charge Lyle Jameson like a mad bull, knocking him down but in so doing receive a mortal dagger to the rib cage. She saw DiSesa and Otto and the rest of the loyal crew mount their own suicidal charges, throwing themselves at the enemy. She saw them set upon and cut down by the well-armed crew of the *Hafgufa*. She saw cruel blades cut into the flesh of unarmed men. She calmly turned toward herself, twelve feet below. She saw herself screaming. Poor girl, she thought, she does not know how helpless she looks. Then she saw herself being pulled away from the massacre by the man in the black hammock. He was on deck now, trying desperately to pull her back into a cabin. There was nothing left to see on deck. Only tentacles of blood reaching and ensnaring the men of the *Albatro*. She decided to float back down and follow her body.

27

The man from the black hammock half led her, half carried her to an aft cabin beneath the quarterdeck and closed and bolted the door behind them. He sat her down on a chair facing a low table that was awash with papers and empty wine bottles and went to a chest in the back of the cabin, rummaging and finding an unopened bottle of wine. As he approached the other side of the table and seated himself opposite her, he absently threw her a blanket with which she numbly wrapped herself. He placed his palms to his forehead, smoothed back his hair, and took a deep breath like he was trying to collect himself. Then he slowly grasped the bottle he had placed in from of him and very deliberately, as if he was trying to force his hands into steadiness, he began a twist of the wine screw into the cork.

"Who are you?" Grace asked, trying to regain control of her faculties.

"My name is Bergeron," he replied in perfect Italian.

"Who are you?" she repeated.

"Ah, a better question." He grunted as he pried the cork

loose of the bottle. "You want to know who am I in the context of all this ..." Bergeron waved toward the deck.

Before he resumed speaking, he sighed. "I suppose I can draw the loose connection for you. I am a banker. I am Swiss. With the full vested authority of my banking house, I finance projects and enterprises in the name of progress ... This hell ship started out as one of these projects, but as you can see, we've gone clean over the rails. And you, well, you have picked the lock on Pandora's box."

As he concluded he took a deliberate gulp of wine. Grace was still grasping for reality and for words that would allow her some purchase, some means to understand what had just occurred. *Lucca. Lucca is dead.* A sickening feeling twisted up through her gut, and she struggled to breathe. *Lucca, Lucca, oh God, Lucca.* She felt weak and let her head loll forward. She swayed but did not fall off her chair.

"Why?" she finally managed and looked directly at Bergeron.

"Why? Why what?"

"Why did this happen!? Why did they kill us like dogs?" Grace screamed and started to sob.

Bergeron looked at her with sympathy and wondered if he could possibly explain the *why* to this poor, wretched child shivering in a blanket on this torrid Arabian night. He noticed she had some stealthy flicker of intelligence behind her tears, so he decided to give it a try.

"OK," he said and cleared his throat and started calmly, gently. "I'll give you the *why*. I suppose this particular story starts with a canal, but make no mistake, this story has been told a thousand times with the simple substitution of canal for silver mine, marble quarry, parcel of fertile land, wife of neighbor—anything a desirous hand may grasp at. This is the abridged story of the Suez Canal as told by a humble, unbiased observer of the indefatigable laws of nature and inevitable subjugation of humans by better-armed humans."

As he drained his cup again, Grace took a real look at him for the first time. He was fair skinned and blond with a dark stubble that brought some masculinity to an otherwise feminine face. He was a half head taller than Grace and looked perhaps fifty years of age, but he could have been much older. He spoke as an intellectual, and he spoke very rapidly. He looked like he would have carried himself well had he not been half drunk.

"You know the the Suez Canal as a triumph of modern engineering and an expedient to transcontinental commerce. From the colors your ship flew, I would venture you've been through it a few times. Back when it was just a lunatic's ideation, the Brits spurned the project, so my esteemed banking house provided financial backing to the French, who took on the development project with gusto. However, it was the Khedive of Egypt who made the project possible, and as such, the Egyptians took the majority share of the Suez Canal Company with the French taking a minority position. It was also the Khedive of Egypt who provided the brute force ... hundreds of thousands of forced laborers over the course of ten years of hard toil were required to get that canal dug. The project concluded twenty years ago, and now no one can remember life without it. We cut seven thousand kilometers off the trade route and in doing so forged a European throughway to Africa, Arabia, the true Indies, and the South Pacific. Now we can share *progress* with them." Although he breathed this last sentence sardonically, it was apparent that he took some measure of pride in the development itself.

"And so we generated some *progress*. Lower costs of trade, less dangerous shipping routes, improved access to foreign lands, and along the way we enriched a few men like your father—yes I know of the man. But we also created a choke point and a toll of immense value. Imagine every ship that passes through the Suez paying a small fortune for the convenience and safety of a better route to the the riches of the Indies. The Egyptians and the French started to grow wealthy, rapidly. Now pay attention. Shhhhh. Can you hear it? Here come *the laws of nature!*" He gestured dramatically as he once again filled his cup.

As he laid out the entanglements of global politics he took a pause now and again, seeming to marvel at the brilliance of it all, as if he were inspecting the inner-workings of an intricate machine. He gazed into the machine with wonder, but before full-fledged admiration could take hold, he was pulled back by something. Perhaps what pulled him back was the cruelty of it and the disregard for the lives snared and gnashed between the gears.

"Remember, I told you the Brits did not partake in building of the Suez? Well, that did not stop those devils from wanting some of the spoils. The laws of nature. The laws of human nature. There may be moments, even periods, of exception, but there will always be a reversion to the law. The biggest, most meanest ape eats the choicest fruits. In our case the ape is Great Britain, and they aim to appropriate, annex, assume, and arrogate all they can. Can you guess what is going to happen? Around the time the Suez is completed and its success is apparent, the Egyptians start to have financial trouble. Financial trouble, you say? I say financial trouble indeed. It starts with Egyptian cotton supply shortages, but no matter, the trusty British Empire backstops Egypt, and the Khedive becomes a debtor to Her Majesty. But the next year's harvest is even worse, and cotton prices do not increase with the Egyptian cotton scarcity as expected because of the timely return of American cotton. The American Civil War was over, you see, and the

American South had recovered. The good Khedive of Egypt must declare bankruptcy, and he sells 44 percent of the stock in the Suez Canal Company to Great, Great Britain. This transaction occurred just over five years after the completion of the canal. As you might imagine, the Khedive is distraught. Ten years of sweat and blood, a population put to the grindstone, and for what? Perhaps the Khedive is too distraught and does not play good royal subject very well. He is deposed and replaced with a bumbling but subservient son. It only took the Brits three more years to get full control of the Egyptian share after local unrest gave them cause to seize the remaining stake."

"What does this have to do with ... us?" Grace asked, though she realized as soon as she said it there was no longer an *us*. She was the sole survivor of the *Albatro*.

"The man out there, our dastardly captain, is Lyle Jameson. They call him Wild Lyle because he apparently stuffed a dagger down a man's throat after losing a game of cards on the Black Sea. Of import to our story is the fact that he is a cousin of Leander Starr Jameson. Do you know this name?"

Grace shook her head.

"The nicest thing you could say about Leander Starr Jameson is that he is the capable lackey of Cecil Rhodes. Do you know who Cecil Rhodes is?" he said, almost patronizingly.

"I have heard of Cecil Rhodes, the diamond tycoon," Grace said.

"Oh, but much more than diamonds, my dear. Much, much more than that. Cecil Rhodes is the snarling bulldog of the British empire, who, in return for total autocracy of Southern Africa, has done unspeakable things in the name of the Union Jack. Who do you think set pestilence and conflagration about the Egyptian cotton fields to tank the price of cotton and put the Khedive under financial pressure? From what you saw today, do you think these men could be capable of the same civil unrest that allowed the final Suez ownership position to change hands? If you are still wondering how this sordid tale weaves its way into the yarn of the *Albatro*, consider what you and your unfortunate friend saw in the hold of this ship. What did you see?"

"Men. Men chained up."

Bergeron nodded gravely. "Yes. The cargo of this ship is holding 120 African souls. Slave labor shipped from East Africa to Egypt, transported by the lackeys of Mr. Rhodes. Britain needs men to irrigate the Egyptian desert. The Brits now have a keen interest in Egyptian cotton after buying up tracts of farmland on the cheap. Cecil Rhodes, for his role, gets the unconditional support of the British Empire to continue his rogue political experiment, and my banking house is financier to the British government. I know it is rather complicated, dear."

Bergeron seemed thoughtful for a moment. "I do not deny that I play a part in this unfair affair. I lend capital, and I grease the machine. I keep the engine of *progress* primed. But I am not pulling the levers." He pulled deeply from his cup.

Grace was glaring at him. He sensed her hatred and said, "Do not append your abhorrence unto me. As I have told you, I deeply regret your circumstances, but I am a bystander. I'm an unaffiliated observer in this. I could have not spoken up at all out there. I could have left you on the deck."

He did not know why he was excusing himself and trying to justify himself to her but he continued. "Blame Malthus, blame Adam Smith, blame John Stuart Mill, blame Her Majesty Queen Victoria, but do not cast that stare at me. You have no perspective on this world. You think Wild Lyle Jameson is to blame? He is not the true evil in this world either. He's a pawn. He's not a leader, he is a prisoner just as you. He is the captain of a ship full of vile men who signed on to pirate and pillage legally. The only way he maintains his post, and his life, is through repeated acts of repugnance and violence. We are all in irons!"

When he finished speaking, he was practically shouting. He rubbed his temples, sighed heavily, then fixed her a hard stare, which she returned.

"You will be raped," he said softly. "I'm sorry, but there is nothing I can do."

"Why?" she asked, expecting him to get back on the pulpit. But he did not.

"I'm sorry. It's not fair."

They broke eye contact after a full minute of searching. Grace was searching for some deliverance from this hell, and so was he. They both decided they could not help each other.

Just then the cabin door shuddered three times from the forceful knock of a barbarian at the gate. A knot welled up in Grace's throat.

Bergeron lurched to this feet toward the door, which he half opened, releasing the stinking breath of Wild Lyle Jameson. Yellowed teeth in bloodied gums were exposed, and a wolfish smile formed slowly on a face that not even a mother could love.

"Let's 'ave the girl then, Bergeron," said Wild Lyle, trying to peer over Bergeron's shoulder.

"We'll be returning her to her father for due reward," stated Bergeron flatly. "You'll have your share, and I'll have mine."

"That's fine," Wild Lyle said. "But I want a turn at her." He made to shoulder past Bergeron, but Bergeron, though the more slender man, was prepared and stood firm. Wild Lyle looked at him with surprise and terrifying amusement.

"No, sir," said Bergeron, a little surprised at his own voice. Then he surprised himself further by saying, "I intend to have a turn at her first."

Grace had maintained her position huddled in her chair

with her back to the cabin door. She slowly turned her head to present an ear to the conversation. Lyle's head was cocked, and he was staring at Bergeron scornfully.

"Thus is my ship," Lyle said.

"It's my purse," Bergeron returned.

Wild Lyle put his face a half inch from Bergeron's and said, "You'd spit on me if I didn't have forty murderers at my back, wouldn't you? Cause I'm not a bloody gentleman?"

Bergeron did not reply. Lyle twisted his face to the right and left, still keeping only a half inch between their faces, "Cause I don't have a bloody top coat, and my hands are rough?"

Then Lyle, in his best imitation of cut-glass English, a stark comparison to his own cockney, put his hands on his hips, took a slight bow, and said, "Would you like me to slit your throat for you, sah?"

Bergeron said nothing and tried to control the pounding fear building in his chest.

"You 'ave one hour with her," hissed Lyle, and he turned and continued to laugh maniacally as he left, dragging his dagger along the side of the bulkhead.

Bergeron closed and bolted the door and turned to Grace. "Well, I bought you an hour," he said, noticeably relieved to be free of the encounter. He sat back down heavily into his chair.

Grace could still not get a read on this man, but she decided to take a chance. "You need to help me get off this ship. My father—"

"Your father has nothing of interest to me," he said as he peered into his wine cup.

Grace tried a different tack. "The foul deeds done here today will become known."

"There are knowns, and then there are *knowns*," Bergeron said thoughtfully.

"Will you admit that if the exact deeds done here today

were *known* and given credence, your reputation would suffer, as would that of your banking house, as would that of the great Cecil Rhodes?" said Grace, setting her trap.

"If the deeds were substantiated, then yes, of course."

Grace now sprung her trap. "You are all fools with your drink. But when you sober up, and when Lyle starts thinking clearly, he will kill me. How could he let me return to my father? He would trust me to keep a secret? He would trust that I would not expose every gory detail to my father about the pillage of his property and the slaughter of his lifelong friends? You sit and you preach, and you explain how this perfect machination of politics allows for the perfect execution of evil, and you explain your role as the bystander. Unless you help me escape, I am dead and you are no bystander to my murder, sir. I am here. Not nameless, faceless collateral damage done in a foreign land. Your abstinence will condemn me to death."

This was not a revelation to Bergeron. Somewhere in the back of his heart he knew she was not leaving this ship alive. Lyle was dumb but not stupid. A ransom would never work. Bergeron thought of his predicament and smiled to himself. She was forcing his hand. Help her or be a murderer? Help her and get murdered. His self-preservation urge was strong but dulled by the alcohol. How long would the guilt stay with him if he turned her over to Lyle? Alcohol would help that pass.

He looked again at Grace. She was staring right back, eyes bright and unshackled from duress. When he had led her into his cabin and away from the massacre, he had presumed she was a scared child. She had since shed her cloak of meekness just as surely as she shouldered off the blanket she had been wrapped in. He saw a woman who was breathing fire.

"Maybe you'd like to know why I am here on this ship?" he offered.

"You're here because you financed an irrigation project in

Egypt for the British government," Grace said heatedly and impatiently. "You're bringing slave labor to Egypt."

"Yes, that is true. We financed an irrigation project to make the Egyptian cotton fields profitable again now that they are owned by the British, but I was going to tell you why *I* am here. I am a principal in a prestigious Swiss banking house. Why would I come on a voyage like this one? Why would I, a gentleman, be on a hell ship bound for the inferno with Lucifer himself at the helm? Would you like to know?"

"No," said Grace. "I don't care."

"I'll tell you all the same. Normally our firm would hire a trusted agent cut from a rougher cloth than I to accompany a voyage like this one, but I decided I wanted to get out of Geneva. My wife left me. I decided I needed to leave Geneva after she left me."

"I think she displayed sound judgement," said Grace.

"Our only daughter died. She was nine years old. She fell off a horse and broke her neck. We were riding together. It drove a wedge between me and my wife. She believed I was not displaying an adequate amount of grief."

After a long moment of silence, Grace asked, "Are you telling me all of this because I am dead anyway?"

"I'm telling you this because if I decide to help you, I'd like you to know it's because I'm just as lost as you are in this obscene moment, in this obscene life."

Grace blinked. Bergeron forewent his wine glass and made use of the bottle, polishing off it's remaining third. He wiped his mouth, slapped his thighs, and said, "OK, let's get off this boat."

"OK," she said warily, studying him for his intentions. Her heart beat faster, and she realized she did not have much choice but to trust this man.

"You have no choice but to trust me," he said, reading her thoughts. "The men will be drinking 'round the forecastle. We will now have the cover of darkness. We will hear them, and they can hear us if we are not careful. I'll gather some provisions and lower a skiff down the starboard side. Meet me outside this cabin in ten minutes." He jerked his thumb behind him to point at a chronometer in the corner of the cabin.

"I need to get something before we leave," she said.

"Impossible," he said as he turned to go. "All the spoils of the *Albatro* will be under lock and key in the ship's hold."

She made to argue, but he shook his head and hissed, "Ten minutes," then left through the cabin door.

Ten minutes later they had removed the canvas boat cover from the skiff and were silently lowering the boat over the side, letting the rope slide from their hands a foot at a time. Then they lowered the provision sacks Bergeron had pilfered from the ship's stores. Bergeron turned to help Grace over the rail, but she had already nimbly begun her descent, rappelling with a line she had fastened to a deck cleat. She landed silently onto the tiny craft and contemplated shoving off quickly and leaving Bergeron behind. She decided against it as there was the possibility of him raising the alarm. She also acknowledged that the additional manpower would be helpful as this little fifteen-foot rowboat would need to traverse over fifty nautical miles to make landfall. She set about putting the oars into the oarlocks, and as soon as Bergeron's feet hit the floorboards, she maneuvered the skiff's bow away from the *Hafgufa*'s hull and toward open water. Bergeron settled into the coxswain seat, and Grace started rowing in the sculler seat, her back to the bow. She dipped the oars silently and made her pulls deep, slowing her motion when the oars resurfaced to stifle their sound. Soon the swaying sight of the *Hafgufa* passed from her view and only the moonlit movement of the Red Sea remained. She rowed for what felt like an hour, all the while in silence. She focused her mind on her stroke and did not let it wander. She felt that if she broke from her methodic pulling, all the terrors of the day would catch her. She could not let herself be caught, not by the physical terrors of the *Hafgufa* nor the emotional reminders of the slaughter of the *Albatro*. Of her crew of brothers. Of Lucca.

After two hours, a fair breeze glided up from the east, astern of the skiff. Grace spoke for the first time. "Is the canvas boat cover in the boat or did we leave it behind?"

Bergeron stirred. He was half asleep. The wine and the hour of evening had caught up with him. He groped behind his seat and said, "No, it's here."

"What do we have for tools? Do we have a saw?"

Bergeron rummaged through the provision sacks, blinking his eyes forcefully to inspire wakefulness. He produced a rigging knife with a serrated blade and handed it to Grace. Grace paused from her rowing and inspected it. Bergeron inspected her. She seemed to be deep in thought. Though she contemplated the knife, he could tell she was working out the mechanics of something and weighing probabilities of success. She was a fascinating creature. Only hours ago she had witnessed the massacre of her crew and probably her closest companions, but nevertheless she was operating with the cold calculation of a professional survivalist. Only hours ago she had been trembling under a blanket, and now she was Washington crossing the Delaware. And what beauty she possessed! She sacrificed nothing of her femininity with her display of strength and skill in her operation of their rowboat. He felt his eyes repeatedly drawn to her hands. They were the hands of a woman, no doubt, but they were tanned and capable and had a confident power to them. All of a sudden, she was using those hands to unscrew one of the oarlocks. She had apparently made up her mind and leapt into action, bringing both oars inside the boat. When she had freed the oarlock she started working it into the bow of the skiff such that the ring was parallel to the floorboards instead of perpendicular as it was on the gunnel. She then snapped her fingers at Bergeron and pointed to the canvas boat cover. Bergeron hastened to comply and gave her the canvas. She set about cutting up the cover, puncturing small holes in the edges and then threading a small line, sewing parts of the canvas together.

Without looking up she said, "While I'm doing this, why don't you take that rigging knife there and start sawing one of the oars. It's an eight foot oar; give me three feet on the paddle side and five feet on the handle side."

"You want me to saw our oar in half? How will we row?" Bergeron asked, quite surprised.

"Why row when you can sail? Breeze is up. Don't cut it in half, I want a three foot piece on the paddle side and a five foot piece on the handle side." When he did not immediately stir, she looked up and urged, "Quickly now!"

Bergeron started the painful process of sawing at the oar with the rigging knife. While he was working at that, Grace took the other oarlock and placed it in the center of the skiff's stern rail. "A guide for our rudder," she explained. She then lashed the canvas, now a triangular sail cloth, to the oar that Bergeron was not busy with. After creating a divot under the oarlock placed at the bow, she stepped her mast and stood the oar with the attached canvas straight up at the bow of the boat. When Bergeron, now sweating from exertion, handed her the five-foot piece of oar, she was able to lash it to the bottom edge of the sail, creating a boom. By tying a line to the mid part of the boom, she now had a mainsheet with which she could trim her mainsail.

"Switch places with me," she instructed Bergeron. "I want you to hold the mast in place. She is not so steady."

Grace went to the stern and placed the short section of Bergeron's oar into the oarlock. She dipped the paddle side into the water and was thus able to steer the skiff with one hand. Her other hand manipulated the mainsheet, and the rowboat, bursting from its cocoon, was now a jury-rigged sailboat running downwind.

As Grace knew, the skiff was without a keel or daggerboard, and the flat bottom would prevent them achieving any point of sail closer to the wind than a broad reach, but the little craft would perform well enough when the wind was at her stern. The exertion involved in the sawing of the oar had left Bergeron fully awake and fully sober, and he now had a proper command of his mental faculties. The magnitude of his audacious decision to flee the *Hafgufa* had settled on him.

"I take it you have some idea of where we are headed?" he asked Grace, hoping they were not cutting a random course.

"If the breeze keeps up, we'll make land in six hours, more or less."

"And then?"

"And then it's a four or five day's hike south to Massawa."

"Why not go north to Suakin? It would be a two-day hike, or maybe less."

"That would be the obvious choice, which is why we will not choose it. Also, there is an Italian army garrison in Massawa that would offer us greater protection. There is a man there that will help us. He's the father of ... a friend. His name is Ferrando."

Bergeron was considering further argument in favor of Suakin on account of their meager provisions, but Grace's face had darkened, and she had spoken with such firmness that he decided to leave it alone. What an adventure this was becoming, he mused to himself.

28

Four days later, Grace and Bergeron entered the city gates of Massawa on foot and were immediately introduced into a shouting corporal mixture of a marketplace that was alive with the sounds of barter and the smells of grilled meats and salted fish. Some of the smells Grace identified brought forth memories of Mediterranean markets, and she even recognized some of the spoken tongues above the clangor of the crowd. She had expected Massawa to be an African city, and while the impossibly African combination of arid humidity hung over the marketplace, it seemed oddly ... Italian. All the treasures of the African interior were sold—elephant ivory, zebra hide, ostrich feather, lion's mane—but merchants were also hocking cured meats, sun-dried peppers and tomatoes, sacks of grain and fava, and cigars. She saw a man taking a machete to a wheel of hard cheese and a young woman hand cranking a coffee grinder. Where she expected huts were cafes enclosed in stone, and where she expected to hear exotic vernacular was the lingua franca, Italian.

"Colonialism, Grace," Bergeron said, seeing her confusion. "Invasion of the *Italianos*."

Grace found a merchant who was boasting of his fresh moray eel in sing-song Italian and backing up the claim by holding the wriggling creature above his perspiring bald head.

"Sir, where is the Italian Army garrison?" Grace asked loudly enough to be heard over of the din of the Massawan commercial district. The man used his eel to point to farther down the main drag.

"Follow the blue sashes, *mio tesoro!*"

Grace and Bergeron walked farther into the city, seeing more and more blue-sashed Italian soldiers, until they came to a grand structure with two layers of trussed marble arches supporting a grand dome that shone metallic and proffered up an Italian flag at its summit.

They dismounted and walked through lofty wooden doors into the vestibule.

There was a desk manned by a soldier with a long nose and sleepy eyes. He looked up and did not speak until they had traversed the distance between door and desk, footsteps echoing in the cavernous room.

"What is your business?" he asked plainly.

"We are Italians," said Grace. "We need to speak to the highest-ranking Italian official in the city."

"That would be the colonel," the soldier said slowly, all the while glancing dubiously at Bergeron. He then looked back at Grace and added even more slowly, "But. What. Is. Your. Business?"

"We need to find someone and deliver an important message," said Grace, growing frustrated.

"The colonel has a country to run and a war to wage. He is the most powerful Italian on this dreadful continent, and you'd like me to grant you an audience because you have an important message for someone important?"

Grace fished for something beneath her shirt and brought out a gold signet, which she slammed on the table. "My name is Grace Ligoria of Ligoria Trading Company. We have two score vessels making us the largest merchant fleet in Italy. If you don't know the name Ligoria, then get someone who does." Grace spoke her last words with such venom that the sleepy-eyed soldier now seemed wide awake. He asked them to wait one minute and disappeared through another grand doorway.

Moments later he returned with a spindly soldier whom he conversed with in hushed tones. They stopped about fifteen feet from Grace and Bergeron. and he called to her. "Your name is Grace Ligoria?"

"Yes," she said.

"Come with me to see the colonel. Your friend must wait here."

Grace followed the tall but youthful-looking soldier up a spiral staircase and into a smaller yet no less grand antechamber, and he motioned for her to continue on into a room that he indicated was the colonel's office. Thanking the tall soldier, she pulled open the door to the office, which looked to be directly beneath the building's resplendent dome. She entered, and what she saw nearly took her breath away.

Sitting behind a desk of carved oak was a man who looked like the specter of Lucca with two more decades of wear. The man was handsome and wore his shaggy jet black hair the same way Lucca had. He was smiling at her in a way that she well knew.

She could only assume she was in the presence of Colonel *Enzo Ferrando*.

This sight, and the realization that she had to tell this man of Lucca's death right here and now, was too much for her, and she broke into spasming sobs. The man rushed around from behind his desk and held her, telling her it was OK and to be calm. At first this only made her sob more hysterically. Soon she settled down, and he led her to a chair in front of his desk.

When she was finally recovered, she looked up at Enzo, and it was obvious that he was being as patient as he could but also experiencing terrible anxiety over what she was about to say. She decided to just say it.

"Lucca is dead. He was murdered."

Enzo's brow contorted in confusion, grasping for comprehension of the words that had left her mouth and hung in the air, resonating off the dome and all the polished surfaces of the elegant stateroom.

He looked away abruptly, and she saw his jaw clench rigidly. He took a breath and turned back to her. He asked her to tell him everything, which she did. She spared no details, including her love for his son. She told him exactly how Lucca had died.

He did not interrupt her and asked no questions, save one.

"What was the name of the ship that attacked you?"

When she told him, he nodded with a trace of recognition. She was studying him now. Most observers might say he was taking the news fairly well, but she felt that she knew him, and to her it was clear that something had changed. Something deep and as old as Abraham. Something permanent.

He was now writing something and looking down as he spoke. "In four days time, the *Castelfidardo* will berth here in Massawa and you will be able to get passage back home to Genoa. You will be protected. It's captained by Geraldo Al-Dapo, an old friend."

After speaking the words "old friend," he looked up sadly and asked, "What is an old friend but someone who knew you in better days?"

Grace did not know what to say.

"Your father has been very kind to my family," Enzo said. "Please give him my warmest regards."

And now Grace did not know what to do. All she knew was that she felt an immense, all encompassing exhaustion. She felt her lip tremble again. "I'm ... I'm so sorry, I—"

"No, no." Enzo held up a hand and kindly silenced her. "You've been through more than I can imagine. You need rest. Lieutenant Tassoni, the tall man outside, he'll see to it that you get food and clean bedding. You're safe now."

Grace nodded and exited the office, respectfully closing the door behind her. Enzo sat quietly for a moment. His recurrent sensation was surfacing, and he felt himself hauled brutally through bramble patch and thorn bush and mud by the invisible lead around his neck.

He pulled out his old Colt Dragoon revolver from the holster he still kept on his hip. He tried to remember Al-Dapo's sentiments when he had gifted it to him five years ago. *Good for killing savages.* Something like that. He looked at the gun for a long time.

"I'm a little nervous," he said aloud.

"I know," said Anita, who was sitting on his lap. Her apparition was stroking the back of his scalp with her fingers and brushing away his hot tears. "I'm here."

He lifted his revolver to his temple and grasped at the invisible lead. Then pulled out the slack in the line.

* * *

GRACE AND TASSONI reentered the vestibule and approached Bergeron while he spoke casually with the sleepy-eyed soldier. Then a thunderous boom seemed to quake the very walls of the building. The dome swept up the boom and stretched it into a reverberating roar that sounded like a wild beast of the plains rumbling into the distance.

Tassoni and the soldier looked at each other wild-eyed and sprinted back up the spiral staircase. They were followed by dozens of armed guards. Grace started to run to the staircase, too, but Bergeron held her back.

"There's nothing you can do."

Grace turned to Bergeron. "What happened? Why would he—"

"Grace! Grace look at me." Bergeron grabbed her shoulders. "The *Hafgufa* got those slaves from Massawa. We got the slaves from here. From him."

She felt her world slide sideways, and she tried to steady herself against the grievous blow this realization had dealt her. She pushed his arms away and slapped his face with all her might. "He thought he was responsible for his son's death ... You let me tell him!"

"He had a right to know the truth," Bergeron said, recoiling from the blow. "And I did not know how he would react. I did not know he would take responsibility unto himself."

Grace was breathing heavily, and she spoke with pure animus. "There are some men in this world that take responsibility unto themselves. I'm not surprised that concept is foreign to you."

"He takes responsibility when the pain returns to his doorstep," Bergeron said calmly.

Grace thought about planting her knife squarely in his rib cage, but she wasn't sure she could locate a heart to pierce. She felt heavy. Like a gull that finally ceases flapping against the wind and feels invisible forces spirit it back toward the earth. She was as tired as she'd ever been in her eighteen years.

29

Eleven days after Grace embarked for Genoa and three days after the burial of Enzo Ferrando, a dead man walked through the gates of Massawa. His footsteps were random, and his breathing was ragged. He wasn't noticed immediately, and he staggered through the crowded market-place until one by one the barterers, the buyers, and the beggars saw him and stopped what they were doing. Once they caught sight of the dead man walking among them, their daily cares fell about them like the forgotten toys of a child. The entire marketplace stood and stared as if turned to stone.

Soon the Massawan marketplace was completely quiet save for the haggard footsteps of the dead man until he, too, stood still. He seemed to notice the hundreds of sets of eyes peering at him, and he grew uncertain. The crowd's silence turned to whispers, and they craned their necks to get a better look at the dead man. The whispers grew deafening.

"Could it be?"

"It's him, back to life."

"It's the colonel."

"What witchcraft is this?"

The excitement grew, and the crowd grew. Those on the outskirts wanted a view of the dead man and pushed toward the spectacle. The crowd surged inward onto the dead man. The dead man, now panicked, spun around looking for an escape from the faces and the hands that were grabbing at him.

Just then the discharge of a pistol jolted the collective attention to a large, hulking man bulling his way through the crowd. The man held the pistol above his head. The big man fired into the air again and was given enough berth to get to the dead man, whom he threw over his back and carried out of the marketplace, all the while firing his pistol and shouting at the crowd to disperse in a guttural Italian.

Once they were clear of the crowd, the big man set the dead man down and urged him to follow him. After noticing that the dead man could not keep up, the big man resumed carrying him, and they wound through side streets and alleys until they were sufficiently alone. The big man then set the dead man down once again and used a massive leg to casually kick in the door of a boarded-up house. After confirming the house to be empty, he brought the dead man in, sat him on a chair, and thrust a wineskin into the dead man's hand.

The big man then fetched his own chair and drew it up close to the dead man.

Then the big man spoke softly. "They think you are Enzo Ferrando. I know you are not Enzo Ferrando, despite the resemblance, because Enzo Ferrando was a man I knew well."

The dead man brought the wineskin to his mouth weakly and took a sip. Then he said through parched lips, "Was?"

"What?" the big man asked.

"You said *was*. You said Enzo Ferrando *was* a man you *knew* well."

"Yes. Enzo Ferrando is no longer among the living."

The dead man slumped in his chair and started to shake pitifully. The big man recognized these convulsions as a display of grief. Then a larger wave of realization washed over the big man, and he sat back in his chair.

"You're his son," the big man muttered.

Lucca managed a nod.

"My name is Zagranos Pasha. I served under your father. You could say we were friends."

Lucca brought the wineskin to his lips again. He then looked up at Pasha. Pasha was so big, he could not help but loom. In any other state, Lucca would have been terrified of Pasha. The man had eyes that could go dead, a face that could go blank, and hands that could quite effortlessly crush windpipe and bone. The middle of Pasha's face was occupied by a large, disfigured nose that couldn't decide which way it wanted to slant. Above his nose perched a Cro-Magnon brow that seemed built to withstand blunt force trauma. But Lucca was too numb to be terrified. "How did my father die?"

"We'll talk about that later. Much to talk about. First, I think we change that bandage. Let's have a look at your neck."

Lucca allowed Pasha to peel the bled-through cloth off his neck, taking some tissue with it.

Pasha whistled and said, "It looks like you got your throat cut, boy. Luckily for you, someone did a shit job of it. Still, needs to be sewn up properly. I'll find a medical man. Stay here."

When Pasha returned with a doctor, he found Lucca sleeping in his chair and the wineskin empty.

Lucca woke up some hours later. He found he was wearing clean clothes, and he had been moved to a straw bed in the same house. Pasha was in the corner, carving something with a long knife. He turned to Lucca when he noticed him stirring.

"The medical man said you need to keep changing the

bandages. If it gets infected, you'll have trouble amputating." Pasha chuckled to himself.

Lucca felt his neck and found he could feel the stitching through the bandage. He then sat all the way up and look over at Pasha. "I'd like to know how he died."

"He died by his own hand." Pasha sighed without looking up from his carving. "Probably the only hand that could have felled him. I don't profess to fully understand the act, but I know it was not an act of cowardice. That man was incapable of any act of cowardice. He was the closest thing to an immortal that we had among us."

Lucca was shaking his head. "I don't believe it. Why would he just kill himself? What drove him to ... to do it?"

Pasha gritted his teeth and let out a longer sigh. "I was told that Enzo Ferrando had been given news of the destruction of a merchant vessel crewed by his son. No survivors."

"No survivors?" Lucca's lungs grasped at air, and his mind immediately leapt to Grace.

"Obviously my information is not accurate, as evidenced by your presence. I'm looking at a survivor. Maybe there are more. How did you survive?"

"Swam," said Lucca as he laid back down and closed his eyes.

"What happened?" asked Pasha.

"Sorry. I'm not sure I have the energy to relive it just now." said Lucca, still with eyes closed.

"I heard pirates."

Lucca did not respond.

"Dishonorable way to earn a living, pirating. Dabbled in some privateering myself, which is different than pirating, but even there honorable men were not to be found. Even when you sail for a sovereign nation, gold is the goal and glory just an afterthought ... OK. I can see you'd like some rest. I'll be back at sun up to check on you. Shitter is in the next room over."

Zagranos Pasha vanished into the night, leaving Lucca alone. Lucca had not seen his father in five years, but the man had never been far from his thoughts. They wrote to each other periodically, but more importantly, Lucca had always felt his father's presence. It was the presence of a guardian. He had felt his father on the deck of the *Albatro* as the bosun's knife slid across his throat. He had felt his father as he swam for two days, using the stars to finally find the shore. He had felt his father when he dragged himself up the beach and pleaded with a native to bring him some water. His father had always been the presence sitting in the chair at the edge of his bed. No matter what nightmares Lucca dreamed up, he could always wake up to his father, sitting there, ready to make everything right. Where was his father now? He could not feel him.

"He left me," Lucca said to the empty room. He had never been more angry.

And then there was Grace. And Bartolo and DiSesa and the crew of the *Albatro*. But especially Grace. No survivors? He thought of the hundreds of tortured souls in the hold of the *Hafgufa* to be sold in captivity. He thought of his five years on the Albatro, working, laughing, learning, loving. Five years erased from existence like they were turned to steam. How could this happen? Where was his father?

30

Lucca woke up the next day to the smell of frying pork. It was a delicious aroma, and Lucca realized how famished he was. The impressive bulk of Zagranos Pasha was crouching over a small cooking stove in the corner. He was working sausages around on a griddle with a two-pronged utensil that looked like a toy in his massive hand. The relative sizes of the big man and the little stove were of comedic proportions, and Lucca may well have laughed had not the memory of his current condition returned to him. His troubled mind could not hold sway over his stomach, however, and when Pasha served up the blood sausage and biscuits, Lucca ate wolfishly.

Pasha nodded approvingly at Lucca's appetite and stated, "I'm working on getting you some boots. In a day or two, you may be ready to travel."

Lucca's attention was consumed by the consuming of his breakfast. His face was not six inches from this breakfast, thus minimizing the distance that food needed to travel from plate to mouth.

Pasha continued on, "Now that your father is drinking mead in Valhalla, there is nothing left in Africa for me, so I could take you to Genoa on my way back to the Balkans. In fact, I ended my contract with the Italian Army the day your father died and have been hanging around for the next ship out of this hell hole. What say you?"

"Why would I go to Genoa?" asked Lucca without looking up from his plate.

"Well, isn't that your home? Don't you have some family there?"

"No. No siblings. Mother's dead."

"Ah, yes. I knew that about your mother. Enzo wouldn't shut up about it, actually. Anita was his wife's name, same as Garibaldi's. And your name is Loki?"

"Lucca."

"Lucca it is. He wrote to you sometimes, isn't that right? Did he ever mention me, Zagranos Pasha?"

"No."

"Well, maybe not by name, but in his letters did he mention anyone who fit my description?" Pasha straightened himself up.

"I ... don't believe so," Lucca said uncertainly, now looking up from his food.

"He never mentioned a seven-foot-tall mercenary who saved his ass more than a couple of times?" said Pasha, looking at Lucca incredulously.

"The mail can be ... unreliable. It's possible I missed that letter."

"He never mentioned the man who helped him avenge his father's killers?" Pasha cried, throwing up his hands. "Your grandfather's killers?" Clearly agitated now, he stood up in a huff and paced the little room, which only allowed for three of his massive strides.

Speaking to the ceiling, Pasha wailed, "What is the purpose

of heroic deeds if they are not sung about? Where are the bards? Where are the Virgils and Homers?"

"Clearly, there were many important things that my father kept from me. I did not know my grandfather was avenged until you just said so. So then, it does not surprise me he would forgo mention of a great friend." Lucca offered this to console Pasha, but he said it with absolute honestly. Apparently, there were many things he did not know about his father. Another bitter disappointment.

This did comfort Pasha noticeably, and he set about picking at his own breakfast before saying, "Well, as you said, the mail service is not so reliable."

After a time of silent eating, Pasha renewed the conversation. "So where will you go, Lucca?"

"I don't know. Not Genoa. There is no one there for me." He did not add that there was someone there in Genoa, Grace's father, that he could not bring himself to see. Not yet. Nor did he wish to burden Greta Nonna.

"Well then, you'll accompany me to my home in Albania," Pasha suggested in a triumphant manner. "Some hiking in the mountain ranges and you'll be cleaned out and reborn, ready to deal the world a savage blow! You can meet my sisters. Two of them are still maids."

Lucca could not imagine a woman version of Pasha and did not want to, but somewhere else, anywhere else, sounded better than here. He agreed to accompany this Zagranos Pasha.

31

Lucca was still weak and had developed a hacking cough that shook his entire reduced form, but within two days time he was able to accompany Pasha to the Port of Massawa and board the British Sloop *Taliesin*. They made their way to the port through a ferocious storm that had rushed up from the south and pelted Massawa with horizontal rain. At midday the sky was black as coal, and the sprightly giant and the sickly youth were provided excellent cover as they walked down the main street. The only soul they met was a street merchant busy boarding up the windows of his shop against the storm's rage. The merchant did a double take and recognized the dead man even against the rain and howling wind, but when he approached the pair, Pasha knocked him down and told him he was ugly.

As if a supernatural sign, the wind was at their backs, ushering them down the street, up the gangway, and out of Africa.

Lucca had expected Pasha to procure their passage with two steerage tickets, but when Pasha pulled a handful of gold coins from his pockets and stuffed them roughly into the captain's hands, he realized that steerage was not how Zagranos Pasha intended to make his exodus from the dark continent.

The *Taliesin* was a wooden sloop repurposed and rechristened from the Royal Navy for trade and civilian passage. *Taliesin* would stop at Suez, Port Said, Cyprus, Athens, and the Port of Dürres, where they would disembark.

"It ain't a fancy Cunard liner, but this will do," said Pasha upon opening the door to their cabin.

Yes, this will do, thought Lucca as he fell into the silk-sheeted lower bunk and into a profound slumber.

Lucca and Pasha both woke up several hours later from a knock on the cabin door. Lucca opened his eyes to find the upper bunk about six inches from his face and looking like it was starting to buckle; such was the weight of Pasha on the top bed. Lucca slid out of his bunk and opened the door to find a man in a white Eton jacket who formally informed Lucca that supper would be served in the main dining room in one quarter of one hour. Lucca nodded, and the man bowed and left. When Lucca turned back to the cabin he found Zagranos Pasha out of his bunk carefully pouring a bottle of red wine into his wineskin pouch. Pasha then uncorked a different red, which he poured into the wineskin as well.

"Ready for dinner?" Pasha asked, smiling.

32

While the *Taliesin* had left Massawa and the southerly storm in its wake, the pitch and sway of the ship in open water caused Pasha to bounce into the wall of the passageway with every step as he walked to dinner, all the while stooping under the low-hanging ceilings. Lucca, who had his sea legs, did everything he could not to laugh as he followed Pasha to the ship's main dining room.

The *Taliesin* was a passenger vessel converted from a navy ship, so the dining room was more humble than the steam-powered luxury ocean liners currently cruising the seas, but a chandelier glittered above a room full of crisp white tablecloths and porcelain dinnerware, and Lucca thought this must be the fanciest room he had ever been in.

The man with the Eton jacket guided them to a table on the opposite side of the room, where Pasha sat with his back to the wall looking more ridiculously out of place than an ostrich in an osprey nest. Lucca was looking forward to seeing Pasha's giant hands operate the delicate silverware that spanned the entire place setting.

Pasha, looking very much the barbarian at royal court, winked at Lucca and took a long pull of his wineskin. He had barely brought it down when Eton Jacket came back to take their order.

He had started to rattle off the specials of the evening when Pasha held up an enormous palm and interrupted him, saying, "Oysters and beef, my good man. Three dozen and a side each of your choicest cut. That is what we shall be having."

Eton had a long nose, from the top of which he looked down at these obvious intruders into high society, and offered them what he thought be fitting accompaniment to their galling presence.

"Would the *gentlemen* like a few pints of ale with their meal?" Eton said in a nasally voice. The queer emphasis on the word gentlemen did not go unnoticed.

"No, that won't do, my dear boy," Pasha replied with a sly smile. "Just because we are at sea does not mean we must eschew proper drink. I'm sure you can rummage around back there and find us a Muscadet Sèvre-et-Maine to complement the oysters."

Eton stiffened like someone had doused him with cold water. Lucca was impressed with the order's effect on the snobby waiter and felt a pleasant pang of pride in his breast as his new friend demonstrated there may be more to a mercenary than met the eye.

The waiter maintained his composure and turned to leave with a small bow.

"Garcon!" Pasha called after him. "That's *sur lie*, not *surly*."

Lucca may not have understood the pun, but he laughed at Pasha's pleasure with his own joke. He felt himself start to relax, an almost alien sensation for him. When it was served, the dry white wine was crisp and seemed to spread a soft effervescence all the way through to his extremities. Lucca's hacking cough had dissipated almost entirely. The oysters were briny to perfection, and the decadent dinner was doing well to lighten his heavy state of being. He was even enjoying the company of this strange savage Zagranos Pasha.

Pasha was enjoying himself immensely and had the waiter running to and fro with fresh and empty wine bottles, which Pasha supplemented with his own wineskin.

After Lucca had himself consumed a few glasses of wine, he asked Pasha to tell him about his father. Pasha slowed the pace at which he was chewing his beef and nodded, expecting that Lucca would be asking exactly that question. Pasha finished his mouthful and dabbed his face with a napkin of brilliant white that contrasted starkly against his sunburnt face. He then cleared his throat and leaned over the table in a conspiratorial manner.

"Where to begin ... Considering your father was not comprehensive in relating to you his full history—as evidenced by the fact you had never heard of me—I will start toward the beginning of his ascension to the most powerful Italian in Africa. Of course this is less impressive considering the general standing of Italy in the totem of European nations and the general importance of Africa in global affairs, but still no mean feat for a dockworker who could barely seat a horse. But the Fates did tap Enzo. I have been on too many battlefields to not see the intervention of divinity when it occurs."

Lucca spoke up. "I don't follow you."

"Well, where did I lose you?"

"Fates. Divine intervention. Are you saying my father was touched by God?" Lucca searched Pasha's face for permission to laugh at the hyperbole. But Pasha did not give it.

"I said tapped by the Fates. I see the doubt on your brow, boy. Remember, I have lived the length of your life and more with a weapon in my hand. I know a little something about death and desperation. You think God visits in on tea parties and debutante balls?" Pasha waved his hand at the room as if making the point there was no God in sight and continued.

"You think he presides over tedious trade negotiations or the hearings of bureaucrats? You'll find God where you find extremes. He'll be in the tent with you at Waterloo, holding you down as the hack surgeon saws off your frostbitten foot. Only when the stakes are at their highest does a man show his worth. Remember that, Lucca. Piety is for the birds. Courage and honor in the face of the business end of the bayonet is the true test of soul. That's God's test for us. And if you want to find him, you know what you have to do. Great battles earn divine attention, and courageous acts earn divine favor. Remember that, and you'll be taken care of in the afterlife."

Pasha paused to empty his wine glass, snap at the waiter, and undo the top few buttons of his shirt as if the room was starting to get too warm for him.

He began again. "So yes. I have seen the extremes that this life serves up, and I have seen, with my own eyes, the willful actions of Enzo Ferrando when beset by life's extremes. I do believe your father was tapped by the Fates, and from what I heard, I believe your grandfather felt the tap as well. So did Henry V of England. Roland. Leonidas. Take your pick."

"I see," Lucca said cautiously.

"And by the way, I'm not so sure there's only one God," added Pasha. "I've been giving this much thought."

Although Lucca felt that he was getting to know this man better, he felt no closer to uncovering the particular type of madness that was ailing him.

"Where was I in my story of your father?" Pasha asked as he rummaged around for his wineskin.

"You were toward the beginning," Lucca replied.

"Yes. Galliano Battalion had taken Massawa. It was a bloodless conquest, mind you. The Brits handed it over to the Italians for some devious reason. I suppose it testifies to the value of Massawa at the time. It was a sure-as-shit hole of a place, but a decent amount of trade ran through there. Back then the five companies of Galliano Battalion were led by a bureaucrat called Cristofori. Colonel Cristofori. Maybe your father mentioned *him*. I believe he fancied himself a political strategist but never came close to the dirty parts of war until his end. Massawa is not a terrible seat for the Italian presence in Africa, but back then it only existed within the walls of the port city. The market where I picked you up did not yet exist. The concerning part about Massawa, though, was the fact that an enemy could walk right up to the port city walls and knock the door down without much trouble. We needed outposts to extend into the interior so we wouldn't be battling in our front yard."

"Who were you fighting?" Lucca asked.

"Who were we fighting? The goddamn natives, of course. Didn't your father tell you anything about what he was doing?"

"So the Eritreans?"

"No, those were our allies. We were fighting the Ethiopians." Pasha paused and then nodded to himself. "Yes, the Ethiopians. I'm pretty sure we were fighting the Ethiopians, though it really makes no difference. They all respond the same way when they have a few holes punched in them. Rebel, royalist, infidel, Turk. Holes is holes.

"OK," nodded Lucca.

"OK, I'll continue. There was a run-down fort settlement called Sahati about one hundred miles inland from Massawa, which was a four or five day's march with provisions. This fort would at least allow us to take the fight deeper into the interior and not put the Italian trading port at risk. It was decided that two Galliano companies would occupy the old fort, shore up its defenses, and commence raids into enemy territory. It was natural that First Company and Fifth Company were selected for the mission; First Company for its fighting and raiding prowess and Fifth because some poor bastards were needed to build up the walls."

"You were in First Company?" asked Lucca.

Pasha eyed Lucca as if he was asking a question that he knew the answer to but saw no guile on the boy's face. "Of course," replied Pasha. "Well, I was originally in First, then I moved to Fifth Company under your father when the Fifth was slowly becoming an outfit to be proud of."

"He was head of Fifth Company, the builder company?"

"That's right. Enzo was a captain and the head of Fifth. Captain Vittori was head of First Company. Vittori was one of the few bonafide soldiers in the Italian Army. One of the best horsemen I ever saw, and I rode against the Roşioris on the Russo-Turkish front. He didn't much like me, as it turned out, but I will concede he was a man of honor."

"Did the Fates tap Vittori?" Lucca inquired.

"Ha! No. The Fates fucked him in the eye. But we are skipping ahead. Between the two companies we had over 180 men, about twenty horse, no cannon, and no idea what was waiting for us in the wastelands of Africa. I remember first getting to Sahati and telling Enzo we should burn it down and start over; such was the shape of the place. But we set to work, building up the fortifications and making the place steadfast. I remember toiling like a slave in that heat, and it brought on a thirst like nothing I've experienced before. My tongue was like the desert sand. I remember walking to the water basin and finding it dry. I walked over to the captains, Enzo and Vittori, and they were speaking in controlled but concerned tones. When I asked them about the water, Vittori didn't even look at me, but your father replied curtly that the supply wagons from Massawa were three days late and we were running low on all provisions, not just water. I told them immediately it was the Ethiopian raiders who had picked off our supply wagons and probably had us surrounded, but Vittori told me to get back to work."

"That afternoon we sent out five scouts. Only two came back and brought with them some concerning news. It seemed, as yours truly had predicted, that our supplies were cut off and we were surrounded by an Ethiopian force that could be upwards of ten thousand troops. Ten thousand to our 180, only half of those real warriors! So as I said, some concerning news. Low on provisions, numbers against us, and little chance of reinforcement. You can see how this was shaping up as the stuff of legends."

It seemed to Lucca that Pasha had developed a glint in his eye. Lucca had to admit this Pasha was a fine storyteller. His passion and his vivacity had Lucca transfixed.

"Won't say that we felt all was lost, ho no! We had guns, ample ammunition, a battle-proven commander in Vittori, and most important of all, territorial advantage. The Sahati Fort, for all its ramshackle appearance, was superbly located smack in the middle of a vast clearing atop a gently sloping hill. We could see any invaders for a half-mile out, and there was no cover until the tree line, which was a half mile in each direction. Provisions were a problem, but I've drank horse blood before and didn't half mind the taste."

Pasha took a deep gulp from his wine glass as if the thought of horse blood had actually piqued his thirst. Lucca got the impression that others in the main dining room of the *Taliesin* were bending their ears in the direction of the big man's tale.

"Of course the cowards attacked at night. They came on foot and on horseback, howling like demons, and by the light of my rifle muzzle I could see war paint and terrible tattoos. But we were ready for them. We rained down bullets like hellfire, and when the sun came up, we saw four hundred of those savages strewn about the sand. The wind already had them partially covered. On our side we only sustained a dozen injuries, and the result buoyed our spirits and steeled our hearts for the next bout, which we were sure would come the following night. But it didn't. Nor did it come the next night. Nor the next."

"They were starving you out?" Lucca asked.

"It wasn't hunger that plagued us so much as thirst. The rations were down to a half cup a day, and our urine was so concentrated at that point that it was beyond drinking. We would run out of water within four to five days. The officers and the senior enlisted men got together to discuss our options. One option was floated where we would all sneak out by night, try to break the line, and make it back to the protected walls of Massawa. The problem was, just as any invaders were completely vulnerable in the area from fort to tree line, so too would we be. We only had enough horse for a fifth of the men, so the odds of even getting to the tree line without being picked off were slim to none. Plus there was the matter of the injured men. They could not make the trek even without the cannon fire. We resolved to select a small group of riders who would try to break through the Ethiopian's eastern line with speed and ride like hell to Massawa, where they would be able to alert the colonel who could muster the rest of Galliano Battalion and whatever other reinforcements could be raised from the Eritreans. It was a suicide mission. Naturally your father volunteered, but everyone including Vittori knew him to be absolute shit on horseback, so he was passed over. I volunteered, but there was nary a big enough horse to seat me that could make pace, so I too was passed over. There were other volunteers, but it was obvious Vittori would be leading this mad dash, and he did. Vittori and seven of the best riders of First Company reigned up just before sunrise. Vittori gave command of Sahati Fort to

Enzo while on horseback and ordered the east gate opened. The eight riders plunged into the soft light of the desert, whipping, beating, coaxing, pleading with their horses to maintain an unsustainable pace. They needed to make the tree line, then there was hope of running through a handful of half-asleep savages and boring on through to Massawa. The charge was a beautiful thing. Vittori at the front, his back parallel to the earth like a damned jockey, whipping his horse with everything he had. When they were halfway, we few on the wall started to hope. When they were two-thirds to the tree line, we started to grip on to each other; such was our apprehension."

At this time the majority of the other diners had stopped their private conversations and were listening to Zagranos Pasha. Pasha was half standing now, using his arms to simulate the whipping motion of Vittori on his horse. But just as Pasha was reaching the apex of his excitement, he sat back down in a huff and spoke in a subdued fashion.

"And that's when the guns opened on them. The fire came from their left, right, and forward. One by one the riders fell under the rain of artillery. When the smoke and dust cleared, we counted eight riders, eight horses. No one reached the tree line."

Pasha took a wine break and wiped his brow, surprised to find he was sweating. He did not notice or did not care that he was the center of attention until Eton walked over and asked whether Pasha could keep his voice down so as not to disturb the other diners. After Pasha assured him that he would not disturb the other diners in a most sincere display that Lucca suspected to be conscientiously over the top, Pasha continued his tale.

"Back at Satahi Fort, all eyes turned to Enzo. He had command, after all, and we were in quite a situation. Our best horses and best riders did not have what it took to make it out alive, and 170 odd men were scheduled to die of thirst before the week was out. I would not say that your father inspired a whole lot of confidence either. He did not take the death of Vittori well and was almost unapproachable for the remainder of the day. He would pace around the inner courtyard, only pausing to break something or shout at someone. He was rage and frustration incarnate. When he finally cooled down, the only people he wanted to see were the Askari twins, the princes. Did I tell you about them? Well, there were these two twins, Akele and Makele, and they were the sons of the Eritrean warlord chieftain who was helping us fight the Ethiopians. I guess Enzo had picked up some of their Tigrinya language because he was conversing with them and drawing things in the sand for several hours until the sun went down. During this time I could see the rest of the men getting increasingly agitated, especially those of First Company, who had just lost their leader and were now under the command of a dockworker. I wouldn't use the word *mutiny*, but there was certainly agitation, mixed with dehydration, mixed with fear. I stepped in and reminded them of Enzo's stock, of the Old Bull Antoni Ferrando. Even though I was not an Italian, that seemed to cool heads. I implored them to at least wait for Enzo's plan. But when Enzo gathered us together, even I was dismayed at his plan.

"Enzo's plan was to send two riders out of the south gate at dawn. Sound familiar? I thought so too. But as Enzo continued to detail his plan, heads started to nod. The riders would exit the south gate because south was the most proximate bearing to the tree line, and in all likelihood, more sparsely manned than the Ethiopians eastern front. They would be expecting us to try to break through toward Massawa, where we had reinforcements, by going east. To the south lay ... sixty miles of desert. But after that? The Askari chieftain's stronghold, our

Eritrean ally. The riders would be Enzo himself and Akele. Makele was to stay at Sahati Fort. As it was later explained to me, he wanted Makele to stay behind with us and remain in danger as a way to better leverage the Askari chieftain to help rescue us. This time, unlike the prior attempt, there would be covering fire. The hope was we could keep the Ethiopians' heads down long enough for the two riders to slip through. The only question asked of Enzo was, Why him? We knew he was terrible on horseback, and why should he be needlessly discarded if the plan failed? His answer was 'because it is my job.' And that was that."

Up until this point, Pasha had done a decent job keeping his voice down in the dining room, and as a result the other patrons, having been hooked into the tale, drew their chairs closer to Lucca and Pasha's table in order to hear, their meals forgotten.

"Dawn came and we brought forward the best two horses we had left, which I will say was a sad display. The men were severely dehydrated, and the horses fared even worse. Enzo reigned up, and he gave his final orders. He gave command of the fort to a string bean called Tassoni, with orders to surrender if he fell. The outcome of surrender in the African Horn was a coin toss. Sometimes it would mean ransom back to civilization in exchange for weapons, gold, or exotic timber. Sometimes it would mean death and dismemberment—and it would not be death *and then* dismemberment either. But those were Enzo's orders: to surrender the fort if he fell. I think that's why he gave command to Tassoni instead of me. With me, we would have fought to the last man. Thermopolis, the Alamo, and a whole lot of dead savages. But those were his orders. As he gave the orders, I could see he was getting some nerves. He was talking much faster than usual, and his eyes were wide with a madness I had not seen from him. He put us in our positions and then trotted with Akele to the south gate. Every man who could stand was on the wall with a rifle ready to provide covering fire like his life depended on it."

Pasha was standing now at his full height. His passion was back, and no damned waiter would tell him to lower his voice.

"The south gate opened, and the son of the Old Bull and the son of the chieftain erupted out of the fort like demons up from the nether. The two riders surged forward, whipping their horses as 170 lives hung in the balance. I could tell Enzo was riding on the razor's edge of control. It was a hard sight to describe. How do you describe two men working like hell to prevent your destruction when you're safe behind a wall?"

Lucca could see that Pasha's eyes were wet and he had gotten emotional. Pasha steadied himself and gripped the table for support before resuming.

"The instructions were to commence with covering fire when the riders were halfway to the tree line. It felt like an eternity, but commence we did. We gave the tree line everything we had and then some. By that time the element of surprise was gone, and we were shooting and hollering as fast and loud as we could. They were three quarters to the tree line when the enemy cannon fire started. We saw the cannon fire before we heard it. The silent salvo struck fear in our hearts. We saw the ground all around the riders become perforated, and great mounds of dirt shot up twenty foot high. And we saw Enzo fall. We saw his horse falter, and we saw him go over the top of his reigns. One hundred and seventy hearts, all beating together, sunk like stones. Many moaned and looked away. I did not, and for that I was rewarded because what I saw then was sweeter than any earthly nectar. Enzo fell from his horse, and without arresting his momentum, he rolled and leapt at the horse of Akele who was still mounted, riding at full speed. Emerging through the chaos, though the air was thick with smoke and gunpowder, I saw Enzo pull himself up on Akele's horse to sit behind his brother at arms. We watched, astonished, as the two men atop one horse made the tree line. Covering fire was then useless, and I traded my rifle for my war horn and blew until my lungs gave out."

As if on cue, Pasha, right there in the dining room, withdrew a curved ram's horn about the size of Lucca's forearm from one of his inner pockets. Pasha, in the main dining room of the *Taliesin*, took up his war horn and produced a blood curdling *Haaaarrrrooooooooooo*. The sound made the hair on the back of Lucca's neck stand up and caused an uproar all around them. But Pasha was not done with his tale and not to be deterred, so he lowered his war horn and pressed on with the story. To Lucca's surprise, the other diners, though frightened, appeared eager for him to continue.

"We heard the discharges of Enzo's great pistol in the distance and assumed they ran into enemy troops. We heard it again and assumed he got the better of them. The men at Sahati fort were ecstatic, as you can imagine. We once again had hope. But hope dissipates rapidly when you are dying of thirst in a desert wasteland. The hours went by, and then the days went by. If the Ethiopians had attacked us then, they would have taken us handily. We could barely stand. Then on the fourth day after Enzo's departure, we heard the most beautiful sound: gunfire from the south. It was the Askari chieftain and his own horde of savages come to give the Ethiopians hell. The fighting lasted no more than a few hours. We did our best to pick off any Ethiopians who retreated into our range, but the Eritreans mopped them up without issue. Just beautiful. The south gate was opened, and in rode Enzo himself. The men of First and Fifth would have been crying tears of joy if they could have spared the water."

That was when Lucca realized his own eyes were wet. Pasha

held up his hands, now to the whole dining room, as if to hold their applause. His tone got very grave, and then he continued.

"Unfortunately, this story does not have a happy ending for Galliano Battalion. On the march back to Massawa, not even halfway back, we saw a great cloud of buzzards circling an area known as Dogali. As we approached we were hit with the smell. When we figured out that stench was from bodies, and the bodies were from the rest of Galliano Battalion. I remember Enzo getting down off his horse and retching. I understood why. It seems that Second, Third, and Fourth Company of Galliano had been on the road to our rescue when the Ethiopian horde caught them at Dogali out in the open and overran them. This would explain why the Eritreans had such an easy time with the Ethiopians at Sahati. Most of the Ethiopian force had shifted to attack the vulnerable portion of Galliano. That massacre is called the Battle of Dogali, though it was not much of a battle. Seven thousand versus less than ten percent of that number."

The dining room was very quiet. Even Eton was respectful of the silence that now pervaded the room. Even the rocking of the ship seemed to have grown more gentle.

"Colonel Cristofori was among the dead, and because Enzo was the highest-ranking Italian military man left in Africa, he took command. Soon after he was promoted to colonel, reinforcements arrived with Gatling guns. The rest of the story, well, it was woe to the Ethiopians. The African Horn saw the full wrath and power of Enzo Ferrando."

Pasha stood up, still seemingly oblivious to the attention of the entire dining room, and carefully laid gold coins on the table. He then put a hand on Lucca's shoulder. "Let's get some rest."

33

That night Lucca woke himself up with a hacking cough. He also woke Pasha.

"We should get you to a medical man when we get ashore," said Pasha, half asleep.

"Zagranos?" Lucca whispered from the bottom bunk.

"Yes, Lucca Ferrando?"

"I need to find out if there are any other survivors of the *Albatro*. My ship."

Pasha paused for a long moment, then finally said, "Then we should go see the Fruitbat."

"A fruitbat?"

"*The* Fruitbat. A man and a fellow Albanian. He is the smartest man I've ever met. He has a network of spies."

"Why is his name the Fruitbat?"

"His name is actually Vreto, but everyone calls him the Fruitbat because he has big ears and he hangs upside down when he is doing his thinking."

"And you think he would know something about the *Albatro*?"

"It's possible. It's his job to know things. He is running a revolution, after all. Now try and get some sleep." Pasha yawned and shifted in his bunk.

Soon Pasha was snoring profoundly, but sleep would not come to Lucca. He got out of bed and padded quietly to the cabin door, then down the passageway and up to the deck. The salt air quickened his heart as it always did, but there were no stars in the sky. He took from his pocket the scrimshaw razor that Grace had given him. Dark ideations passed through his mind but were gone as quickly as they came. The razor had saved Lucca's life. When he had fallen from the *Hafgufa*, his hands were still bound, and he would not have made the long swim to shore if he had not been able to cut through them.

Lucca thought about the story Pasha had just told him and could not make sense of it. His father had taken his own life. His father, the hero, the conqueror who had clamped on to life so hard that he could not be unseated. It made less and less sense, and Lucca wondered if he had ever truly known his father. These were the final thoughts haunting his mind as he dozed off there on the deck.

34

Over the next few days, Lucca's health deteriorated, and his hacking cough grew more violent. Zagranos Pasha found a doctor among the passengers, and Lucca was diagnosed with pneumonia. Lucca grew feverish and could not leave the cabin. Pasha kept watch over the boy and changed his neck bandages even as the fever dreams gave way to fever nightmares and Lucca ranted and raved.

"There is a fire on this ship," Lucca informed Pasha one day. Lucca had dark circles under his eyes and a pallid coloring to his flesh. He was shivering under a mount of blankets.

"I think you are hallucinating," said Pasha uneasily.

"Can't you see the smoke coming up from the floorboards? Can't you smell the ash?"

"I cannot."

"It makes little difference. The sea is also on fire."

"How can the sea be on fire?"

"Only the surface. The depths will be calm and cool. We must dive under." Lucca made a pathetic effort to get out of his bunk, but Pasha pressed him back down.

"You need to rest, Lucca Ferrando."

Lucca nodded weakly and shut his eyes. Lucca's fever broke as the *Taliesin* was pulling into the Port of Dürres. The pneumonia remained, but Lucca had enough energy to go up on deck and stand next to Zagranos Pasha as they pulled into the medieval-looking harbor. Lucca had a blanket wrapped around his shoulders, and Pasha was smoking a long chibouk pipe.

"Good to be home again," Pasha said and took a deep breath. "I have long been dreaming of good Albanian meat stew. The finest in all the world. I bragged so often to your father about our stew that he told me he would come visit and try it for himself if I would only shut the hell up about it."

"And you believed him? You are a fool for trusting him." Lucca surprised himself at how much acid there was in his words. He was surprised at the anger he found lurking in his heart. He had been damning it up for a long time, and he felt the cracking of the dike.

Pasha stiffened. "Of course I believed him. He was a man of honor."

"I don't believe my father was a man of honor," Lucca said darkly. "And what do you know of honor? You are a mercenary and a killer. You romanticize the most horrible parts of human nature. You justify the evil deeds of men like my father. You sing his song well. But who sings for the men he kills? Who sings for the *Albatro*? You are not a man of honor. You fight for fortune. You fight for the country of highest bid."

Pasha grew very quiet. Lucca realized he had just dealt Pasha a blow more savage than anything he had ever received in his many battles. When Pasha finally spoke, he sounded distant and sad.

"Say what you will about me, but I resent your commentary on Enzo Ferrando." Pasha took a deep sigh and continued in a small voice. "It is true that I don't fight for a country. Albania is under Turkish control and not yet a nation; it is just an idea. A soul without a body. Fighting for a country is a luxury. I have to fight for something more abstract. One day we may cast off the oppression and have ourselves a nation. "

Pasha turned to walk away, but Lucca caught his massive arm.

"Zagranos. I'm sorry. I have not been myself lately. I'm sorry for those words."

Lucca had his mouth open like he was searching for something else to add but ended up closing it and looking down. Zagranos pulled him in and the two men embraced. When they disembarked from the *Taliesin*, they went directly to the city stables, and Pasha purchased two horses: a lively looking palfrey for Lucca and a massive charger for himself. Pasha explained to Lucca that these horses had shorter legs than the Arabian breeds because they were meant for mountain riding.

And into the mountains they went to find the one called the Fruitbat. Lucca was firmly impressed by Pasha's skill on a horse and marveled at the way he seemed to be so in tune with his animal and the rough terrain. For his part, Lucca was doing all he could to remain seated on his overeager palfrey. The terrain was varied and at times treacherous with thick wooded areas, rocky ledges, and deep marshes, but the horses were surefooted, and in time Lucca grew to trust his palfrey.

After they had been riding for over four hours, Zagranos stopped them and held up a hand. Then he studied the ridge above them and yelled something in a foreign tongue that Lucca assumed was Albanian. From out of nowhere, four armed men appeared on the ridge and carefully worked their way down to the pair of riders. Zagranos got down off his mount and helped Lucca do the same. Zagranos embraced each of them in the curious way Lucca had seen Turks embrace

—they grasped each other's shoulders and touched foreheads. The armed men looked at Lucca inquiringly, and Pasha offered an explanation that seemed to satisfy them. They were then led on foot to a thick wooded area where one of the men struck the heel of his boot down on something hard. A moment later, a piece of earth gave way, and Lucca could see a man with a lamp occupying the entrance of a narrow tunnel. Two of the armed men mounted their horses and presumably rode off to hide them.

As Lucca was wondering if Zagranos would be able to fit, he found himself being ushered down into the tunnel. Once he was a few paces in, he turned and was relieved to see Pasha right behind him in the tunnel, crouching uncomfortably. Lucca turned back to face forward and started following the man with the lamp who was lighting the way in front of him. He saw old mining equipment strewn around the sides of the tunnel with wooden ceiling supports posted every few feet. Soon the tunnel opened to a very large area that Lucca could only assume was a natural cave. The stalagmites had been cut away from the cave floor, but the stalactites looming overhead produced an ominous aura. The cave was alive with activity that seemed to ignore the looming stalactites; Lucca guessed that over fifty men and women were engaged in some form of work. He saw machinists and welders working on rifle barrels. Seamstresses were working with red-and-black cloth. Groups of men were huddled around maps and leafing through correspondence.

"A rebellion factory," Pasha said into Lucca's ear. "Follow me. I know the way to the Fruitbat's office."

Lucca followed Pasha out of the main cave and into a curved hallway that looked to have been carved out centuries ago by an underground river. They passed a small alcove where two shirtless men were beating on another man who was tied to a chair. Lucca was standing dumbly outside the alcove when the two shirtless men turned to notice him. Before they could say anything, Pasha pulled Lucca along.

"Don't you mind that. That's the interview room. Come this way." Pasha led them further down the natural passageway.

"Zagranos, do I call him Fruitbat? Mr. Fruitbat?"

Pasha chuckled. "I would not recommend that. Call him Mr. Vreto. That would be the closest thing to his real name. Few of us use our given names anymore. Do you think I was born *Pasha*—the Turk name for high commander? I was born a brigand. I took up *Pasha* when I took up with the Bashi-Bazouks, and that was many years and many loyalties ago."

Finally the pair came to another, larger alcove. A single lamp was strung from the middle of the room, and it illuminated a lone figure bent over some machine and pecking away at it. The man was stick thin and smoking a long cigarette. From the smoky haze of the room, it looked as if he had been chain-smoking for weeks. The man turned, and Lucca could see he was even thinner than Lucca first thought. His clothes seemed to hang off him like a scarecrow after the birds had carried off all the straw. Around him were stacks and stacks of newspapers of all regions and languages. It looked as if he was fortifying himself with printed word.

"Hello, Zagranos Pasha. Come in." The Fruitbat beckoned them in with a bony hand. He had thick, round spectacles, and through a trick of the light and haze, they combined with his large round ears to give the appearance of four circular orbs glowing in alignment.

"Hello, Vreto," Pasha said. "What is that little machine you have there?" He pointed at the hunk of metal in front of the Fruitbat.

"It is called a typewriter. It allows me to write with typesetting. Allow me to demonstrate." The Fruitbat hammered away at his machine and then snatched the paper that had been extruded from the top, handing it to Pasha.

Pasha read the words typed neatly on the page. "WHO IS THE BOY?"

Pasha cleared his throat. "Oh, ah, excuse me. This is Lucca Ferrando. He is the son of Enzo Ferrando, my commander during my stint on the African Horn."

The Fruitbat was now studying Lucca intently. "Zagranos. Would that make him the grandson of Antoni Ferrando, the Old Bull?"

"Indeed it would," replied Pasha.

There was a pause in the conversation as the Fruitbat took off his glasses, cleaned them, and lit another cigarette. When he spoke, he was looking directly at Lucca and his words were spoken kindly.

"This organization has been called many things. It can be thought of as many things. I think of it as a school, and I think of myself as a student. What do we study? We study revolution. We study the history of freedom from oppression. What I have learned in my studies is that there are many ways to topple a government. There are many roads to Rome, as long as Rome burns. Of course, I have studied the life and work of Giuseppe Garibaldi and the revolution that unified Italy. So of course I know of your grandsire, the strong right arm of Garibaldi. I even know of your father, and I have tried, through Zagranos, to garner your father's support in our cause, but Zagranos has thwarted my efforts. Maybe it is that Zagranos has some misplaced loyalty to your father and he thinks that I would have corrupted him. I use the past tense because I am aware of his death. I am sorry for your loss." The Fruitbat took a long pull of his cigarette and looked at Lucca expectantly.

"Thank you, Mr. Vreto." Lucca said cautiously. He was wary of this man.

Pasha cut in. "Vreto, it is not that I don't want to do my part, but it would have been a wasted effort. Enzo Ferrando was incorruptible."

"It's alright, Zagranos, I believe you," said the Fruitbat. "No one here questions your loyalty, old friend."

Lucca, surprising himself with his boldness, asked the Fruitbat a direct question. "After you overthrow the Ottoman Empire, what will you replace it with? What are your ideals?"

The Fruitbat was slow to answer. He leaned forward in his chair and exhaled smoke from his nostrils. "Once the beast is slain, then and only then can we hammer our spears into spades and rebuild. If we use the spear for spadework, we dull the edge. We need to stay sharp if we want to kill the beast. Said more bluntly, we are not the architects of a brave new society. We are the demolition crew. If Albania has to exist in a smoldering pit after the fall of the Ottoman Empire, so be it."

Lucca felt uncomfortable as the Fruitbat brought his gaze to Lucca's neck bandage.

"What can I do for you, Lucca Ferrando, son of Enzo, son of Antoni?" the Fruitbat asked.

Lucca looked at Pasha, who nodded at him encouragingly. Lucca began, "My ship, the *Albatro* was chased, boarded, and sunk by blackbirders in the Red Sea. The ship that sank us was called *Hafgufa*. I was cast overboard, and I do not know what became of my crew. I was hoping you heard something."

Upon hearing this, the Fruitbat leaned forward in his chair and started muttering to himself with his cigarette in his mouth. "My, my, my." Then, without looking, he reached at a stack of newspapers on his right and deftly pulled out a paper from the top third of the stack. He then handed Lucca the newspaper. The newspaper was written in French and said

Journal de Geneve at the top. Lucca's French was not great, but he could decipher the main article on the front page, "The Slaughter of the Albatross."

The Fruitbat spoke up. "It seems there is at least one other survivor and he, she, or they are in Geneva, Switzerland. That is the only publication I've seen so far to publish the event."

Lucca spread the paper on the ground excitedly and was on all fours trying to read it as fast as possible.

"Someone else survived!" Lucca shouted, and Pasha clapped him on the back heartily. Then Lucca stood up and looked at Pasha. "Pasha, I must go to Geneva."

The Fruitbat spoke again. "I have two words of caution for you, Lucca Ferrando. First, I can see you are not well. Your throat looks infected, and it is a long, hard ride to Geneva, especially as it is now winter. Zagranos can ride with you as far as Bosnia, but I have some business for him to take care of there, and you'll be on your own crossing the Alps."

Pasha looked like he knew exactly what dark business the Fruitbat had for him, and he only nodded. Lucca also nodded.

The Fruitbat continued with no humor in his voice. "My second word of caution: very few outsiders see the inside of this place and leave freely. Zagranos Pasha has vouched for you, and so you are our honored guest. It goes without saying, however, that if you were to reveal the location of our little operation here, I would have to ask Zagranos to hunt you down."

Lucca looked at Pasha, who offered him a disturbing smile.

"I will tell no one, of course," Lucca said firmly.

The Fruitbat nodded. Then he said, "Would you like me to write to the *Journal de Geneve* and let them know there is another survivor and to expect you in the next month? Presumably they will coordinate the reunion."

"Yes, please. Thank you very much Mr. Fr ... Mr. Vreto," Lucca said.

The corner of the Fruitbat's mouth twisted in a small smile. "Good luck, Lucca Ferrando."

35

As Lucca and Pasha stooped and crawled their way back out through the tunnel, Lucca could not help letting a little bit of hope creep back into his chest. He dared not fully acknowledge it as he believed a disappointment would kill him. Even still, he found his legs working better and his breathing easier. When their horses appeared, Lucca was able to mount up himself, and they rode north without stopping for three hours. Pasha kept a respectful silence, allowing Lucca to be alone with his thoughts. A survivor in Geneva.

The pair rode hard for four days, staying at wayside inns at night and stopping only to water the horses by day. On the fourth day they reached the Bosnian border, the point where Pasha would accompany Lucca no longer. It started to rain as they stabled their horses and ducked into a wayside inn where they would share their last meal together. Lucca had grown quite fond of the giant Albanian and realized he would be very sad to see him go. Lucca, his legs sore from the riding, walked gingerly to an open table and sat himself down. Pasha sat down a few moments later with two mugs of ale, two bowls of steaming broth, and a map, which he unfolded between them. Pasha smoothed the map flat and produced a pencil.

"Now listen carefully, Lucca. I will explain the best route to get you to Geneva without getting your eyeballs frozen or your throat reopened by bandits." He started drawing on the map. "Instead of heading west to Milan and crossing the Italian Alps in the dead of winter, you want to cut north through Austria. Ride to Innsbruck and take the Brenner Pass, a much better route this time of year. That puts you in eastern Switzerland, and you can then ride southwest to Geneva on good road."

Pasha then folded the map, presented it to Lucca, and started tucking in to his dinner.

"Pasha?"

"Yes, Lucca Ferrando, what can I do for you?"

"You never told me how you helped my father avenge my grandfather's killers. I suppose I should know. Just in case I never see you again."

Pasha nodded and used his sleeve to wipe his mouth after polishing off his ale. "Yes. In truth it was a tidy thing. At the time of this little adventure, your father could have had the entire Italian Army in Africa at his back, but when he heard word that the three hero-killing bastards had surfaced, he only had me accompany him. I suppose it could have been on account of me being in the employ of the army instead of conscripted since this little assassination adventure wasn't exactly official Italian Army business ... Or he could have chosen me because I'm rather good at punching holes in people.

"Anyway. After years of hiding, we heard the three cowards would be attending some sort of political function in Protenza in support of a fellow named Depretis. We took a fast ship to Naples and rode hard for two days. We arrived in Protenza at night, just before the meeting. There must have been three hundred people there, and the trouble was we had the three names but we knew not the faces. We didn't know what these bastards looked like, and we were afraid that if we started asking questions they would scare and run off into the night. Your father had a clever idea, though. He snuck over to the grand podium before the council or whatever convened and got hold of the meeting agenda and penciled in the three bastards' names on the list of honorees. When it came time to honor the honorees, the first bastard's name was read, and he stood up proudly, allowing us to put a face to a name. If only he had known what he won! When the second bastard's name was called, he stood up, too, but more warily, and he shared a look of concern with his honored companion. Maybe your father wasn't so clever after all, because when the third name was called, all three of the bastards realized the game. The third man never stood up. We made the first two, but sure enough they set out like bats out of hell. One riding hard to the east, the other to the south. I went south, and your father went east. I caught my man in half a day and had him bound and gagged real tidy. With the right steed, and it must be a proper beast, I can out ride any damn Italian. Your father, a shit horseman despite his exploits on the African Horn, took two full days to run down his bastard. It took another three days for your father to double back and meet me where I was holding up with my prisoner. I'm not sure why your father was taking so long, but at least he got his man."

Pasha took a moment to pause. He had a glint in his eye that made Lucca uncomfortable.

"It was all real tidy. I remember your father walking into the barn where I had this bastard bound and gagged. He didn't even give me more than a glance. With a steady step he just walked over to the bastard, whose eyes were getting wider with each of those steps. He then drew and gave the bastard one between his saucepan eyes. He had holstered and started walking away before the body even slumped to the ground. And that was that. He didn't tell me much about the bastard who had run east, but I think he was done in a very similar fashion. Now you know."

Lucca wished he felt shocked by hearing that his father had committed two cold-blooded murders, but he was not. When it was clear Pasha was finished speaking, Lucca asked, "What about the third man?"

"I told you, the third man never stood."

"But you said you helped him avenge my grandfathers killers. I thought that meant all of them."

"Well, I did help. Just because we didn't get all of them doesn't mean I didn't help. I suppose he's still out there somewhere, if he hasn't shit himself in fear so badly that he's died of dysentery." Pasha shrugged and then seemed to remember something quickly. He started searching around in his pockets and then produced a thrice-folded envelope.

"Here are the three names of your grandfather's killers. Two are crossed out. One left, as you said." Pasha handed the thrice-folded envelope to Lucca.

Lucca accepted the envelope hesitantly but did not open it.

"That's why he never told me," Lucca said. "He wasn't finished."

Pasha carefully packed his pipe and mused to no one in particular. "Yes. It was a tidy thing but not how I might have done it if it was me that was thirsting for vengeance. I think I might have inflicted a little more pain—you know, drawn it out a little more. I would have of course made sure the scoundrels knew who I was before I did the deed. I would have said something menacing and final before I pulled the trigger, too, like *Rabid dogs must be put down!* or something of that nature."

Pasha went to light his pipe, but Lucca snatched the match from him. He struck it and then held the thrice folded envelope under the flame until the fire had consumed it greedily.

"That's how it is then," said Pasha, raising his eyebrows, surprised but not unamused.

"I have none of my father's hot blood in me, Pasha," said Lucca just before he lapsed into a fit of coughing.

"I don't like the sound of that cough, Lucca. You could wait until spring to cross the mountains."

Lucca shook his head. "You know I cannot. I know that at least one person from the *Albatro* is alive. Finding them is the only thing that matters to me now. Pasha, I need to speak to you about money. You have paid for my passage thus far, and I need to borrow the palfrey. I promise I will pay you back as soon as I come into the means."

Pasha waved him off. "You owe me nothing. I owe a great debt to your father. Consider it recompense. Besides, I'm rich. I've made a fortune fighting for countries of the highest bid." He winked at Lucca and puffed on his pipe.

"You are a good friend, Zagranos Pasha."

Pasha seemed to bow his massive head under the weight of the compliment.

Lucca raised his mug of ale for the first time. "To Geneva!"

"I hope you find what you seek, Lucca Ferrando."

36

The next day Lucca started early and rode north until both he and his palfrey needed rest and water. He had started to bond with the animal, and he felt a mutual respect building in the creature. It was a fine animal, and Lucca decided he would buy her from Pasha if he could get the money together. Lucca surprised himself by having thoughts like these, normal thoughts that would occur to normal people. He took it as a positive sign.

After watering at a cool stream but before he mounted up, he studied his horse. She was of a sorrel-roan coloring. From afar she was a washed-out copper-red, but when mounted, a rider could clearly see the distinct red-and-white hairs that colocated to coax out the roan coloration. She was not a tall horse, no more than fifteen hands, but she had a muscular neck, and Lucca was impressed by her vigor. In fact, Lucca spent more energy reining her in than spurring her on. As he mounted up, he resolved to let her spread her wings.

As they restarted their amble north, Lucca filled his lungs with the crisp air. It was getting colder already, and soon they would be getting higher. He noticed the palfrey's breath, in time with the rhythm of the hoof falls and visible in the cold air. He loosed the reins and gave her a squeeze of encouragement, and she sprang forward into a gallop. The gait was smooth and fluid, and Lucca felt his own movement aligning with the horse's. The hoof falls occurred so close together that Lucca could only make out three distinct beats. Three sounds where four hooves struck ground. Three syllables, like Geneva.

North they rode. The palfrey seemed to be getting stronger by the stride, and Lucca gave her all the rein she needed. She charged ahead with joy like she was nipping at the tail of autumn. The tail of autumn gave way to the wet nose of winter, and a dusting of snow started to wreathe the road. The heady pace of the horse and rider continued for days, only stopping for watering and to camp upon wind-sheltered rocks where Lucca would barely have the energy to build a fire and spread his bed roll before sinking into sleep. His last thought at night and his first thought at morn were the same: Geneva.

The snow continued to deepen. The road itself was no longer visible, but the tree lines shaped their path, and the palfrey galloped with a confidence that Lucca did not care to bridle. Geneva. The snow was fluffy and light, and the palfrey's motion would kick up the stuff like ocean spray. Lucca was reminded of the *Albatro* under full sail knifing through the Mediterranean. As the snow grew deeper, the world grew quieter. All the sounds of nature were wrapped up and muffled by the white blanket that stretched as far as Lucca could see. Even the hoof falls of the palfrey were muffled so that a ringing quiet hung in the air. Again Lucca was pulled into a memory of the *Albatro* and the calm before the storm that nearly sank them.

Just after breakfast on his third day of riding, Lucca started to make out the unmistakable enormity of the Dolomites, regal with their ragged peaks. He could make Brenner Pass that day if the weather held. The palfrey seemed to sense this and was surging through the snow with a wild energy. The horse's enthusiasm was infectious, and Lucca did not rein her in. He used her energy to temper his deep weariness and rode hard into the white expanse, all the while chanting his eternal mantra, Gen-e-va.

Then like a fog horn ripping him from a peaceful slumber, he felt the horse jerk and falter under him. He heard an audible crack, and the palfrey tried to catch herself, but her front leg could not bear the weight of their momentum, and the horse was driven down into the earth. Lucca flew over the reins and onto the road, landing hard on his shoulder.

The snow took some of the impact out of Lucca's collision with the ground, and he was able to sit up and look back at his fallen animal. The horse tried in vain to stand, but one of her front legs was badly broken. She tried again and faltered and lowered her head on the ground. She was still breathing heavily, and her breath obscured Lucca's view of her eyes. He crawled over to her through the snow. His shoulder screamed, but he was able to lift her head onto his lap. He petted her neck and gave her water. He felt that she was in a high degree of pain. A flick of Grace's razor and it was done. He felt the warmth of her life spread over his trousers and watched it turn the white snow into steaming red slush. It was so quiet there. It had started to snow, and he could no longer see the Dolomites. Everything was muffled. He couldn't even hear himself say "Geneva." He told himself he had best get going as he would have to get to Geneva by foot. First he might rest a bit, he told himself. It was so quiet.

37

Lucca awoke with a start. His head hurt something awful, and he had to blink several times to sharpen his blurry vision. He found himself in a clean, white hospital bed, and there was a man shrieking on the other side of the room. The room was a ward lined with other clean, white beds, and at that moment the shrieking man was standing on one of these beds and crying, "Moynier! Moynier! Moynier!" at the top of his lungs. He was the picture of aged agony with a great white beard and wild white hair that matched the starched white sheets he stood on. Nurses and orderlies were gathered around the man's bed trying to calm him, subdue him, and finally strap him horizontally to that same clean, white bed. The man continued with his pitiful cry of "Moynier!" though his shrieks soon died down to whimpers. Lucca saw that one of the nurses remained by the man's bedside to mop his brow with a wet towel. With the excitement now ended, Lucca drifted back into the sleep of the dead.

When Lucca awoke once again after an unknown interval of darkness, he was surprised to see this same man sitting on a small stool at the side of his bed. Lucca immediately sat up, somewhat disturbed by the idea that this old man could have been watching him sleep for any amount of time. But the man was nose deep into a dense-looking tome, and upon seeing Lucca wake, he shut the book and looked at Lucca with kindly eyes.

"Buon Giorno," he said. His white hair was now combed and kept.

Lucca nodded suspiciously. He then became conscious of a much larger bandage on his neck and brought his hand up to inspect it.

"Don't touch that," the man said quickly. "Doctor's orders. You are fresh out of surgery."

"Where am I?" Lucca asked. "What is this place?" His voice was hoarse, and speaking felt like swallowing shards of glass.

The old man's eyes crinkled into sympathy, and he said, "You're in a hospital in Heiden. Heiden is a small town in Switzerland."

Lucca gave the ward a full look for the first time. It was a hall, long and wide with tall glass windows between each of the ten beds that lined each side of the room. It was a wing that let in light from both sides, and the light seemed to play off the long, billowing curtains of white veil that caressed the window panes. The floor was marble, and suspended from the ceiling was a crystal chandelier.

Lucca looked back at the man sitting attentively at the side of his bed. "I had surgery?"

"Yes, you certainly did, and it was all quite a spectacle. I am sure the doctor will return shortly and elucidate all, but I do believe you were suffering from an infection that required the removal of rotted tissue around your neck. I do know that they found you in a sorry state. Flo, the nurse, told me that you were found sprawled across the road, half-dead with a horse next to you that was full-dead. After they found you and brought you here, you must have laid there on this bed for a week, spasming and coughing and muttering about Geneva. Then, just when the Doctor thought you were strong enough for surgery, you escaped! Well, it's not as though you were being held prisoner, but your bed was empty. They found you staggering down the road, asking the way to Geneva. You were not completely naked, but your hospital gown only covered your front. In the end, the doctor got his way and did get that rotted tissue out of your neck. I suspect he saved your life."

Lucca shifted his weight and groaned. The kindly old man nodded with recognition and pity. "Bed sores. Those will heal, I'm sure. Decidedly painful in the meantime."

Lucca was indeed in pain and processing information at a snail's pace, but when the old man said the word *Geneva*, all the circumstances of his present state came flooding back to him.

"I need to get to Geneva," said Lucca, more to himself than the old man, and he started to mentally prepare himself to get out of the bed.

"Why?"

"Someone ... is expecting me ... at the headquarters of the *Journal de Geneve*."

"Well then, we shall write them a letter informing them of your present condition and provide them instruction to revise the point of rendezvous. I happen to know the chief editor there, and he used to know me. We shall write to him this instant, and he can relate the particulars to your friend. What do you think of that?"

Lucca blinked. "OK ..." He was thankful for the old man's help because he did not believe himself capable of standing.

The old man was up as soon as Lucca consented, and he hurried to the other side of the ward to gather writing materials. He returned with a fountain pen and a clean sheet of paper.

"Very well. You shall dictate, and I shall be your loyal scribe. Now we shall address the envelope to our chief editor of the *Journal de Geneve,* but to whom shall we address this correspondence? Dear ...?" the old man prompted.

Lucca looked at the old man for a long time. He was thinking about how he could possibly be sitting in this strange hospital bed talking to a man who in all probability could be crazy as a loon. Lucca then had the uncomfortable thought that he too might be crazy as a loon and this beautiful hall could be a lunatic asylum. Apparently he had ridden his horse to death, and through the skilled hands of an unknown surgeon, narrowly avoided death himself. He then decided that this old lunatic taking his dictation was one of the least crazy occurrences in a long time.

Lucca cleared his throat. "Dear ... shipmate."

After scratching at the paper with his fountain pen, the old man nodded his head in encouragement and Lucca continued. "I, Lucca Ferrando, am here in ..."

When Lucca paused, the old man helpfully offered to insert the present location. Lucca then cleared his throat again. He grimaced as he did this, and his hand once again went to this neck. The old man noticed this and called out to the nurse. A red-headed nurse of middling age clicked over the marble floor to the two men. She was plump and had watery eyes.

"Flo, could you get my young friend here some warm tea with some honey? It's for his throat."

"Of course," she said and smiled at them both. During the time the tea was prepared, Lucca and the old man waited quietly. The old man appeared utterly content. Clearly he was a gentleman. Was he being politely patient, or was he truly at ease?

Once a cup of tea was brought, drank, and placed carefully on the bedside table, the dictation continued. "I am recovering from a surgery and unable to travel to Geneva. I will be well soon but unable to travel for several days ..."

The old man cleared his throat. "Might I suggest saying that you are unable to travel for several weeks? Not only do I believe that to be a more realistic prognosis, but this will instill the necessity for your correspondent to make his or her way *here* rather than wait several days for you to resume your journey *there*."

"OK, let's go with weeks then." Lucca thought for a moment and then said, "Could you ask them in a polite way to just come here?"

The old man nodded dutifully and continued to scratch at the paper. After he concluded his work, he gave the letter to Lucca, who read it over twice and then handed it back.

"We shall send this posthaste! Flo!" The old man handed her the letter with instructions, and she clicked away.

"Who are you?" Lucca asked the old man as soon as the nurse had left with the letter.

"Ah, yes. I realize I have you at a disadvantage as I now know your name. May I call you Lucca?"

"Yes."

"Lucca, I am a patient here. I used to be Henri Dunant, but you can just call me Henry and that will be just fine."

Lucca wondered at Henry's choice of words. How could he have once been someone else? He decided to ask a different question that was also on his mind. "What ails you?"

"I'm afraid I have a rather dire case of eczema."

"I see. I'm sorry."

"Well, thank you, but it's nothing compared to your case. As I said, you've been quite a spectacle here at our quiet hospital in the Swiss mountains. Usually it is I who am the spectacle. In fact, that's why I came over today. I wanted to apologize."

"Apologize for what?" Lucca asked.

"Although I have no recollection, Flo informed me that I had one of my fits last night. If you slept through it, all the better, but you would have heard some screaming and witnessed some unbecoming conduct to be sure. It seems that these fits or spells come upon me sporadically. I suspect it is engendered by some dark recall of the past."

Henry then pushed himself to his feet. "Well, Lucca, I am very pleased to meet you. I will let you rest, but maybe, if your throat is able and you yourself are amenable, you could tell me your story tomorrow. I seem to know less and less each day, but I do know that you have a story. I should very much like to hear it."

"Thank you for your help, Henry," returned Lucca, "but I'm not sure I want to relive it." Henry nodded and walked away.

38

The next day, the nurse came over to Lucca's bed and prodded him gently. "Lucca, we are going for a little walk."

Lucca was awake, but he did not think he was up for a walk and displayed his doubt plainly.

"We have to get you up and moving. I'll help you, and we can take baby steps. We have a beautiful garden here, and although it's cold, the mountain air is good for you."

Lucca winced in pain as the act of standing put pressure on his sores. The nurse assisted him, and together they walked slowly to the tall glass-paned doors at the end of the hall that opened to the garden. The garden had a walkway that was enveloped by a wooden pergola wrapped in old vine. The walkway led to a gazebo in the middle of the garden. The gazebo was not a hundred feet from the tall glass doors, but by the time Lucca got there, he was winded and sweating from the exertion. Henry joined them at the gazebo and shared pleasant commentary about the Swiss Alps and hiking trails that he had known as a young man.

Henry offered to walk Lucca back to the hospital, and Lucca accepted his arm, leaning on him for support. When they were about halfway, Lucca looked up to see a figure in the doorway. She was blonde. When she saw him, she came running at a dead sprint. Lucca lurched forward to go to her, but his feet would not react, and Henry had to catch him. Grace was there a second later, and the two locked each other into the deepest embrace.

Then they both started talking and crying at the same time, which led to joyous laughter.

"I don't understand," Lucca said. "How did you find me? We only sent that letter yesterday." He held her tightly to make sure she was real.

"When you didn't show up at the *Journal de Geneve,* I thought something must have happened and you'd be in a hospital."

"But how did you know I was in *this* hospital?"

Grace smiled broadly. "Because you weren't in the twenty-four other hospitals I checked."

Grace and Lucca made their way inside. Grace was peppering Lucca and the nurse with questions about his health. Lucca could not take his eyes off Grace for one second. He no longer felt his bed sores or any other bodily pain. When the nurse left to bring some tea with honey, Lucca and Grace sat next to each other on his bed, arms wrapped around each others' waists, heads touching.

"Are there other survivors besides us?" Lucca asked. Grace shook her head.

"What happened to them?"

"Lucca, what I saw on that ship will haunt me forever. I envy you that you were not there to witness it. I will just tell you that it was a slaughter."

"How did you get off that ship?"

"I met a man with half a heart, and he helped me escape."

Lucca raised his eyes to hers.

"Don't worry, Lucca, you have nothing to worry about. He accompanied me to Genoa. When I got to Genoa, I found that my father had passed away and my brother had seized control of the company. I suspect my father's passing had been hurried along by my brother."

"I'm so sorry, Grace."

"It's alright. I've decided my father's legacy can take a new form. We can start a new trading company. This man who helped me escape, he is a banker, and he is providing the financing for a new ship. I journeyed with him to Geneva, and he has helped me enormously, including the publishing of the article you read in the *Journal de Geneve*. We will take delivery of the ship within a week. It will be our ship, Lucca."

"Grace. I'm not well."

"But you'll get well, Lucca. You'll get well in no time at all. This is what Bartolo would have wanted."

Lucca tried to smile at her. "I admire your spirit, Grace. I wish I had some of it. I'm sorry for your father. I also lost mine."

Grace drew a deep breath and took Lucca's hands in hers. "Lucca, I need to tell you something." Grace started and stopped several times, and then she started tearing up.

"What is it?"

"Lucca, it's about your father. I feel responsible for his death."

"Grace. He killed himself. Only he is responsible for his death."

"I met him before his death. I gave him the news of ... of your death."

Lucca looked down and then at Grace. "Grace, he would have found out the *Albatro* sank and the crew was dead from someone else, and the result would have been the same."

"But someone else telling him would not have known it was the *Hafgufa* that caused your death."

"I don't understand, Grace."

"Lucca. He felt responsible for your death. Those slaves were Ethiopians. Your father provided the *Hafgufa* with their slaves."

Lucca unwrapped his arm from Grace and sat quietly on the bed with his hands in his lap. His eyes were closed, and he was trying to get himself to breath normally. Grace was watching him with deep concern.

Finally Lucca spoke. "Grace, you bear no responsibility. My father alone ..." Lucca could not finish his sentence and just sat there shaking his head.

Grace did not know what to say. She put her arms around him, and they were still for a long time. She broke the silence. "Lucca, I have something for you." She reached into a bag she had brought with her and pulled out a big leather-bound portfolio. It was his sketchbook.

"I was able to retrieve it from the *Hafgufa* before I escaped," she said, holding it out to him. Lucca did not reach for it, so she set it on his bedside table. She then made him lie on the bed, and she lay next to him in an embrace.

"I thought I lost you," he said.

"I'm here," she said.

Over the next few days, Grace took the care of Lucca into her own hands, and little by little he made progress. On the third day, Lucca made it to the gazebo with only a little help from Grace, albeit the walk was painful and slow.

"Lucca, you're not well enough to travel yet, but you will be soon. I need to get to Venice to take delivery of our ship."

"Grace, I'm not ready to go to sea."

"We don't sail for a month. You'll be more than well by then."

"Even if I'm well, I'm not ready to go to sea."

"Just focus on getting your body well, and your mind will follow. We'll sail on the twenty-first, one month from today. The salt air will cure all. We belong out there, and we will never get our lives back from inside this place. You'll be in Venice on the twenty-first, or do I need to come back here and carry you?"

Lucca smiled but did not speak. She left the next morning.

39

Lucca groaned as the nurse turned him to his side to get clean sheets under him.

"Almost done, Lucca," said the nurse. "Be brave for me." She was dexterous and practiced, and she replaced the old sheets with brightly starched ones in under ten seconds.

"I've also brought some of your tea here, Lucca." She pointed to the steaming cup on his bedside table.

"Thank you, Flo," said Lucca.

The nurse giggled, and she fluffed Lucca's pillow and placed it behind his head. "Flo is actually not my real name. It's Zosa. Mr. Dunant calls me Flo after Florence Nightingale."

"This Henri Dunant," Lucca said quietly. "Is he ... mad?"

Zosa stiffened, and Lucca could tell he had touched a nerve. "He is most certainly not. No madder than you or me, anyway. He has experienced much heartbreak, and he is a gentle soul. I wish fame had never come to him in the first place."

"He is famous?" Lucca asked.

"Why yes, of course. You have not heard of Henri Dunant?"

"I confess I have not. Though I am just a deckhand on a merchant ship. Or, I was."

"Well that man there ..." They both looked across the wing at Dunant, who was sitting on his bed with his back to them. "That man there is the founder of the Red Cross and the architect of the Geneva Convention."

"Then what is he doing here?" Lucca asked.

"That is a long, painful story, Lucca. He will have to tell you himself, but in my opinion he is suffering from heartbreak. He worked so hard for them, and they turned their backs on him."

"Who is *them*? Who turned their backs on him?"

"All of us," said Zosa. And that was all she would say. She left Lucca to contemplate this, but returned a few minutes later with a book.

"If you would like to understand him better," said Zosa, handing him a slim volume, "you should read this. It tells of his experiences at the Battle of Solferino." The book was old and worn from many readings and bore the words, "*A Memory of Solferino* by Henri Dunant.*"

Lucca accepted the book and looked up at Zosa. "My grandfather fought at the Battle of Solferino."

"Then I am even more surprised you have not heard of Henri Dunant. Come, you can read later. Now you must get some rest."

"Zosa?"

"Yes, Lucca?"

"Could you ask Mr. Dunant if he would like to come speak with me? I am not so tired."

"Of course, Lucca, I'll ask him," said Zosa, walking off.

A few moments later, Dunant was seated next to Lucca's bed, and Lucca was telling his story. He started from the very beginning and withheld nothing. He told of his father's rebellious act that had first caused the separation of the Ferrando family. He told of his first days on the *Albatro* and his five years at sea. He told Dunant of Bartolo and DiSesa, and he told of Grace. He told Dunant what he remembered of the *Hafgufa* pirates and how he managed to swim and crawl his way to Massawa only to find his father dead by his own hand. He told Dunant what he had learned of his father through the mercenary Zagranos Pasha. He told Dunant that his father was not the man he had known as a boy. The telling of his story was painful yet cathartic, and Lucca felt a lightening of the burden he had been carrying. Dunant proved to be a fine audience, saying nothing but saying everything with his empathetic eyes. When Lucca finally finished his tale, the two men sat in silence for some time.

"You're in a lot of pain, Lucca," said Dunant.

Lucca felt his lip tremble, and a wave of emotion wash over him. He tried to say something, but his voice broke. All he could do was nod.

"Lucca." Dunant inched his chair closer to Lucca's bed. "You may not be ready to hear this, but I shall tell you anyway. The source of your pain is the hate you hold for your father. I think you judge him harshly, and—"

"I think I judge him justly," Lucca interrupted.

"Be that as it may, the hate will consume you. Look what hate has brought me, Lucca. Three decades of bitterness and despair. It haunts me still. For Christ's sake, you heard me screaming the name of an old adversary in a bout of madness. This agony of mine does not have to be your path. I used to believe that I was a force of good in this world. Now I am just an unworthy old man."

"Forgiving my father would mean pardoning his sins," Lucca said flatly.

"No, I don't believe that is so. Forgiveness is about understanding the man, not about condoning the act."

Dunant left Lucca alone with his thoughts. Out of restlessness Lucca picked up the book Zosa had given him, stole a glance across the hall at Dunant, and started reading.

The next morning it was Dunant who woke up to Lucca at his bedside. Lucca had pulled up a chair and was patiently waiting for Dunant to wake up. He had *A Memory of Solferino* in his lap. Dunant was happy to see Lucca until he caught sight of the book in his lap.

"Where did you find that old rag?" he asked.

"Zosa gave it to me," replied Lucca.

"She did, did she?" said Dunant, looking annoyed.

"Mr. Dunant, I have something to ask you."

"Please, call me Henry, Lucca."

"Were there many men like you at the aftermath of Solferino?"

"Like me in what way? There were many people who provided aid to the wounded and dying."

"Were there any others who you remember dressed in linen suits, as you were?"

Dunant looked puzzled and chuckled a little. "No, I suppose I was the only one garbed in that outlandish fashion. I had come straight from Algiers."

Lucca did not chuckle and was dead serious. "Mr. Dunant, do you remember a man—he would have been a large man. You, or another man in a linen suit, found him dying of thirst. He had his boots stolen right off his feet by pillaging peasants."

Now Dunant was serious, and he stiffened slightly. "Call me Henry, and yes, I do. I remember this man as clearly as the day I met him. We were able to help him to a hospital and luckily his life was saved ... That was not in the book."

"Mr. Dunant. I believe that man was Antoni Ferrando. My grandfather."

Dunant was regarding Lucca with high skepticism. "The chances of that are—"

"You gave him water, and he gave you a flag."

Dunant leapt up and pulled a large trunk out from under his bed. He flung it open and rummaged around feverishly, finally producing a neatly folded triangle. He unfolded the triangle to reveal a white flag with a red cross on it.

"That is the flag of Genoa," Lucca said quietly, incredulously. "My grandfather's flag."

"This flag ..." Dunant started and stopped, collecting himself. "This flag was the basis for my design of the Red Cross symbol."

"Mr. Dunant, I have to thank you."

"Thank me? For what?"

"I would not be here if not for you. If my grandfather had died that day, my family would never have existed. Your work has helped millions of faceless people, and they may never know who to thank. But I do. Thank you, Mr. Dunant."

"Call me Henry, Lucca, please."

"But you are Dunant, and you always were and always will be."

The two men shook hands.

40

Lucca woke into his dream. He was sitting upright in his hospital bed, but in his lucidity he knew he was still dreaming. The hospital wing was the same but bathed in a soft reddish light. And there, sitting beside his bed, was his father, Enzo Ferrando. Enzo was seated, elbows on his knees, and looking down at his hands. Lucca could not see his face. Lucca addressed him, but Enzo did not look up.

When Lucca finally woke into the brightness of the day, he thought about this ghostly visitation for a long time. What gnawed at him most was that he couldn't see his father's face. Lucca tried to summon that face up from his memory, and it dawned on him that after five years he was starting to forget what the man had looked like. He was still thinking about his father when Dunant came over to his bed.

"Lucca, I hope you do not mind, but after you told me your story, I made some inquiries. It turns out I still have a bit of influence left with the Italian king. It took some doing, but I've arranged for someone to come here to meet you. I hope you don't mind."

Dunant led him gently through the pergola that led to the small gazebo in the center of the garden. There was a young man sitting there. When he saw Lucca and Dunant approach, he stood, and Lucca could see the man was tall but not large. His lankiness immediately reminded Lucca of DiSesa, and Lucca felt a sharp pang in his chest. When they arrived in the gazebo, Dunant introduced the young man.

"Lucca, this is Lieutenant Tassoni of Galliano Battalion. He served under your father. He has traveled a long way to see you, and it was not easy for him to secure leave for such a journey. Lieutenant, this is Lucca Ferrando, Enzo Ferrando's only son. I will leave you gentleman to talk. Thank you again, Lieutenant."

Lucca sat down and waited for Tassoni to speak. Tassoni cleared his throat and began. "Please forgive my plain speech. I'm not an educated man."

Lucca said nothing, and Tassoni continued. "As Mr. Dunant said, I served under your father for about five years and got to know him well—Sorry, I must say you sure do look a lot like him."

"But I am not like him," said Lucca flatly.

Tassoni looked like he did not know how to respond but then nodded in understanding as if Dunant had told him this would be how Lucca might respond. "He was a great man, Lucca."

"Are you going to tell me how he killed savages by the tens of thousands? Are you going to tell me how he was a man of honor who sold hundreds of no-good savages into slavery?" Lucca's voice was still weak, but he put an unmistakable edge on it.

Tassoni looked down once again and shook his head sadly. "No. I wasn't going to say that. I could say that many people are of the belief that those men we put into slavery had it coming. They were not innocents; they were prisoners of war and the very men who had slaughtered Galliano Battalion at the Battle of Dogali. But I wasn't going to say that. I was going to talk about a latrine."

"I do not understand."

"Before Enzo Ferrando came to Fifth Company, the company that I was posted to, we were the dregs of the battalion. We were a joke. They even put the Fifth Company barracks right next to the latrine. The smell of shit was what we woke up to, and it was what we laid down to at night. Soon after joining Fifth Company, you would feel so immersed in shit that, well, we started to believe that we were shit. We believed we were shit, and that was the way it was. Then your father came. The first whiff of shit that hit his nostrils was the last. Within ten backbreaking hours we had that latrine moved far away and downwind of our barracks. We could taste clear air again. Your father was certainly not a perfect man. But we live in a world of shit, no? You cannot stop men from shitting, but maybe you can get out from under it."

Tassoni shifted in his seat and pointed at a small wooden chest near his feet. "I brought his personal effects. I will carry them inside for you."

Lucca said nothing and just stared past Tassoni. Tassoni took the chest and got up to walk back toward the hospital. Before leaving he said, "Lucca, I'm sorry for your loss. The highest compliment your father ever paid me was when he told me that I reminded him of you."

Tassoni then walked toward the hospital, carrying the chest as one would carefully carry an infant. He stopped halfway through the pergola and cocked his ear, then turned his head back to Lucca. He had thought that he heard the words "thank you," but he could not be sure. Lucca was sitting perfectly still, staring into the distance.

41

It was a long time before Lucca came in from the garden. The sun had set, but the low light was holding as if it was not yet ready to say goodbye. He hobbled into the hospital wing through the tall garden doors, stopping to rest several times before he reached his bed. As he sat down on the side of the bed, he caught sight of his old sketchbook that Grace had brought him. He took it and opened randomly to a page toward the beginning. It was a portrait of his father wearing an easy smile. Like a plunge into warm water, he felt all the memories and senses and smells of his father gush over him.

42

One month later, Grace Ligoria was aboard the *Albatro II*. The ship was docked in Venice. She had just finished cleating off the halyard she had run up the mast. She arched backwards, stretching away the stiffness that followed the day's labors. Her crew had worked with industry, and they would be ready to set sail the following day. She did a double take as soon as she spotted him on the dock. He was tall and lean. He wore an easy smile, and under his arm he carried a bunch of bananas. Her helmsman had arrived.

43

Henri Dunant went on to win the first-ever Nobel
Peace Prize in 1901 for his role in the founding of
the International Committee of the Red Cross and
the establishment of the Geneva Convention. The Nobel Prize
was started from the fortune of Alfred Nobel. Nobel acquired a
fortune that can be attributed to the invention and commercial-
ization of dynamite.

When death darkened Dunant's door four years later, he
welcomed her in as an old friend and bade her sit a while. They
sat and talked for a time. She nodded politely as he talked
about hiking in the Jura Mountains as a young man. He told
her how he would occasionally hike by the light of the moon as
it shone down on Lac Leman. He had even cut a few trails. He
was proud of a switchback trail he cut into the mountain that
let hikers avoid a treacherous ridgeline. He explained to her
that with time and the many footfalls of young hikers, the
switchback he cut became the preferred path, and the treacherous line had all but vanished into overgrown forest. She

listened respectfully, but she knew all of this. And when it was time to go, he stood up and put on his coat and his hat. She gave him a little smile of encouragement and straightened his lapel. He held the door for her, and they left together.

44

Cape Town, South Africa — 1894. Seven years after the sinking of the *Albatro*.

'Wild' Lyle Jameson was not so wild anymore. He was landed and part of the new South African gentry that grasped firmly to the coattails of one Cecil Rhodes. Lyle's cousin Leander Jameson had seen to it that Lyle's work in the furtherance of the South African cause was rewarded handsomely. A man like Lyle Jameson, who would not quibble and bray when something dark needed doing, was an esteemed commodity in the Rhodes regime. Miner uprisings? Clashes with the Boers? Lyle Jameson was a man to meet violence with righteous violence and not a man to quibble or bray.

Lyle was at this moment surveying his reflection in the bathroom of a ballroom. He had grown a mustache like his dear cousin, and combined with new dentures to hide the ravages of scurvy, he had achieved the near look of a gentleman. His baldness, spackled with sun blotches from his days at sea, was instantly ameliorated by a bowler hat. He had even worked to temper his accent. He straightened up and finished his gin. No, Lyle Jameson would not quibble if something dark needed doing, and on this night, something dark did need doing.

Lyle walked out of the lavatory, nodded his way through the ballroom, and stepped into a coach waiting for him outside.

"The Alabaster Pub," Lyle barked at the coachman. The coach lurched into movement and sped along a freshly paved road.

Cape Town is coming along, Lyle thought to himself as they passed the newly built opera house. He was angry that he had been forced to leave the ballroom just as the night was picking up. He had seen Rudyard Kipling chatting excitedly with Cecil Rhodes. *Why do these damned Boers always insist on making deals in queer gutter pubs on the edge of town?*

After ten minutes time, the coach lurched to a halt on an unpaved road outside the Alabaster Pub.

The night was hot and sticky. Lyle stepped out of the cab and immediately slapped the side of his neck, killing the mosquito attempting to take his newly noble blood. He walked up the two stairs to the pub entrance, but before opening the door, he felt for his trusted dagger now tucked into his boot.

Upon entering he saw a barkeep at the back of the room, a few sleepy patrons on the left side, and a grand fireplace to his right. The fireplace, of stately English design, was terrifically out of place in sub-Saharan Africa. The only other figure was a large man sitting at the long center table in the pub. The man was barefoot and using a paring knife to clean the dirt under his toenails.

Lyle approached the barkeep.

"I'm looking for a man named Botha," he said. He addressed the barkeep loudly enough that the whole pub could hear. The barkeep shrugged and apologized. He did not know a

Botha. Lyle surveyed the pub again, walked over to the big man cleaning his feet, and asked if he was Botha.

"I'm not Botha," the big man replied. "But sit. Share a drink with me while you wait for your friend."

Lyle Jameson sat at the table but refused the drink. "I have business to attend to. I'm not here for drink."

The big man held up his palms to indicate acquiescence and went back to his feet. Lyle put his hat on the table and readied himself to wait on this damned Boer politician.

After a few moments, the big man put down his paring knife, put both feet on the floor, and slid over to the middle of the long table so he was facing Lyle Jameson. Lyle looked up with a mixture of disdain and annoyance.

"What would you say to a friendly wager?" the big man asked.

"I'm here on my business. I suggest you give mind to your own."

"A friendly wager," the big man said. "Hear me out." He produced a large gold coin and flipped it into the air. It landed between them on the wooden table.

Lyle studied the big man's face. Clearly it was a face that had some hard living beaten into it. "Let's hear the wager. But I'll give you fair warning. Don't be fooled by the topcoat. If you cross me, I'll run a blade 'cross your throat."

"The wager is simple. You listen to my telling of the story of Ana Maria and Ana Paula. If you don't feel any emotion upon my completion of the story, you win this gold coin. If you show emotion, I win. But you must be honest."

Lyle scoffed at the silliness of the wager. "And what do you win?"

"I win nothing."

Lyle made up his mind that he would be taking that coin no matter what. "I'll listen to your story. Proceed."

The big man cleared his throat and began. "This is the true story of Ana Maria and Ana Paula, two darling cousins. They lived in Spain, and as eight-year-old children, they were alike in every way. They dressed the same, they did their hair the same, they were diligent about their chores and their prayers, and they were inseparable friends. I should say, they were alike in every way except one. Ana Paula had a fatal disease, and the families knew she would never reach adulthood.

"Ana Maria and Ana Paula would always play together by the church pond every day after their chores were finished. One day Ana Paula did not show up to the pond. Ana Maria waited by the pond and then left for her home, hoping to see her cousin and her best friend the following day. The following day came, and Ana Paula did not come out to play. Ana Maria went to Ana Paula's house and knocked on the door. When her uncle, Ana Paula's father, came to the door, Ana Maria explained that she had not seen Ana Paula for two days and wanted to know if she was OK. The father promised little Ana Maria that Ana Paula was fine. That night he went to Ana Paula's room and asked her why she had not gone out to play with her cousin. Ana Paula told her father, 'Father, I am Ana Maria's only friend. I will be gone soon and she must learn to make new friends.'"

The big man looked at Lyle Jameson expectantly.

"So did the bitch die?" Lyle said and snorted, chuckling to himself and reaching for the gold coin.

But the big man grabbed his arm. Lyle glared at the man in a fury and tried to yank his arm free, but the big man had a tremendous grip.

The next few seconds seemed to happen in slow motion. Lyle reached with his left hand down to his boot, grabbed his dagger, and thrust it at the big man's neck. He saw the big man's other arm come up and grab his dagger arm at the wrist. He felt his left forearm, his dagger arm, torque horribly, and he heard the sickening crack of breaking of bone. His useless arm released its grip on the dagger. The big man took possession of it in a flurry and moved like a windmill, arching high up and driving the dagger down through Lyle's right hand and through the wood table, effectively pinning Lyle Jameson to the spot.

Lyle Jameson roared with anger and tried in vain to use his broken arm to pull the dagger out of this hand.

"You asked me what I stood to win, You should have asked what you stood to lose," said Zagranos Pasha.

Lyle's face was twisted with roiling rage, and he spat and hollered, "Who the bloody hell are you?!"

Zagranos Pasha calmly got up from the table and made his way to the fireplace. He carefully picked up a hefty, wrought-iron poker and turned back to Lyle Jameson.

"Why, surely you see that I'm an instrument of divine retribution. Or ... or maybe I'm just a good friend of one of your victims. In any case, rabid dogs must be put down."

Zagranos Pasha carefully lined up his swing with the contorted, disbelieving face of Lyle Jameson, and with a loud grunt, the Beast of the Balkans swung the wrought-iron poker with all the might and avenging energy of an Old Testament reckoning.

THE END

HISTORICAL FACT VS. HISTORICAL FICTION

Members of the Ferrando family, Grace, Bartolo, DiSesa, Bergeron, Lyle Jameson and yes, even Zagranos Pasha, are all fictional. Many real, historical figures are invoked in Terribilita including Garibaldi, Depretis, Crispi, King Umberto, Cecil Rhodes. The character Colonel Cristofori and the real Cristofori share a name, a rank, and an untimely demise, but not much else. Cristofori's personality and penchant for bureaucracy is purely a work of fiction. The only significant character in the story who actually existed was Henri Dunant.

Dunant's character arc stays true to the history of the man. He rises high through almost accidental fame, then experiences one of the greatest falls from grace ever, only to be redeemed in his final act with a Nobel Peace prize. The inspiration for this book actually came from reading obsessively about Dunant's life and wondering what he was doing and thinking during his decades of despair and isolation. To draw this out, I resolved to create a fictional character to go and meet this enigmatic humanist whose accomplishments still impact our lives today. The book germinated from there. If interested in going deeper, *A Memory of Solferino by Henri Dunant* should be the next stop. Dunant's primary source account of this grisly conflict in Northern Italy is not only well written and engaging but also responsible for galvanizing Europe into a humanitarian effort that would result in the International Committee of the Red Cross and the Geneva Convention.

Another fascinating historical gem that intersects with the story is the Battle of Dogali. In *Terribilita*, when Enzo and the remaining men of Galliano Battalion's First and Fifth Company manage to escape Fort Sahati, they come upon the aftermath of the Battle of Dogali where their countrymen had been massacred by the Ethiopians. In 1887, Colonel Cristofori led a battalion of Italian soldiers, supplemented by Eritrean Askari, to reinforce Fort Sahati. Along the way they were ambushed by a force of over fifteen thousand to their five hundred (*Source: Warfare and Armed Conflicts: A Statistical Encyclopedia of Casualty and Other Figures, 1492–2015, 4th ed*). Excepting some escapees, nearly all were slaughtered. For many Europeans of the era, this event was considered the epitome of Italy's colonial folly. If you find yourself in Rome, stop and see the *Piazza dei Cinquecento*, a square that honors the five hundred who fell at Dogali.

During Bergeron's drunken rant in the cabin of *Hafgufa*, he speaks extensively about the Suez Canal and its dark origins, especially the brutal confiscation of the canal ownership from Egypt to England. The immutable facts are that Egypt, in a state of bankruptcy, sold the canal rights to England. Whether or not Egypt's economic troubles were fueled by English greed as a means to acquire the canal rights is less certain. What is certain is that hundreds of thousands of Egyptians were put to toil for years on end (some estimates show over one hundred thousand dying during the course of the project) to construct an asset that was stripped away in less than the time it took to build.

UPCOMING BY BEN WYCKOFF SHORE

The Old Boys of the Balkans (Working Title)

Reunite with Zagranos Pasha as he returns to his home country of Albania after a long exile. Pasha, now a much older mercenary, wades into a world he only half recognizes as he struggles to find footing in a region bursting at the seems with ethnic and political conflict. The Balkans are a forever fascinating region, but it doesn't get much more exciting than the turn of the century and the build up to WWI, the Great War.

To receive updates, drop us your email at
cinderblockpublishing.com/contact

Or email us at cinderblockpub@gmail.com

We shall not spam.

ACKNOWLEDGMENTS

Thank you to my mother, Jenny Shore, for her steadfast support of me and this project. She would read my drafts aloud to allow me greater perspective in the editing process and to entertain a willing audience, Peter and Sam.

The child is father to the man. If the man (the author) in question has any semblance of literary skill it should be credited to a childhood where reading was encouraged and promoted. Literary promoters of the first order include the families Gocksch, Sudano, and Brockway/Johnson and many great teachers.

Lastly, thanks to you, the reader. By purchasing this book, you have generously (or unwittingly) participated in a wee bit of philanthropy. A portion of the profits from sales of Terribilita will go to the American Red Cross for Disaster Relief.